LOVE'S CHALLENGES

As bride-in-name-only to the dazzlingly handsome and wealthy Lord Humphrey Dewesbury, Joan had certain obstacles to overcome.

Joan had to still the wickedly wagging tongues of society, and make them sing her praises instead. Joan had to beat the beautiful and fashionable Lady Augusta Ratcliffe, who was determined to take Lord Humphrey from her, at Augusta's own game of intrigue and enticement. Joan had to win over Lord Humphrey's highly hostile parents, who were very much on Augusta's scheming side.

But the greatest challenge of all was Lord Humphrey himself, who insisted on loooking at Joan as a proper wife and not as a willing woman. . . .

GAYLE BUCK has freelanced for regional publications, worked for a radio station and as a secretary. Until recently, she was involved in public relations for a major Texas university. Besides her Regencies, she is currently working on projects in fantasy and romantic suspense.

SIGNET REGENCY ROMANCE
COMING IN DECEMBER 1991

Mary Balogh
Christmas Beau

Margaret Westhaven
The Lady In Question

Dawn Lindsey
The Barbarous Scot

A CHANCE ENCOUNTER

Gayle Buck

A SIGNET BOOK

SIGNET
Published by the Penguin Group
Penguin Books USA Inc., 375 Hudson Street,
New York, New York, 10014, U.S.A.
Penguin Books Ltd, 27 Wrights Lane, London W8 5TZ, England
Penguin Books Australia Ltd, Ringwood, Victoria, Australia
Penguin Books Canada Ltd, 2801 John Street,
Markham, Ontario, Canada L3R 1B4
Penguin Books (N.Z.) Ltd, 182-190 Wairau Road,
Auckland 10, New Zealand

Penguin Books Ltd, Registered Offices:
Harmondsworth, Middlesex, England

First published by Signet, an imprint of New American Library,
a division of Penguin Books USA Inc.

First Printing, November, 1991

10 9 8 7 6 5 4 3 2 1

 REGISTERED TRADEMARK—MARCA REGISTRADA

PRINTED IN THE UNITED STATES OF AMERICA

1

LORD HUMPHREY was in a black mood. It was time to make good on a long-held understanding and offer for the hand of his godparents' daughter, Miss Augusta Ratcliffe.

The Earl and Countess of Dewesbury had been fast friends with Lord and Lady Ratcliffe for decades. When the viscount was five years old, Lord and Lady Ratcliffe had been blessed with the birth of their only daughter, and in the excess of celebration that followed, the Earl of Dewesbury had expansively suggested a closer tie between their families, thus bringing about the understanding that upon reaching his majority at five-and-twenty, the viscount would offer for Miss Augusta Ratcliffe.

The young viscount had not then understood the implications of what was being said over his head. As he stared down at his future wife, reddened of face and shrilling at the top of her lungs, his prominent feeling was one of fascinated revulsion. Through the years his feelings for Lady Augusta Ratcliffe had changed only slightly, and not for the better.

Lord Humphrey detested Miss Ratcliffe. She had always played off her airs against him and treated him with the smug possessiveness that one usually reserved for a pedigreed lapdog.

Lord Humphrey avoided his intended as much as was humanly possible during their respective childhoods. When the time came for him to be sent off to school, he welcomed the opportunity to leave Miss Ratcliffe behind; and later, when he had established himself in London society, he had felt himself even freer of her cloying presence.

But ever since Miss Ratcliffe had first taken her bows into London society, it had become rather more difficult to ignore her existence. It did not take long before the circles in which they both moved became aware of Miss Ratcliffe's possessiveness and of his lordship's tangible dislike of her. It became quite an amusing thing for the society to watch, especially when it somehow became known that the viscount was bound by familial duty to offer for the lady.

Of late there had even been bets laid in the clubs regarding when the offer would be made.

Lord Humphrey had celebrated his upcoming twenty-fifth birthday by getting thoroughly drunk. He had been unusually ripe for any outrageous scheme put to him by his cronies. Perhaps he hoped to either get himself killed or at the least become so completely inebriated as to inspire permanent amnesia. The result had been two wild days of carousing, horse races, and fisticuffs—from which he came away sporting a purple bruise across one cheekbone—culminating in a raucous party hostessed by a set of demimondaines.

Lord Humphrey vaguely recalled attempting to drum up a duel over some lovely's charms. He had quite charmingly announced his ambition of putting a period to his now-damned existence. However, none of his friends had taken his aggressive declarations to heart and so he remained alive and whole, somewhat to his disgust.

Now dusk was falling on his last day of freedom. His head was pounding and his acute discomfort was not aided by the motion of the speeding phaeton.

He was driving down from London to his country estate. In the morning, with the coming dawn and grim sobriety, he would continue on to the family seat, where he expected to be congratulated by his parents on his upcoming nuptials, and from thence to the Ratcliffe Manor to formally ask for the hand of Miss Ratcliffe.

In his coat pocket was a special license obtained the week before by petition from the Archbishop of Canterbury. At his feet was a small valise packed with the bare essentials required by a gentleman traveling over the weekend without his valet.

Lord Humphrey intended to have the disagreeable business done and over with without spurious delay and false celebration. He had no intention of playing either the dignified fiancé or the happy bridegroom, and so he would tell everyone. He wanted the knot tied that same weekend in the privacy of the family chapel, without the added gall of fanfare and wedding breakfast afterward. He knew that his insistence would cause general dismay and even anger in some quarters, especially with Miss Ratcliffe. However, he felt that if he was to be forced into a distasteful marriage, it would at least be done in the manner he wanted it.

Afterward, he would return at once to London. Miss Ratcliffe could do what she damn well wished, he thought grimly.

Through the pounding haze that encompassed his mind, Lord Humphrey reflected bitterly on the chains of honor that had bound him to a loathsome future. The understanding between himself and Miss Ratcliffe was concocted before either was of an age to understand. He had been brought up in the belief that the informal agreement between his parents and his godparents was irrefutable. He did not want to marry at all, but any lady would be infinitely preferable to the bride chosen for him.

Unfortunately, Miss Ratcliffe did not return his distaste. He knew beyond a shadow of a doubt that the lady would not set him free of the obligation. Miss Ratcliffe, too, had been raised with the idea that her future was neatly tied up and she had on frequent occasions made known that she quite fancied herself mistress of the huge establishment that would pass to the viscount upon his parents' demise.

Miss Ratcliffe had been on the town for three Seasons. Lord Humphrey had hoped that she would find someone more to her liking, but with the passing of each Season Miss Ratcliffe had remained unattached. Miss Ratcliffe was never backward in informing him how many and whose offers she had turned down in preference to the one that he had yet to voice formally to her. There was always an arrogant coyness in her voice on these occasions that never failed to set his lordship's teeth on edge. Lord Humphrey had felt himself to be regarded as little more than a pet on a chain, never allowed to stray far or to express himself against the wishes of his mistress.

Lord Humphrey was so occupied with his angry thoughts that as he rounded a bend in the narrow road, a small shadow passing in front of him did not immediately command his attention. Before he was aware of its happening, his carriage had nearly bowled straight over the pedestrian. The small figure flew to one side, narrowly avoiding the oncoming phaeton's wheels.

Appalled and shaken, Lord Humphrey pulled up his team. Hastily snubbing the reins, he leapt down from his phaeton and ran back to the side of the road where the woman had flung herself aside to escape the rush of his carriage. His worst fears were assuaged somewhat when he saw that she was moving. "I am so frightfully sorry. I say, are you quite all right?" he asked anxiously.

"I believe so. At least, I think so," the woman answered in a somewhat dazed manner.

"Here, let me help you out of the ditch. It is the least that I can do," Lord Humphrey said, jumping down into the ankle-deep water. He was completely unheeding of the mud spattering onto his exquisitely shined top boots. The viscount bent to put his hand under the woman's elbow. She allowed him to help her to her feet, but suddenly she cried out and abruptly sagged against him. Not quite sober, Lord

Humphrey staggered with the unexpected weight. Recovering himself with some difficulty and thoroughly alarmed, he exclaimed, "What is it? Are you hurt?"

The young woman bit her lip. She raised her eyes fleetingly to his. "My ankle. I must have twisted it when I leapt into the ditch."

He saw even in the poor light that her face was unnaturally white and that her eyes held a sickened expression. "Up you go, then," he said brusquely. Without further ado, he swept her up into his arms and staggered unsteadily out of the ditch. Breathing heavily at the exertion, he deposited her inelegantly onto the seat of the phaeton. The young woman righted herself, her color somewhat recovered and heightened by his unexpected gallantry. She readjusted her bonnet with a slightly shaking hand.

Lord Humphrey climbed up beside his passenger and picked up the leather traces. "I shall drive you to your destination, if you will but give me the direction," he said.

She did so in a low uncertain voice, apparently mistrusting his driving ability after the exhibition that she had so lately been privileged to. But drunk or sober, Lord Humphrey was accorded to be an excellent whip. He kept the team to a decorous pace and after a few moments his passenger was confident enough to loosen her death's grip on the seat rail.

Lord Humphrey glanced over at the young woman. "I am Lord Humphrey. I was not paying as close attention to my driving as I should have been, or I would have seen you in time. I most humbly beg your pardon, Miss . . . ?"

"Miss Joan Chadwick," she supplied. After a pause, she said, "Your apologies are accepted, my lord. It was foolish of me to have been on the road so late in the evening. I do not wonder that you did not perceive me in the dusk."

It struck the viscount as an odd thing, indeed, that a young woman should be walking alone along a country lane so late. "What are you doing walking at this time of evening?" he asked curiously.

"I was returning to the place where I am staying after being to the village on errands,'' Miss Chadwick said briefly.

Lord Humphrey's curiosity was not satisfied, and if anything, it was heightened. Miss Chadwick's activities posed a welcome diversion from his own despondent thoughts and he pursued the topic of her errands. ''I have been through that village any number of times and I have never thought of a reason to stop. What errands could you possibly find to do in that sleepy village?''

After an astonished glance for his lordship's unusual lack of civil indifference, Miss Chadwick realized that her escort was somewhat the worse for having consumed spirits. Strong drink was something she knew very little about, but she had often heard woeful tales about the odd effects it had on some individuals, often causing the person to be unusually tenacious over some notion or other. She therefore decided to set aside her natural umbrage at the viscount's nosiness and answer him fully and simply so that he would not persist in his questioning.

Lord Humphrey learned that Miss Chadwick was the daughter of a vicar. Her father had died, and as the vicar was a widower with little to his name but a few published works, she had had no alternative but to seek refuge with an old family friend until she could gather her resources together enough to earn her own living.

''I hope to find a post as a needlewoman or as a governess. That is what I was doing in the village, sending in an advertisement to the London *Gazette* in order to find a suitable position,'' she said.

Lord Humphrey was struck by the gloomy future that Miss Chadwick had outlined for herself. It was nearly as bleak as his own, he thought blearily. He cast a thoughtful glance at his slim companion. Miss Chadwick appeared to be a well-bred and well-educated young woman, who would certainly be quite wasted in such positions, and he said so.

''I don't think that will do for you, my girl. You'd be bored silly within a week of mending someone's dirty laundry. As for working as a governess, you'd be sent packing in a fortnight," he said frankly.

"Sir!" Miss Chadwick was taken aback and somewhat piqued at what she construed as a slight against her abilities. "Why, I hardly think that you are any judge to say such a thing, my lord. I am perfectly capable of teaching in any number of subjects, being quite conversant in Italian and French and—"

"You need not rattle off your qualifications to me. After all, I am not dangling a governess's post in front of your nose," said Viscount Humphrey with asperity.

"No, you are not," Miss Chadwick replied. She remained silent for a moment, during which she struggled to gain firm control of her feelings. "However, I do take gentle offense at your unwillingness to see that I should make an excellent governess."

He threw a harried glance at her. "What I meant was, you've an appealing face, Miss Chadwick, too appealing to suit a governess. Even in this light, anyone can see that."

Miss Chadwick was once more reduced to silence. She did not know whether she should be flattered or amused by the backhand compliment. She said finally, "Perhaps that is so, my lord. Nevertheless, one must do whatever is necessary to get on with one's life, and in the best possible style that is open to one. Do you not agree, my lord?"

Lord Humphrey was frowning, as he had been for several moments. While he conversed with Miss Chadwick an odd notion had popped into his head that had gradually begun to take possession of his mind.

Now, at Miss Chadwick's words, he slewed his head around. His eyes held obvious surprise and some other indefinable emotion, almost a suspended excitement. "Lord, I don't know why I did not think of it before," he murmured.

He suddenly smiled with such charm that Miss Chadwick was dazzled. "Miss Chadwick, you are precisely right. One should arrange one's life in the best possible style open to one. I most humbly thank you for opening my eyes to it before it became too late.''

"Whatever are you talking about, my lord?'' Miss Chadwick asked, understandably confused.

Lord Humphrey whipped up his team. "I cannot think of the least objection to it, actually.'' He turned to his passenger and regarded her with a somewhat anxious air. "What say you, Miss Chadwick? Can you think of any objections?''

"No certainly not,'' said Miss Chadwick, not really attending as she eyed with misgiving the increasing speed of the team. She gripped the seat rail again. "My lord, I hesitate to point out something that is most likely of little consequence to yourself, but I do have an inordinate fear of fast carriages and—'' She suddenly saw a landmark whip past. "My lord! You have missed my turning. The house is down the lane that we just passed.''

"Oh, we have no need to stop. It would only result in questions and an unnecessary delay. We shall go straight on, I think,'' said Lord Humphrey coolly.

Miss Chadwick eyed his lordship in growing alarm and perplexity. "My lord, I don't know what you mean. But I do know that you promised to set me down at my doorstep after running me down in the lane. Pray do turn your horses around and take me home.''

The viscount did not slow his horses as she would have expected him to. "Home? Pah, you cannot call it that. Why, you've as good as admitted you are there on sufferance only until you are able to find a position of unending drudgery. I have a much better scheme in mind for you than that, I promise you,'' he said.

Miss Chadwick began to wonder what she had gotten herself into. With a sinking sensation she thought she knew too well what sort of future the viscount was referring to. She was not at all worldly, being the much loved and protected daughter of a minister, but she had read and heard enough in her short lifetime to have learned something of the sort of sordid life to which a certain type of woman was condemned. She had no desire to become anyone's mistress. It went against the moral code that she believed in. Besides, she had never even thought of the possibility of marriage without its being indelibly linked to hazy romantic notions of love and a fine upstanding husband.

"My lord, really! I have accepted your apology. There is no need to trouble yourself further," she protested.

She saw that his lordship was not attending to her, having begun to whistle tunelessly and quite cheerfully. Exasperated, she reached out and tugged sharply on his sleeve. "My lord! I have no intention of becoming your mistress, so you may as well have the decency to set me down and allow me to bid you good-bye."

Lord Humphrey threw her an astonished look. "My mistress? What put that maggoty notion into your brain? Miss Chadwick, I intend to marry you at Gretna Green!"

2

UPON LORD HUMPHREY'S announcement, Miss Chadwick, already considerably alarmed, felt that nothing could now rival the turmoil of her emotions. She rather wildly wondered if she shared the carriage with a madman.

However, Miss Chadwick was made of resolute stuff and she did not shrink away from the gentleman now so bent on his driving. She cast a despairing look at the speeding horses and clung tighter to the seat and its rail. In a calm and rational tone she said, "My lord, you cannot have thought. You cannot possibly fly with me to Gretna Green." Her breast swelled with indignation. "Why, we have just met. I have not the least notion of your character, although I can regrettably say that it is much the worse for strong drink. Nor do you have the least notion of who and what I am."

Lord Humphrey barked sardonic laughter. His eyes glittered in the fading light. "I already know that I like you better than Augusta Ratcliffe, and for me that is reason enough to marry you."

"Augusta Ratcliffe?" faltered Miss Chadwick, grasping in appalled comprehension the gist of his lordship's reasoning. "Are you then engaged, my lord?"

The viscount frowned heavily, his eyes still on the surging

team. "No! At least, I suppose you could call it that, might one? It is the most deuced coil that ever I have been in."

Miss Chadwick saw that his lordship was fast sinking into a ruminative reverie. She said gently, prodding, "My lord, if you have promised yourself to this Miss Ratcliffe, then you certainly cannot elope with me. Surely you must see that?"

"I have not promised myself to Miss Ratcliffe. I was never consulted in the least. Our parents did the thing while I stood staring at her in her cradle," Lord Humphrey said bitterly.

"Oh." Miss Chadwick thought she understood the problem. The viscount was suffering from an overweaning sense of honor, and instead of seeing that he must tackle the problem head-on, he was instead reaching desperately for straws and in his inebriated state he had latched on to the ludicrous notion of eloping with her.

As she saw it, she had only to convey to the viscount that he was not obligated to marry the lady that he so obviously detested if he had not actually offered for her. He would naturally be very grateful to her and then no doubt he would sheepishly turn the carriage around and take her safely home. Accordingly, Miss Chadwick bent herself to the task of pointing out the realities to the viscount. "My lord, I gather that you have not actually offered for the lady in question yourself. Am I correct in that assumption?"

The viscount shrugged a brusque assent.

Miss Chadwick smiled as she let out a sigh of relief. "My lord, then you need not wed her. You have only to explain to your parents that you prefer to look about for a bride of your own choosing. I am certain that none but the most tyrannical of parents would actually expect you to make good on a foolish promise exchanged so many years ago. And as for Miss Ratcliffe, she might very well be grateful on her own count to be freed of such an onerous duty."

Lord Humphrey snorted derision. "You don't know Augusta or you would not say anything by half so silly. Augusta has been thinking herself lady of the manor for all of ten years or more, ever since she got her figure. She has turned down scores of offers. She means to have me," he said gloomily. "If I was to cry off as you suggest, the rarest dust-up would be kicked up, and not just by Augusta but also by my parents and my godparents as well."

Miss Chadwick was momentarily silenced. His lordship's misery at the thought of his seemingly unavoidable future was obvious. She said sympathetically, "Oh dear, it is a pretty coil, isn't it? One does hate to be the object of filial displeasure, naturally. I suppose that you cannot appeal to Miss Ratcliffe's finer nature?"

At that Lord Humphrey gave a crack of genuine laughter. He threw an impatient glance at his companion. "Her finer nature! That's rich, by Jove! No, mine is much the better plan. I shall present them all with a *fait accompli*. There cannot be much said once the knot is tied, you know."

Miss Chadwick could think of several things that could be said and none of them either comfortable or complimentary to herself. "My lord, I simply cannot marry you," she said determinedly.

Lord Humphrey looked at her again. There was an anxious expression in his gray eyes. "You have not taken an aversion to me, surely?"

"No, of course not. Why should I?" Miss Chadwick asked, and then she bethought herself of several very good reasons. Her own fine brown eyes kindled with righteous anger. "Though I do not know why I should not, when you have actually abducted me. Yes, and have forced me into an intolerable position where I shall have to explain my tardiness to my host and hostess. Why, I shall be fortunate if they do not condemn me for a forward hussy who actually connived to be run down by your lordship's carriage. Indeed, I shall be fortunate if my reputation survives this adventure intact."

The viscount looked much striken, but then his brow cleared. "No, they won't, for the next time that you have occasion to see them, they will be bowing and scraping and addressing you as 'my lady,' " he said confidently.

A horrible thought struck him. He threw her a stern look. "Mind, I have nothing to say against anyone who is kind enough to take in someone who is a bit down on their luck. But I'll not have a rum set running tame about the place. A visit from these friends of yours once or twice a year is all to which I shall agree. Of course, you may visit them as often as you wish."

Miss Chadwick was pardonably exasperated. "Really, my lord! Mr. and Mrs. Percy are very worthy, but certainly not cut of the same cloth as your own acquaintances. As though I would not have the sense to know that different sorts of company will not mix."

She realized that she had fallen into the trap of sharing in the viscount's delusion. She recovered herself quickly. "In any event, the question shall not arise. I shall not marry you, whatever the state my reputation is left in at your hands," she said resolutely.

The viscount's frown deepened and there appeared a somewhat chilly note in his voice. "I shall not leave you ruined, if that is what you fear. I am no libertine, at least," he said swiftly.

"No, I am sure that you are not. I never meant to intimate such a thing," said Miss Chadwick, appalled by her own inadvertent *faux pas*. She gathered herself together. The viscount had an unaccountable way of rattling her self-possession. She supposed it was because she was unused to the ways of gentlemen and their odd ways of thought. "My lord, I beg you once more. Pray set me down. I should make you a very bad wife, you know. I am not at all fashionable or witty or beautiful."

"I don't want fashion or wit or beauty. I can have all that in Miss Ratcliffe," said the viscount crushingly. He apparently realized that he had not been exactly complimentary. "I say, I do beg your pardon. My tongue seems to run on without my consent. Your features are actually rather pleasing, as I said before. And I am certain that you can be quite witty, since you are something of a bluestocking and all."

"Thank you, I am sure," Miss Chadwick said in a wooden voice.

Lord Humphrey saw that he had deeply offended the lady, and since it was not in his nature to deliberately inflict hurt on another, he attempted to make further amends. "I daresay you would like to be married to me. I am rather plump in the pocket and I wouldn't be stingy with your allowance, you know." He paused to gauge her reaction, and when none was forthcoming, he added, "You could be as extravagant as you chose and I would not breath a word against it. At least I should try not to, at all events."

"Very good of you, I am sure," said Miss Chadwick. She was looking at him now and there was the trace of a smile upon her face.

Encouraged, Lord Humphrey pressed home his point. "And of course there is the advantage of social position. That is what Miss Ratcliffe finds so attractive about me, I suspect. She would eventually be the Countess of Dewesbury and mistress of Dewesbury Court, which is a grand sprawling place. Mind you, I am not all that fond of the older section of the house. It is too damp and dark for my taste, besides being haunted."

"Haunted?" Now Miss Chadwick looked at him wide-eyed. "Surely not!"

"Quite, quite haunted," Lord Humphrey said cheerfully. "Some Tudor ancestor of mine lost his head to the headsman's ax and he has had the bad taste to roam the halls for centuries, his severed head under his arm, while groaning in the most heart-rending fashion."

Miss Chadwick shuddered, her lively imagination calling a vivid vision to her mind. "No, I don't wonder that you do not care for that part of the house." She suddenly recalled the point of their discussion as she watched the last sinking of the sun beyond the hedges. The lateness of the hour brought her renewed anxiety. "I don't care for all that, my lord. Unlike your Miss Ratcliffe, I would be quite content in a small cottage to call my own."

"She is not my Miss Ratcliffe," Lord Humphrey said, revolted.

"I beg your pardon," Joan said meekly, recognizing that she had given grave offense.

"Yes, well." The viscount grudgingly accepted her apology. "I don't care for her overmuch, you see. She treats me much like a pet pug, giving me only an absent pat now and then until she wants something of me," he said by way of explanation.

"How awful. But I know exactly what you mean. I once had a friend—at least, I thought she was my friend. In any event, for a while I was indispensable to her. I was always willing to stand in for her whenever she took it into her head to cast off an old beau in favor of a new one. I was her most trusted confidante and she, mine."

Joan reflected a moment before she sighed. "I was most disappointed in her after my papa died. When I went into mourning, she had not much use for my company. In fact, I did not see her above a half-dozen times after that, and on those occasions it was I who called upon her. I doubt that I was ever missed when I came to stay with the Percys."

Lord Humphrey reached out his gloved hand and put his fingers over her tightly clenched fingers where they curled for purchase under the seat. "You will not be subject to such glaring distress again, I promise you. As my wife, you will naturally be entitled to every comfort."

Joan was shocked by his lordship's intimate gesture, but she was touched as well. It spoke well of his own sensitivity to discern her old hurt and attempt to reassure her. However, she could have wished that his reassurance did not stem from his continued delusion that she was going to wed him. She removed her hand from the warmth of his clasp and reached across herself to grasp the seat railing so that she held it with both hands.

Lord Humphrey felt dimly that something more was called for from himself. He frowned deeply, then his brow cleared. "You did say that you had no objections, Miss Chadwick," he reminded her triumphantly.

"I didn't know what I wasn't objecting to," Joan exclaimed, rather incoherently. His lordship was frowning again, apparently attempting to puzzle out her meaning, and she tried again. "My lord, how can you persist in this foolish notion? Surely you must see that I cannot possibly become your wife. The differences in our stations in life, your own averred commitment to an old family promise, the obvious scandal that must arise out of an elopement—why, sir, the objections against such a union are innumerable. I agree wholeheartedly that it was very bad of your lordship's parents to bind you over to Miss Ratcliffe without inquiring your preferences . . . Well, actually, they hardly could do so if you were indeed in short coats. But it is the height of unwisdom to marry the first available female in order to save yourself from an unwanted connection."

Lord Humphrey laughed recklessly. "Anything is preferable to spending a lifetime with Augusta, my girl."

Miss Chadwick persisted in her efforts to dissuade him, but none of her arguments had the desired effect. Finally she quite lost her temper and she threatened to jump from the carriage if his lordship did not instantly set her down. The viscount rather maddeningly pointed out that she would then have a broken neck in addition to her sprained ankle and he earnestly advised her against such a drastic measure.

Miss Chadwick heaved an exasperated sigh. "I see that you are set on this course and nothing I say will persuade you from it. But at least attend to me this much, my lord. Seek out a lady of your own social standing, one who is compatible to you in ways that I am not by birth or training equipped to become. I beg you, my lord, do think of it."

A mulish set settled across his lordship's countenance. "I

have thought upon it. I consider you most suitable, Miss Chadwick, and to Gretna we shall go.''

She saw that he was not quite rational and she rightfully blamed the strong liquor that he had obviously been privy to. "Then at least think of your horses, my lord. At this rate, you are likely to drive them into the ground," she said with asperity.

Lord Humphrey threw an astonished glance at her. He smiled with what she realized was sincere gratitude. He said in a confiding way, "Damn if I did not give a thought to my cattle. It must be the brandy, you know. I seem not to be as needle-witted as I should be. You are perfectly right, of course. We must switch over the team at some point." He frowned suddenly at the thought. "I had meant to stop over at my estate, but now I quite see that will not do."

"I hardly think that my reputation will suffer much worse than it already has if I was to be seen by your lordship's servants," said Miss Chadwick tartly.

Though she shrank from the obvious conclusions that must be drawn by anyone who chanced to see her in the viscount's company, unchaperoned and her cloak muddied as it was, she was infinitely grateful to know that she would be shortly set down someplace where there would be reasonable ears to hear her request to be taken back to her home.

However, her comforting hopes were swiftly dashed.

"No, it wouldn't do at all to stop there," said the viscount decisively. "Hickham, a proper stiff-rumped butler if ever there was, has known me since the cradle and would instantly send word to the earl and my mother about this escapade, and that would put snuff to it." He nodded. "We'll go to the Swan instead. I have never stopped there, so there is but the slightest chance of running into some acquaintance of my parents' or of my own. It is rather farther than I like for my cattle to travel in one journey, but that cannot be helped at this stage in the game. We should be able to change out my cattle for a decent team that will carry us the remainder of the way."

Joan was all the more convinced of the viscount's inability to reason clearly, though he was showing a remarkable and frightening ability to the contrary when it came to bringing about the conclusion of his fantastic scheme.

Completely talked out, she subsided silently on the seat. She hoped that as the miles passed, his head would clear of brandy fumes and he would finally come to realize the ludicrous nature of his plan.

3

THE CONVERSATION between Miss Chadwick and the viscount never resumed.

The viscount alternated the pace of his team in an effort, Miss Chadwick recognized, to draw out his horses' stamina to the longest possible duration. She hoped that the viscount's uninterrupted reflections were giving his thoughts the desired turn and she held herself as still as possible so as not to divert him.

As the miles unrolled and dusk turned to deep night, Miss Chadwick also had time in which to reflect. Her spirited conversation with his lordship had opened avenues of thought that she had previously repressed, in the knowledge that unfounded hopes would cause her only dissatisfaction.

Her situation was one that was certainly not much to her liking, but seeing no alternative, she had resigned herself to it. Joan knew herself to be ill-suited to go into service. She was far too educated and gently reared to ever fit easily into the hierarchical servants' world. She had thus favored the professions that she had mentioned to his lordship. But now she questioned her own wisdom.

As a young girl, Joan had often entertained the thought of marriage, and like any other young maiden, she had daydreamed of the perfect gentleman with which she would share romantic bliss. But no suitable young gentleman had appeared on her horizon. Certainly she had received a handful of suitors, but none had struck the proper chord with her. Now at one-and-twenty, Joan had quite accepted her spinster status with a matter-of-factness that bespoke intelligence and a healthy grasp of reality. It was that same levelheadedness that had brought her to the unenviable conclusion that she could not remain forever upon the charity of her friends. Instead, she should seek out her own fortunes, and in all likelihood her life would henceforth be spent in the service of others.

However, with the viscount's offer, a fantastic possibility was opened up for her perusal. Joan was not insensible of the incredible changes that would be rendered in her life if she were to take his lordship's intentions seriously. After all, the viscount had taken pains to enumerate some of them, and she could easily envision others. At one stroke, she could exchange the gray servitude and dependence of the governess's life for that of a viscountess.

Miss Chadwick's imagination was an active one, and the visions of luxury and ease that were conjured up for her mind's eyes were dizzying. She was sorely tempted; oh, yes, she admitted that she was most truly tempted to accept his lordship's bizarre offer.

Joan slid a sideways glance at the gentleman seated beside her.

The moon had come up, a great cold orb, making it quite easy for the viscount to see the road. He made use of the silver light by putting his horses along at a comfortable pace.

His lordship's profile was readily defined against the backdrop of the dark hedges sweeping by. The brim of his beaver hat shaded his eyes from her in the uncertain light, but she was easily able to make out his profile. His brow and aquiline nose were well-formed, a pleasing and proper accompaniment to his firmly held mouth and determined chin.

The viscount seemed to feel her regard. He turned his head,

and upon meeting her eyes, he gave a brief smile of acknowledgment before returning his attention to the task of driving.

Miss Chadwick's heart turned over in her breast. There had been genuine warmth and charm in his lordship's fleeting smile. She sighed. The viscount would undoubtedly be an unexacting and pleasant husband. It was a pity that she could not accept his outrageous proposal. For a few moments longer, she allowed herself to toy with the fantasy of becoming the viscount's wife. Her mind whispered that such indulgence could do no harm. Indeed, it would be a pleasant daydream with which to brighten the tedium of her days after she had accepted a suitable post.

Under such reflection and comparison, it was little wonder that the viscount's proposal became steadily more attractive to her. She had already formed a good estimation of his character and his personality. There was nothing to disgust her in either, and certainly what little she had been able to discern of his physical attributes appealed to her, she mused.

Miss Chadwick was appalled by the shocking turn of her thoughts. She could not possibly think of accepting his lordship's ludicrous solution to both their futures. It would be unthinkable to take such advantage of the gentleman.

Nevertheless, by the time that Lord Humphrey turned the phaeton into an inn yard, Miss Chadwick was half-wishing that she had indeed accepted his extraordinary offer. But certainly it was out of the question to take up an offer from a gentleman who was so obviously inebriated and who was therefore not in his proper senses. Miss Chadwick suppressed a sigh. Her renewed resolution left her with a forlorn feeling that she discovered she had difficulty in overcoming.

Lord Humphrey snubbed the reins, calling for an ostler at the top of his voice. When that person emerged from his quarters, rubbing his eyes and yawning, the viscount jumped down from the phaeton. He gave his orders regarding the team before going around the phaeton to offer Miss Chadwick assistance in descending. She practically tumbled into his arms when her ankle would not support her weight.

Joan blushed to the roots of her hair and she was glad of the concealing half-light. "I am most sorry, my lord," she said breathlessly.

"Quite all right, Miss Chadwick," he said formally.

The activity in the small yard had brought out the innkeeper, who alternated between expressions of gratification for his lordship's unlooked-for patronage and his willingness to serve in whatever capacity was within his power.

"Yes, yes," Lord Humphrey said testily.

His head felt as though it was held in a metal vise; yet, despite his suffering, he was quite aware of several things. He held Miss Chadwick firmly against his chest. Her arms were around his neck, doubtless bringing ruin to the excellent folds of his neckcloth, and her warm breath tickled his ear.

He had reason to know that she was trim of figure, but she was no featherweight for all that. What with everything that he had indulged in earlier that day having sapped his strength, and with a pounding head, the viscount was not amused to be kept standing about while some idiot innkeeper flapped his jaw.

His temper acerbated beyond endurance, he snapped, "My good man, do me the service of keeping mum."

Without waiting to see the effect of his rude exclamation, the viscount strode across the yard with his burden, making for the door of the inn.

The astonished innkeeper had instantly complied with the gentleman's wishes. Instead, he took to bowing and scraping with an embarrassing servility as he ushered the viscount and the lady into the inn.

Finally the man could no longer restrain himself and he bleated, "What is his lordship's pleasure? Dinner, perhaps, or a private room?" The man determinedly kept his eyes away from the face of the lady held so closely in his lordship's arms, but his very discretion gave some hint of his thoughts.

Miss Chadwick reddened. She could only hope that the brim of her bonnet hid her renewed embarrassment, but she could not stop herself from an urgent whisper in the viscount's ear. "Pray, put me down!"

Lord Humphrey did not comply. Instead, he regarded the innkeeper with jaundiced eyes. He spoke in his coldest tone. "A private parlor and a late supper, my man, and be quick about it!"

"Aye, m'lord, at once!"

The innkeeper bowed several times, backing away as he did so toward the narrow stairs that led up to the second floor. The viscount followed the contemptible man, making rare work of it as he carried Miss Chadwick upstairs.

Within a very short time Lord Humphrey and Miss Chadwick were ensconced in the best private parlor boasted by the inn. The innkeeper bustled about, a waiter in tow, both carrying serving dishes. Finally the innkeeper pronounced himself ready to serve his distinguished guests with his own hands.

The viscount vehemently rejected the man's suggestion, saying at his most arrogant, "I believe the lady and I are perfectly capable of feeding ourselves." He stared haughtily at the innkeeper and was only satisfied when he saw the door swing shut behind the man's back. "Officious fool," he uttered in contempt.

He turned to Miss Chadwick, whom he had seated on the settee in the parlor. While he dealt with the innkeeper, she had taken the opportunity to remove her cloak and had fluffed her short dark locks with her slender fingers. He saw with a spurt of interest that her figure was as trim as he had suspected it to be when he held her in his arms. He liked her face as well. Her features were regular and her brown eyes expressive and intelligent when she chanced to look up and meet his regard.

With a crooked smile, he inquired, "Shall I carry you to the table, ma'am?"

Miss Chadwick flushed, all too vividly remembering the feel of his arms about her. She said hurriedly, "I do not think that will be necessary, my lord. My ankle is much better."

In proof of her words, she rose, supporting her weight as she did so by holding on to the arm of the settee. But when she incautiously put her foot down to take the first step, she nearly overset with the stab of pain that shot up her leg. "Oh!"

A strong hand slipped under her elbow. "Allow me to escort you to your chair, ma'am," Lord Humphrey said gravely.

Even though the color rose hard and fast in her face again, Miss Chadwick saw the humor in her situation and she swallowed a laugh. If she had been entangled in a romantic interlude, surely her very real handicap would render her completely uninteresting. "Thank you, my lord. That is most courteous of you," she said with matching gravity.

Relying heavily upon the viscount's aid, Joan managed to hobble to the table with a measure of her self-respect preserved. He seated her and she murmured her thanks.

She watched Lord Humphrey go around to the opposite side of the table and drop heavily into his own chair. He wore a deep frown and he passed his fingers tiredly several times over his cleft brows, as though attempting to ease some discomfort.

Joan sympathized but only to a small degree. She had never experienced the aftereffects of strong drink, but she had heard that it was very uncomfortable. Her natural sympathy, however, did not blind her to the very real dilemma that his lordship's overindulgence had placed her in. She asked softly, "Coffee, my lord?"

The viscount glanced across at her from under well-marked brows. His stern expression lightened with the faint smile that flickered across his face. He could think of any number of ladies or gentlemen of his acquaintance who would have obliquely reminded him of his stupidity with a few well-chosen words, if for no other reason than to hold him up to gentle ridicule. His present companion had shown extraordinary forbearance. "Thank you, Miss Chadwick." His voice conveyed more than civil acceptance of a polite gesture of hospitality.

Joan was not certain exactly what the viscount had read into her offer to pour the coffee, but she chose to take his simple words at face value. She was too aware of her own lack of sophistication to pretend skill at divining the gentleman's meaning. She poured coffee for the viscount and for herself.

Miss Chadwick sensed swiftly that the viscount was not in the mood for light discourse, and so she bestowed her attention onto the hastily prepared supper.

She was somewhat surprised to discover that she was hungry. She had been so wrapped up in all that had transpired, as well as her daydreams, that she had not previously realized how hungry she had become. The long drive in the fresh night air had apparently worked on her to good effect. She noticed that the viscount was not behind in doing equal justice to the humble fare of meat pies and braised carrots, shallots, and peas, topped off with a peach tart.

Joan finished before the viscount, and while she toyed with her after-dinner wine, she managed to watch him in an unobtrusive fashion. She took note again of the strength of character in his face, obvious despite his inebriation. He had shed his elegant beaver upon entering the parlor. The hat's shadow had served to disguise him to a certain extent and, she realized, had granted to him more years than he could actually lay claim.

Lord Humphrey was a rather young gentleman and definitely an attractive one, at that. His dark hair was cropped close and crisped about his ears; and his eyes were large and handsomely set above his aquiline nose and firm mouth. The width of his shoulders complimented the perfect cut of his coat and the broad front expanse of white shirt and embroidered waistcoat. Most pleasing of all, whenever his lordship's eyes chanced to meet hers, his gaze, though shadowed with pain, was remarkably steady.

Joan unconsciously sighed and turned her eyes to the fire on the hearth. There was little point in contemplating on what could never be, she thought.

Lord Humphrey looked up at the soft sound. He discovered a pensive expression on Miss Chadwick's face and a sad droop to her mouth as she gazed into the fire. His conscience smote him with unpleasant force. He swirled the remaining wine in his glass. Though he was still possessed of a throbbing head, he had become reasonably sobered by the time he had finished with his repast.

He had indeed had ample time for the reflection that Miss Chadwick had so earnestly wished upon him, and he now rather grimly acknowledged to himself that he had made a pretty coil of it all.

Lord Humphrey was acutely aware of the advantage he had taken of Miss Chadwick. Nay, call it honestly and admit that he had compromised the lady, he thought in self-disgust. He had literally abducted her and carried her off without a regard for the inevitable ruin of her good name.

There was but one way to make amends, he thought.

It was ironic that his honor required him to do the very thing that in his drunken state he had fully intended to accomplish.

Even the Earl and Countess of Dewesbury would find it difficult to dispute the purity of his motives once matters were explained to them. Lord Humphrey grimaced to himself at thought of that particular necessity. And there would still be the issue of Miss Ratcliffe's expectations.

Lord Humphrey's lips twisted. His dilemma regarding that particular lady must take care of itself, he decided. He had not, after all, formally offered for Miss Ratcliffe's hand. If he had already done so, the present situation would have been thrice the *contretemps* that it was and certainly not so easily solved.

The daughter of a viscount, Miss Ratcliffe was a member of the same society as he, and she was aware of that society's rules in matters of honor. He simply had no alternative but to pursue the course that he had so unthinkingly dealt for himself and Miss Chadwick.

Nevertheless, he had a very good suspicion that Miss Ratcliffe would not see it in so reasonable a light. He did not look forward to his reception at the lady's hands when they next met.

4

LORD HUMPHREY set down his wineglass in a decisive fashion. "Miss Chadwick."

She turned her large brown eyes on him, her expression one of mild inquiry. "Yes, my lord?"

It crossed Lord Humphrey's mind that Miss Ratcliffe would have reacted to the present circumstances in a somewhat different manner than had Miss Chadwick. He found it astonishing that there was no hint of anger or disapprobation in either Miss Chadwick's glance or her voice. Such forbearance on her part made it all the more imperative that he put right the rare mull that he had made of things.

"Miss Chadwick, I most humbly beg your pardon. I am at last cognizant of the grave disservice that I have done you this evening," he said gravely. He reached across the table to take her hand.

Joan felt her pulse begin to hammer in her throat. She had not often had such attention paid to her, and it was disconcerting.

"I hope that you may find it in your heart to forgive me, ma'am," he said.

Joan felt tears start to her eyes. She blinked once or twice to clear her sight. So as not to give offense, she ever so gently withdrew her fingers from his light clasp. She knew that it was silly to think so, but when his lordship regarded her just so, what that steady quiet in his eyes, and she felt the warmth of his hand about hers, she could almost believe that he actually cared something for her.

She attempted to make light of the startling things she was feeling. "It has been a rare experience, indeed, my lord. Of course I must forgive you. You have obviously not been quite yourself," she said.

"You are kind, Miss Chadwick, kinder than I deserve," Lord Humphrey said with a twisted smile. He settled back in his chair, his gaze still on her quiet expression.

"I was drunk as a wheelbarrow and I suspect a bit mad as well. I can offer no further excuse for my outrageous conduct. That is done with and cannot be recalled. But the consequences are not," he said. "I have brought ruin upon your head, Miss Chadwick, and for that there can be only one solution. Miss Chadwick, I am obliged to wed you and I hold myself ready to do so at your earliest convenience."

Joan was at once amazed and dismayed, most especially at the sudden leap of her heart into her throat. She stared at the viscount, searching his face for sign of inebriation, but his expression, though frowning, was sincere and his gaze clear and steady.

At last she found her voice. "My lord, we have already discussed this very topic to exhaustion. You have a duty toward Miss Ratcliffe, as you have admitted to me. I do not think the case altered to any degree and—"

"On the contrary, Miss Chadwick," interrupted Lord Humphrey. "Before, you were perfectly correct in your argument. Also, your advice to me that I should not wed the first female to cross my path in order to escape an obligation that I disclosed to you to be an onerous one was quite pertinent at the time. You see, I recall perfectly every word of our conversation. A pity that I did not heed you." He laughed but with little real amusement. "My judgment was clouded, Miss Chadwick. I knew only that I wished to escape and you were fortuitously at hand to serve the purpose.''

"My lord—"

He brushed aside her attempt to interrupt him. "I see now that I acted in an utterly selfish manner, without regard to anyone's wishes but my own, with the result that I have placed myself under a deeper obligation and one that most closely speaks to my honor."

Joan felt her heart beating very fast. "And what is that exactly, my lord?'' she asked in a low voice. Her fingers were trembling and she clasped her hands firmly in her lap where the tremor could not be seen.

Lord Humphrey filled his wineglass. He set aside the bottle and picked up the glass between his long fingers. Swirling the dark wine, he frowned down into it. "You have already spent several hours alone in my company, ma'am. Surely you must realize what that means in the eyes of the world.''

He looked up to meet her eyes and he saw that she did know. He said quietly, "I cannot allow you to bear the dishonor that would be yours were I simply to return you to your friends in the middle of the night, without acceptable explanation. I doubt very much that your friends would be as understanding as you or I would wish."

Miss Chadwick knew that what his lordship said was true. She could not explain away the lost hours. Even if she was believed by the Percys, there would always be that stray doubt that must cloud their perception of her.

Her reputation would inevitably be tarnished, for the tale would become known. Mrs. Percy was a dear soul, Joan thought in despair, but she was also an inveterate gossip. There were the servants to be considered as well. Her absence was undoubtedly already cause for alarm and speculation. If she were simply to turn up safe and whole, but on the viscount's arm, she would discover her name all over the county by week's end. And such tales had a distressing way of following one wherever one might go.

Joan shrank from thought of the sidways glances and

whispers that would forever be cast her way were she to insist that his lordship return her to the Percys. Almost anything would be preferable to that burden, she thought.

The alternative that the viscount outlined was so insidiously tempting, she admitted, half in fear and half in yearning. Already she had been given ample time to compare her own meager plans, which had been borne out of necessity, to what the viscount had offered her while in his drunken state. Her own determinations for her future had come up sadly wanting in the comparison. Whatever else the viscount thought he offered her, as his wife she would have the opportunity of exploring companionship, ease, and hope.

It would be so much easier not to have to endure the shame and the faint hint of scandal that must henceforth attach to her name after this night's escapade. She did not know how far her inclinations had carried her until she whispered, "What of Miss Ratcliffe?"

Lord Humphrey had been watching the various expressions cross her face, and at her question he was surprised to feel himself relax slightly. He had not realized that he had awaited her decision with even the remotest degree of tension.

"You pointed out to me yourself, Miss Chadwick, that unless I formally offer for the lady there is no true binding obligation between myself and her ladyship. The obligation remains but a strong wish of our respective parents until that moment." Lord Humphrey shrugged carelessly. "There will initially be displeasure on all sides for my decision, but I think that eventually our marriage will come to be viewed, if not with enthusiasm, at least with resignation."

Joan made up her mind, and for fear that she would lose her courage if she hesitated even a moment to voice it, she said in an unsteady voice, "Very well, my lord. I shall marry you." She trembled in every limb at her own temerity, but the ceiling did not fall in judgment as she half-expected.

Lord Humphrey left his chair to come around the table. He lifted both of her cold hands and, one after the other, raised her fingers to his lips. He regarded her with a scarce smile. "You have greatly honored me, Miss Chadwick. Thank you."

Joan reclaimed her hands even as the color rose hot in her face. "I suppose that we should continue on our way to Gretna," she said diffidently. She did not know how to act or what to say. It was such an awkward moment and quite unlike what she had imagined it might be to accept an offer for her hand.

At her words, the frown descended once more upon the viscount's visage. "No, it shall not be Gretna this night or any other. We may marry in haste, my dear ma'am, but I shall not have it nosed about that we pleaded our vows over a blacksmith's anvil. A magistrate or a parish priest is the ticket."

"But surely . . . What of the license, my lord?" faltered Joan.

Lord Humphrey's eyes gleamed, irony in their gray depths. "I carry a special license this very moment, my lady. I had meant to have the unpalatable exchange of vows with Miss Ratcliffe take place as soon as possible on the morrow once she had accepted my formal proposal."

"Oh, my," said Joan, quite inadequately.

"Quite." Lord Humphrey laughed, almost cheerfully. "Devil a bit, Miss Chadwick. Her ladyship need never know that I put the license intended for her to such better office. The only possible rub that I see for us now is the matter of age. I am of legal age, being five-and-twenty, but what of you?"

"I am one-and-twenty, my lord," Joan said. A fleeting smile entered her brown eyes. "Quite on the shelf, you see." Her small attempt at humor earned an appreciative smile from the viscount.

Lord Humphrey strode across the parlor. Pulling open the door, he set up a bellow for the innkeeper. The man came running, alarmed.

When the innkeeper learned that his lordship wanted a minister and for what purpose, he was openly astonished.

But almost instantly his expression smoothed. "I shall attend to the matter myself immediately, my lord."

Lord Humphrey bethought himself of another requirement. "The lady should have an abigail to attend her."

The innkeeper bowed. "I shall send up my own daughter at once, my lord." He left quickly on his errands, having already learned that his illustrious guest was short of temper toward any who dared to offer a few superfluous words.

When the innkeeper had left, Joan said, "An abigail, my lord? Surely I have no need of such a person."

"On the contrary, Miss Chadwick. The woman will share your bedroom tonight and lend you countenance when we drive back to my estates in the morning," Lord Humphrey said. He regarded her somberly. "I intend to arrange everything within my power to draw some air of respectability about our runaway marriage, in hopes of confounding some of the flurry of scandal that is certain to arise once it is learned that we have wed, and in such a hole-in-the-wall manner." He smiled at her. "I think that I owe you that much consideration, at least."

"Thank you, my lord." Joan did not know what else to say. She felt it was stupid of her not to have foreseen the same difficulties as the viscount. But then he was member of a much more sophisticated world than was she, she thought. She was indeed grateful to him for considering her feelings and her uncomfortable position.

The abigail who accompanied the returning innkeeper was a buxom country girl. She was rendered speechless by the singular honor of attending to an actual lady. At the viscount's sharp critical glance, she bobbed a quick nervous curtsy and went to stand beside her new mistress.

The innkeeper had the local minister in tow. "I 'ave explained what is wanted, my lord," he said.

"Highly irregular request, sir, if I may humbly say so," the minister said, his considering gaze going from the viscount's countenance to that of the young lady seated at the table. He had dealt with more than one runaway couple

in his time, but this particular pair appeared somewhat older
than had the others. He substantiated that fact with a quiet
question.

There seemed nothing untoward in the relationship between
the couple, the gentleman behaving with all solicitous
propriety in aiding the lady to her feet. The minister noted
that the young woman had a pronounced limp. It spoke well
of the young lord's character for disregarding his intended's
handicap. The minister's natural doubts were laid to rest,
and after assuring himself that the viscount had the proper
license, he proceeded with the brief ceremony.

At the proper time Lord Humphrey pulled the signet ring
off his own finger and slipped it onto Joan's. She had to crook
her finger so that the too-large ring did not slide off.

She was so absorbed by the problem of the ring that she
was caught off-guard when the viscount's lips found hers.
The kiss was fleeting, but nevertheless quite unnerving. She
was blushing fiercely when he drew back.

There was an oddly distant look in his gray eyes as he
looked down at the woman that he had made his wife. He
glanced down at their still-clasped hands and a flicker of
warmth crossed his expression. "I shall get you a proper
ring when there is time," he said.

He turned then to the minister to courteously thank the man
for his services and to amply reward him from his purse.
The necessary papers were signed by the primary parties and
witnessed by the innkeeper and the round-eyed abigail, the
latter thinking that she had never seen anything half so
romantic.

Lord Humphrey requested that two bedchambers be made
ready.

The innkeeper's astonished expression earned the man an
icy inquiry from his lordship regarding the facility of his
hearing. "Not at all, my lord," said the innkeeper hastily,
keeping to himself his opinion of the gentry's way of
arranging matters. "I'll attend to the matter myself."

Within a few moments, Joan and Lord Humphrey were

again alone, the abigail having discreetly retreated into the bedroom directly off the parlor that was to be her ladyship's.

Joan and the viscount stared at each other for several long seconds. They neither could think of anything appropriate to say. At last the viscount offered his arm to her, saying that he knew that her ankle must still be giving her pain. "You must be fatigued as well," he said.

"Yes," Joan agreed as she accepted his escort to the door of the bedroom.

He paused at the door to raise her fingers to his lips. "Good night, my lady," he said quietly.

"Good night, my lord," she said.

Lord Humphrey waited until his bride had entered the bedroom and the door was softly closed before he turned away. As he crossed the parlor and left it to find his own bedroom, his heavily frowning countenance was lent deep shadows by the guttering fire.

5

T HE FOLLOWING MORNING Joan met Lord Humphrey again in the parlor. It was an awkward moment for both of them. They smiled at each other, tentatively, like the strangers that they were, who had been thrown together by a whim of fate.

Lord Humphrey spoke first. "Good morning, my lady," he said diffidently.

"Good morning, my lord," said Joan. She wondered curiously what it would be like to address his lordship by his given name, which she had naturally taken note of during the brief ceremony. She supposed that theirs was not to be a conventional marriage, but still it seemed so awkward to continue calling one's husband "his lordship." But then again, the fact that he was her husband did not seem at all real—rather, some last vestige of her dreaming.

"I hope that you slept well, my lady," Lord Humphrey said stiltedly. He mentally cursed himself for his banality. He could not imagine what had come over him, he who was known for his civil tongue and ease of manner.

"Very well, thank you, my lord."

Joan stared at the viscount, who appeared to her inexperienced eyes as elegant and unruffled as if he had just stepped out from under the hands of his valet. His coat was of an excellent cut across his broad shoulders, his shirt was dazzling white beneath his waistcoat, and his buckskin trousers fit tightly about his muscular thighs before smoothing into the tops of his boots. If there were a few creases in the viscount's coat, if his cravat was a little rumpled from its repeated tying, she did not discern it.

Joan put a nervous hand up to smooth her hair. She felt frumpish. Her gown was wrinkled from the day before, and though she had washed her face and hands and combed her hair before emerging from the bedroom, she felt unkempt and ungainly, and as unlike a new bride as it was possible to feel.

They stared at each other for another lengthened moment. Then Lord Humphrey's ingrained good manners at last took over. He held out his hand to her. "Allow me to seat you, my lady."

She shyly put her fingers into his waiting hand. It seemed perfectly natural to accept his lordship's informal handclasp even though before he had always offered his arm to her. Joan was beginning to understand that several barriers that had marked her position in the world were things of the past.

Lord Humphrey escorted her the few steps to the table, which had already been laid for breakfast, and seated her. He noticed that she did not rely on his support as heavily as she had done the previous evening. As he took his own place across from her, he said, "How is your ankle this morning, my lady?"

"It is much improved, my lord. The abigail wrapped it in wet clothes to reduce the swelling," Joan said. She knew that he could not possibly be interested in such a mundane topic, not when there was so much other to be discussed. She placed her napkin in her lap, a frown pulling her slim brows together.

"What is it, my lady? What is troubling you?"

His quiet question startled her. She looked up quickly. He was regarding her with an alert expression in his fine eyes that she found somewhat disconcerting. The color rose in her face. "I did not know that I was so transparent," she said.

Lord Humphrey smiled slightly. "Perhaps my own doubts and uncertainties make you so, ma'am. We have taken a rather odd turn in the road, I think."

"Yes. That is it exactly," Joan said, with some relief that he understood. She looked at him earnestly. "It seemed much the best thing to do, and yet this morning . . . My lord, what are we to do now?"

"Do, my lady? Why, we shall live out the remainder of our lives in a most companionable and respectable manner. Doubtless we shall have a number of progeny along the way and attend a ghastly number of social functions and generally live up to what is expected of us," he said. He saw that she turned her head away from him and he was instantly ashamed of his own flippancy. "Dash it all," he exclaimed under his breath.

But she heard him. Her brown eyes rose quickly to his, then dropped again to her plate and the meager breakfast that she had served herself.

Lord Humphrey pushed aside his own breakfast untasted, suddenly revuled by the ham and eggs and biscuits that not seconds ago he had been ravenous to taste.

She gave a small jump at the sudden forceful movement and she sent another fleeting glance up at his face.

The viscount sighed. "My dear ma'am, it was not my intention to sound so unfeeling. The truth of the matter is, I am very nearly at a standstill in this business. I do not regard the matter of our marriage itself as the stumbling block, but rather the speculation that must arise because of it. I want to get through the business as smoothly and painlessly as possible, but I do not yet see my way clear as to how it can be done."

"Scandal," she breathed, and nodded. "Yes, I understand that. You have married a nobody, all of a sudden and without announcement, when probably everyone has been expecting you to come up to scratch for Miss Ratcliffe for ages. It will look very bad for you, won't it?"

"Yes," agreed Lord Humphrey, regarding her with some sense of surprise. He had not expected her to grasp his unenviable position so readily, nor had he expected her to restrain her anxieties over her own predicament. But, then, perhaps she did not quite fully comprehend the difficulties and discomforts that she must certainly overcome before she was fully accepted as his legitimate wife, he thought. Voicing his reflections, he said, "I have done you nothing but ill turns since I first ran you down in that lane."

"Oh, I don't know. You talked a great deal of nonsense, of course, but one thing struck me as particularly penetrating." She smiled, inviting him to share in her own gentle amusement. "I would *not* have made a very successful governess. I am too used to having my own freedoms and I fear the charges put upon me in such a situation would have tried my patience most unbearably."

"I am glad to have been of some service, at least," he said, also smiling. But he as quickly sobered. "My lady . . . Dash it all, would you object overmuch if I called you Joan? It is deuced awkward as it is without maintaining a false formality."

"Not at all, my lord," Joan said, her heart picking up speed in that ridiculous way it had suddenly started.

"Good. And I shall be Edward to you, if you please," he said firmly. She inclined her head in acceptance and they shared another smile, this one more open than the one before. "Right. Since that is settled, we must now decide what our course shall be. I thought last night that I would simply take you back to my estates, accompanied by that dratted abigail, of course; but I see now that won't quite do."

"Won't it?"

Lord Humphrey shook his head. "It would seem far more respectable if you were introduced to the household in a less shag-bag manner. The servants will talk regardless, of course, and will pass the tale to members of my parents' household. I'd rather they talk about something else than your lack of baggage and whatnot."

"Oh, I see." Joan bit her lip. She had not thought of that, though it had not been many minutes earlier that she had longed for a change of dress. "I must write the Percys about my clothes and belongings. I suppose that we could not remain here at the inn until my things arrive?"

"Decidedly not," said Lord Humphrey, aghast. "I do not intend to remain in this dismal place a moment longer than necessary."

"Well, then, we must go someplace else. I am open to suggestions, my lord, for I am left totally without family and I have no particularly close friends. At least, none that I would wish to trust to this imbroglio," Joan said. She eyed him hopefully. "Surely you have someone that you may trust? A sister, perhaps, or—"

"You have hit upon it, Joan," exclaimed Lord Humphrey.

He had noticed that she had not made use of his Christian name as he had bade her, but he thought he understood. He was himself experiencing difficulty in adjusting to his status as a married gentleman and the end of his bachelorhood. Already he felt the weight of his new responsibility. It would naturally take time for her to become comfortable with her own changed circumstances. Of course, he had the advantage of her in that he had been prepared that very weekend to wed in any event, he thought with irony.

"I shall take you to my grandmother," he said. "Black-hedge Manor is not far from here and I rather suspect that she will be most happy to take us under her wing. She is a wicked old woman, whose greatest pleasure is pricking the pretensions of others, I think."

"Shall I like her ladyship?" Joan asked, a faint smile curling her lips. The question that had most readily come to mind was whether the viscount's grandmother would like her, but one could not ask that, of course.

"Oh, I don't know. I suspect that you might. She is not given much to airs and talks most readily to nearly everyone. But you shall judge for yourself." He spoke cheerfully and with a note of affection in his voice.

Joan realized that he had a real regard for his grandmother, and that heartened her. She had not understood before how very bereft she was feeling. She had only the viscount's goodwill to rely upon, to guide her and sustain her when she would meet his family, and possibly Miss Ratcliffe.

She suspected that she would not be allowed to forgo the latter doubtful pleasure if matters were indeed as the viscount had related to her. She had gathered a fair notion of both Miss Ratcliffe's physical attributes and her character from what the viscount had said of the lady: She was beautiful, arrogant, spoiled, and willful. Joan did not think that she would care for the lady and she knew with certainty that Miss Ratcliffe would despise her.

Joan had also formed a guarded opinion about the Earl and Countess of Dewesbury. She hoped that the viscount's inebriation and his natural depression had misled him in explaining his parents to her; otherwise, she had a shrewd notion that her own addition to the family would never be quite accepted.

As for the viscount's grandmother, she rather liked what his lordship had said about the lady. She was herself of a quiet and, on occasion, of a retiring nature. Joan had always admired the natural vivacity of others and what she regarded as the admirable quality of social polish. It was something that she had never had a true opportunity to develop.

As the vicar's daughter, she had naturally been invited to various neighborhood dinner parties and other social events, but she had always been of a small flock of young ladies and she had not thought that she had stood out in any way. It was for that reason that she had been astonished and humbled that the reigning beauty of the neighborhood had singled her out for particular attention.

She had thought over the matter for some time before voicing her puzzlement to her father. "I do not understand why Clarissa seems so taken with my company, Papa.She is not near so friendly with the other girls as she is to me," she had said.

Her father had regarded her with a gentle smile in his eyes. "My dear child, I wish that I could say with honesty that this friendship has come your way due solely to your admirable qualities. But I think you to be too intelligent to believe me."

Joan had sighed, for her father had but underscored her own suspicions. "Clarissa uses me for a foil and, I think, a diversion for those beaux that she does not wish to encourage."

"Yes, child, I fear that is so."

"But I do not mind it so very much," she had said quickly. "I do have such fun when I am with her. Clarissa can dazzle and entertain everyone about her in such a way that I would be most sorry not to be one of her circle."

The vicar had frowned slightly. "I hope that you will not be terribly disappointed if her friendship for you proves fickle in the end, child."

She had jumped up and kissed him lightly on the top of his balding head as he sat in his favorite chair. "Oh, no, how could I be? I have my eyes open. And I have more faith in Clarissa's good nature than you appear to have, dear Papa."

But Joan had been disappointed, and bitterly so. She had discovered that along with her father's death had died her own small claims to gentle society. Without guardian, without dower or inheritance, she had become a charge upon the parish and hardly one whom a young lady of pretension wished for as a companion. Her friend Clarissa had made it plain in a not-to-subtle fashion that she was no longer the welcome companion that she had once been.

Joan also discovered that her assumption that she would have any number of places to choose from in which to reside was false. The vicar had easily been a favorite among the county's small society and Joan had expected to be able to remain in the neighborhood. She received kindness and sympathy from her father's parishioners, but none had come forward to offer her a permanent place in their home.

Times were difficult and the charge of a young woman, who was neither family nor servant, would be a burden on any household. Those whose minds the notion did cross were reluctant to voice their impulse, for once the offer was made, it could not possibly be withdrawn.

None harbored dislike for Miss Chadwick; on the contrary, she had always been a welcome addition to any informal dinner party or romp for the young people. But that was quite a different thing from providing for a young woman until she married or her future was otherwise settled.

Joan realized fully the loneliness of her position when she had gone to visit her father's gravesite a bare two weeks after his untimely death. It had been a cold day, the sky a harsh gray and threatening more snow for that evening. The grave was covered in icy white crystals and against the snow someone had pressed a wreath of holly and bright-red berries.

She stared at the fresh greenery and suddenly started to cry. It was like a wellspring was released. She had stood quite motionless, the tears sliding down her wind-bitten cheeks, and between her sobs she had gasped in the cold searing air.

When it was over, she had known quite clearly that she could no longer remain in the neighborhood. She had been allowed to stay in the small house that she and her father had thought of as home, but before many more weeks were out, there would be engaged a new vicar who would require the house for himself and his family.

Her naiveté had led her to assume that she would quickly establish herself and make herself useful in one of the many households that her father had served. That comfortable invitation had not materialized, and she saw no reason why the offer should come now.

Joan had walked back to the parish house, meeting above half-a-dozen acquaintances on the way. Her heightened senses had enabled her to see what she had been previously blind to: she was greeted with courtesy and sympathy, but there was a hint of embarrassment and hurry as well. Her

continued unaided presence in the neighborhood was a
reproof to the vicar's flock and one that they could
undoubtedly do without.

That evening Joan had written the Percys, who could at
least be depended upon to shelter her for a time. When she
had received their reply, she had boarded the mail coach
without fanfare or the well wishes of one whom she had
thought to be her friends. Thus she had left the only home
that she had ever known and taken the first step toward an
unknown destiny, her naïveté tempered and her eyes more
discerning.

Now as she thought over and weighed what her reception
might be at the hands of the viscount's various family
members and his acquaintances, she decided that she would
vastly prefer meeting his grandmother first. Perhaps, if the
lady was anything as the viscount had painted her, she would
be able to gather to herself the courage that she would need
to face the others' certain disapproval.

Lord Humphrey had watched the various expressions cross
her face. He had held his tongue, content to eat his breakfast
in the silence of her reflections. He had also watched the
dainty way in which she ate her own meal, approving of a
natural grace of movement and a lack of greed in her
manners. When she seemed to halfway nod to herself,
he decided it was an appropriate time to bring her back to
an awareness of her surroundings. "A penny for them."

Joan looked up at the viscount. Her husband, she corrected
herself. She must begin thinking of him in such terms or the
whole thing would become a hopeless mess. "I was but
thinking of meeting your grandmother, and the rest. I feel
very uncertain of my reception, you see. And I do not think
that I shall enjoy making Miss Ratcliffe's acquaintance at
all," she said.

She had a gift for frank expression, he realized. Lord
Humphrey smiled in recognition of it. "I do not think that
she will enjoy making your acquaintance, either," he said
ruefully and just as frankly.

Her eyes widened and then narrowed in amusement. "I had not thought of it in just that way," she admitted. "How wonderful. I shall not be totally out of water, then."

Lord Humphrey found that uproariously funny and he laughed hugely. "Indeed! I almost look forward to seeing the look on the lady's face," he said, still grinning.

Joan smiled at him, quite genuinely pleased that she had made him laugh. She brushed her mouth with her napkin and set it beside her emptied plate. "I am quite ready to go, my lord, if you are."

"That is my girl," he said approvingly.

He was already rising and so he did not see the swift tide of color that rose in her face. He did not give a thought to his careless endearment or how she might perceive it. Her reaction would have surprised him very much.

The shot was paid and the viscount's own team was reengaged to his phaeton. The viscount solicitously handed up Joan, who took her place in the middle of the seat, while next to her settled the overawed abigail.

The viscount climbed up to sit beside his bride and took up the leather traces. "We shall be at my grandmother's manor house in time for tea," he said cheerfully. He cracked the whip and they were off, bowling out of the inn's small yard onto the road.

6

AT BLACKHEDGE MANOR the viscount's grandmother was experiencing a distinct ennui. She reclined in her favorite chair beside the library fire. A small glass of sherry was easily at hand on the occasional table beside the chair and her feet were comfortably ensconced upon a hassock close to the heat.

Lady Cassandra was two-and-seventy and had once been a great beauty. Time had not dimmed the classic bones of her face, nor the elegance of her movements. Her long fingers drummed on the tabletop as she thought over the contents of the long and involved letter that she had dropped onto her lap with a grimace of distaste. As usual, her daughter the Countess of Dewesbury had managed to bore her to frustration with her crossed and underscored verbiage.

Not for the first time, her ladyship wondered what had she ever done to deserve such a smug, gossipy, and utterly dutiful daughter. She would vastly have preferred a little eccentricity to have cropped up in one of the five children that she had borne, but such had never materialized in any of them and they had all established themselves quite credibly with not one black sheep to tar the family name or give the rare family gatherings a little glitter.

Lady Cassandra was not one to dwell on the vagaries of

life, however. She had long ago become resigned to her own children's lack of imagination and their dull choices of spouses. In recent years she had turned her interested eyes onto the upcoming generation; there were one or two of her numerous grandchildren who had displayed signs of the flaring passion that she had so yearned to see in her own disappointing children.

Her thoughts returned to the subject of the countess's letter, which was the upcoming announcement of the young viscount's nuptials to a very worthy young lady. Lady Cassandra grimaced again, knowing very well what the phrase "a very worthy young lady" meant to her daughter. Undoubtedly the unknown young lady was of good family, socially accomplished, at least of passable looks, and well-dowered. And just as undoubtedly, *I shall detest the girl,* thought Lady Cassandra dourly.

She dispassionately considered what she remembered of her grandson, Lord Edward Charles Peregrine Humphrey, viscount, heir to the earldom and to several estates, whom she had not seen in several months. She was not impressed with what she recalled. Certainly he was a handsome-enough young gentleman, and very correct in his manners and his dress.

She snorted, thinking that it could not be otherwise when the boy's parents were such a stodgy, worthy pair. There was not an ounce of life in the boy, obviously, since she could not bring to mind a single thread of scandal that had ever been attached to his name. And now the viscount was to marry the bride that had been chosen for him twenty years before.

Lady Cassandra decided that she would write her man of business and attach a new codicil to her most recent will, to whit, that her grandson Lord Humphrey was to be deleted from inheritance. Thus far there were nine other such codicils, each bearing the name of one of her dull descendants. At the rate that she was going, she would have the entire company weeded out before ever she expired.

The thought both angered and saddened her, but she stiffened her spine. "So be it, then! I shall leave everything to the gardener or my horse and hounds. At least they show a little passion for life and an interest in the changing of the seasons," she announced tartly to the fire.

The library door opened. Lady Cassandra's butler cleared his throat, but he could not quite disguise the astonishment in his voice. "My lady, Lord Humphrey and . . . a young lady."

Lady Cassandra slewed in the chair to look around it, her fingers digging into the arm for purchase. "Heh? What's that, Carruthers?"

She watched in astonishment as her grandson, Lord Humphrey, and an unknown lady came through the door and approached her. They paused in front of her chair, obviously not quite certain of their reception. They stood quite close together and he held his hand protectively over hers where she clutched his arm.

Lady Cassandra did not even look around at the butler, so riveted was her curiosity. "You may go, Carruthers."

Lord Humphrey waited until the door had closed behind the butler. Then he drew forward his companion. "My lady, I should like to present to you my wife," he said defiantly.

Lord Humphrey's head was raised at a proud angle and his grey eyes held an unwavering challenge that Lady Cassandra instinctively recognized and thrilled to. Her ladyship's glance snapped instantly to the young woman's face. The girl appeared anxious, but she was proud, too, thought Lady Cassandra as a glowing warmth that had nothing to do with the fire spread over her.

Lady Cassandra smiled. She eased back against her chair cushions. "A runaway marriage, I perceive. My dear young sir, I never expected it of you."

The viscount flushed. But his steady gaze did not waver. "My bride, Lady Joan Dewesbury. My lady, Lady Cassandra Catherine Wilmot-Howard, my grandmother."

"I am happy to make your acquaintance, my lady," said the young woman.

Lady Cassandra's hearing was acute. She could detect the slightest nuances in the most casual of comments and with accuracy skewer the speaker with an astonishing insight. Now in the new viscountess's voice she thought she heard a quaver of nervousness, but still, the girl's voice was well-modulated and well-bred. "I hardly think so, my dear child," she murmured dryly.

She was pleased to see that swift color rose in the girl's face, betokening a proper understanding of the unusual circumstances. Lady Cassandra's eagle eyes swept over the girl's modest gown. The merino was decently cut, albeit untidily creased. Its respectable brown shade was most becoming to the girl's unremarkable looks, especially the rare rose that still brushed her cheeks. It crossed Lady Cassandra's mind to wonder why her grandson had not chosen a dazzler rather than this particular young woman, and her curiosity became even more heightened.

There was nothing of the vulgar about the girl, decided Lady Cassandra, and she became quite prepared to receive her grandson's unheralded bride with grace.

She smiled warmly and stretched out her hand. Responding instinctively, the girl put out her own hand and Lady Cassandra took it, drawing the girl toward her. She noticed immediately and with great amusement that upon the girl's slender finger was a heavy and overlarge signet ring, which had been made to fit by the knotting of a tiny square of handkerchief through and through the band. "My dear, you must be tired. Pray sit next to me on this chair," she said graciously, nodding at the chair situated closest to her own.

As her newest granddaughter obeyed her, she turned her head to the viscount and her voice sharpened. "Edward, you may sit there, opposite me, where I may keep a close eye on your countenance while you tell me the whole of this pretty tale. Be forewarned that I shall accept nothing less."

Lord Humphrey flushed again, rather resenting his grand-

mother's attitude but knowing full well that he could hardly
have expected different. As it was, he thought the old lady
had already been remarkably forbearing in her reception of
his bride after the shock that the announcement must have
been to her. Nevertheless, it was not the most comfortable
of positions that he had ever found himself in. "I had not
intended to give you anything but the complete truth,
Grandmama," he said tightly.

Lady Cassandra smiled slightly, the expression in her eyes
mocking him. "Of course you would not. You have always
been circumspect beyond belief," she said.

She was surprised at the flash of temper that crossed her
grandson's face, quickly controlled and smoothed away, and
she wondered suddenly just how thoroughly she had
misjudged the young viscount. She had taken for granted that
he was as correct and as worthy as his parents, never having
seen or heard anything to the contrary. But on the very
evening that she had been reading that he was to wed a young
lady chosen for him, he had come to her with an altogether
different bride in tow.

The unexpected occurrence had quite dispelled Lady
Cassandra's previous feeling of ennui. It quite made one
wish to celebrate, she thought expansively.

With the warm thought in mind, Lady Cassandra inclined
her head in apology to her grandson. "Forgive me, Edward.
You have caught me unaware, but of course I must hear you
out. We shall speak of it over tea, I think." Overlooking
the stunned expression that crossed her grandson's face at
her uncharacteristic apology, she picked up the tiny silver
bell on the occasional table and rang it vigorously.

Carruthers came at once to inquire her ladyship's wishes
and bowed in understanding when she had delivered herself
of several orders, which included not only the serving of tea
but her request to see that bedchambers should be made ready
for her unexpected guests and other provisions for their
comfort. He left again, the door closing softly behind him.

Lady Cassandra turned back to her companions. She was

amused to note that the viscount's eyes had become wary in expression. "Well, Edward? I am waiting for enlightenment."

Lord Humphrey rather reluctantly realized the moment of truth had come. His black brows knit as he thought how best to proceed, and he said slowly, "It is not a tale that reflects well upon myself."

"Nor upon me, I fear," said the viscountess swiftly. She colored when Lady Cassandra turned arching brows and a politely inquiring look upon her.

"You are entirely blameless, Joan," the viscount said, swiftly.

"No, I allowed myself to be seduced by—"

"Seduced! My dear, you shock me profoundly," said Lady Cassandra.

Realizing her mistake, Joan flushed fiery red, then turned pale. Her dark eyes were huge in her face. "No, no! I did not mean seduced in *that* sense, my lady."

"What other sense is there?" asked Lady Cassandra, shrugging carelessly. "Unless, of course, you meant that you did the seducing. I must tell you that in most circles that does indeed reflect very badly upon you, my dear." She did not voice that her own attitudes were more liberal, given that those same beliefs had been molded by a somewhat lurid period of her own past.

The viscount was out of his chair in an instant and planted himself beside his obviously discomfited wife. He laid his hand reassuringly upon her shoulder. Lady Cassandra was astonished by her grandson's protectiveness, but even more so when the girl's hand stole up to meet the comfort of his fingers. The unconscious gesture was most telling, she reflected thoughtfully, and she wondered how long the relationship had been in existence. She felt a sneaking admiration for her grandson, who had apparently learned virtue of discretion very well indeed, for there had not even been a whisper of what had so obviously been in the wind.

Lord Humphrey's gray eyes glittered like cut glass. "You

deliberately misunderstand, Lady Cassandra. There has been no seduction. I persuaded my lady to marry me through unfair means, which she believes that she should have resisted. That's all.''

"And these . . . persuasions, Edward? What were they?'' asked Lady Cassandra silkily. Her eyes had become oddly cold, mirroring her sudden suspicions. She would not have dishonor in the family. If her grandson had done aught to coerce the girl, she would instantly establish herself the girl's protectoress.

"I was drunk. I abducted Miss Chadwick, with the intention of carrying her off to Gretna Green,'' he said brutally.

His grandmother was rather taken aback. It was not quite the distressing revelation that she had steeled herself against; on the contrary, it was quite the opposite. "And had not Miss Chadwick a word to say against this disgusting and high-handed behavior?'' Lady Cassandra asked.

The viscount's lips twitched. "She had several words to say, actually,'' he said ruefully. "But I refused to listen to any of her sensible arguments.''

"No, you did not. However—and it is most reprehensible of me—I did hearken to yours,'' said Joan, glancing up at the viscount with the faintest of smiles on her face. She turned her gaze onto the formidable elderly lady who was regarding her and the viscount so steadily. "I fear that I was not stalwart enough to brave the censure that the time I had spent in his lordship's company would cause for me, my lady. That was the full sum of it, that and that his lordship offered me a far more comfortable future than I had ever contemplated.''

Lady Cassandra was intrigued. "And what had you contemplated, my dear?''

"She was applying to become a governess,'' said Lord Humphrey forcibly. "I told her that she wouldn't last a fortnight, of course. No, Joan, not a word. I've already pointed out that how many languages one speaks has no bearing on the case at all. The plain truth is, my lady, is that Joan is out of the common way attractive. She would have run foul of some lecherous son of the house, and that would have been the end of it.''

"So you naturally decided to save Miss Chadwick from her ghastly fate and carried her off in a most improper fashion,'' said Lady Cassandra, nodding as though in perfect understanding. She raised her brows as she looked over at her grandson's bride, and she asked in a conspiratorial tone, ''My dear, was he too awfully under the hatches?''

''If by that you mean was his lordship the worse for drink and horribly obstinate and unreasonable, why, yes, my lady,'' Joan said, a twinkling light dawning in her brown eyes.

Lord Humphrey cleared his throat, distinctly uncomfortable. ''As to that, I do admit to being four sheets to the wind. Otherwise I would not have run down Miss Chadwick in the road and gotten the notion to marry her at all. Why, I couldn't have, never having met her before.''

''Ran her down! Do I understand you correctly, Edward?'' asked Lady Cassandra. She looked sharply at the young woman seated in the chair beside her, searching for sign of injury.

Joan laughed, shaking her head. ''I was not at all hurt, my lady. At least, it was only my ankle, and it is very much better. I think I was more shaken than anything. I then became quite angry when I realized that his lordship had no intention of letting me down again, so that I quite forgot all about being tossed into the ditch.''

The door to the library opened and Carruthers entered with the tea tray. He approached silently and set out the tea urn and the biscuits.

Lady Cassandra gave a contented sigh. There was a smile in her gray eyes, so like the viscount's own in shape and color. ''I think that I really must hear everything from the beginning. Will you pour, my dear?''

7

LADY CASSANDRA listened closely to the story that she was told. She could accept the account of a chance meeting. Stranger things could occur, as she well knew. However, she thought there was one glaring inconsistency to the narration. "You simply chanced to have in your pocket a special license, Edward?" she asked with exaggerated politeness.

"Er, yes," Lord Humphrey said. He had thought it wisest not to mention the reason behind his journey down from London, but with his grandmother's question he saw instantly how unlikely it was that he should happen to be carrying a special license. He cursed himself for not anticipating it, but he did not offer further explanation. He was strangely unwilling to reveal what to him was the worst part of the entire matter, which had been his drunken conviction that he had to wed in order to escape the detested betrothal agreement to Miss Augusta Ratcliffe.

Joan noticed that Lord Humphrey had glossed over the reason why he had originally insisted upon wedding her. However, she could hardly blame him for being reluctant to appear at any worse disadvantage in his grandmother's eyes. The fact of the hasty marriage was bad enough.

With that one exception, the viscount relayed all of what had led up to the unusual marriage, aided at different times by Joan's soft comments and clarifications.

"So you see, Grandmama, I had to bring Joan to you," said Lord Humphrey.

In the course of his narration, the viscount had risen from his chair and taken a restless turn about the space before the fire. He stood now at the mantel, the reflected heat of the flames casting a ruddy glow over his lean cheeks as he awaited his grandmother's final judgment. He studied her face for clues to what she was thinking, unavailingly. However, if he had been privy to Lady Cassandra's thoughts, he would have been surprised.

Lady Cassandra was very much entertained, though she took care not to allow her amusement to show. It was such a dreadful imbroglio, after all, and one must pretend suitable shock and sobriety. But for all of her somber expression and quiet words, she had experienced quite a burgeoning of affection for her grandson that she had never before thought possible. The young viscount had inherited some dash and spirit, and he was fast becoming one of her favorites.

As for the viscountess, formerly Miss Joan Chadwick, Lady Cassandra approved of her as well. The girl was unworldly, yet at times unexpectedly percipient, and she, too, had a bit of backbone in her. The match would do very well indeed, thought Lady Cassandra, and it was infinitely preferable to the one arranged for the viscount.

Lady Cassandra, without ever having met Miss Ratcliffe, had taken an unreasonable and hearty dislike to that young lady.

The first words that Lady Cassandra spoke were quite different from what Lord Humphrey had hoped for, dismayingly so.

"Edward, before your surprising arrival this afternoon I was reading a letter from the Countess of Dewesbury," said Lady Cassandra. She began to peel an apple with a small sharp knife, her full attention apparently focused upon the task.

Lord Humphrey exchanged a quick glance with Joan. He said quietly, "Indeed, Grandmama? And did my mother chance to convey anything noteworthy?" His lordship's query was casual enough, but the tone of his voice reflected his keen interest in the answer.

Lady Cassandra waved the knife in a vague fashion. "My daughter's letters never fail to bore me to tears. She crosses and recrosses the pages in such an incoherent manner that I am vexed beyond bearing at times."

Lord Humphrey visibly relaxed. He smiled in a reassuring fashion at Joan, who returned it with a quick smile of her own.

"The countess did relate one interesting tidbit, however, and that was that you were shortly to announce your engagement to a very worthy young lady by the name of Miss Augusta Ratcliffe." Lady Cassandra paused in the cutting of her apple as she cast a glance toward her two dismayed companions. "I presume that you are not actually getting up a harem, Edward?"

"Of course not," exclaimed Lord Humphrey, pardonably exasperated.

"Then you shall explain how it is that you have married, however honorbound you were to do so at the time, of course, when you are secretly betrothed to another," Lady Cassandra said blandly. She looked at Joan. "You knew of Miss Ratcliffe, of course."

Joan flushed slightly. "Yes, my lady."

She did not offer further explanation, nor did she attempt to defend herself, which Lady Cassandra liked her for. Nevertheless, Lady Cassandra shook her head and clucked her tongue in a show of disapproval.

"I told Joan of Miss Ratcliffe. She very rightly declined my offer of marriage in deference to my previous obligation," Lord Humphrey said harshly, not liking the inferred slur on a lady whom he considered innocent of any wrongdoing. He eyed his grandmother. The proud look had returned to his cold gray eyes.

"How very sporting of you, my dear," murmured Lady Cassandra.

Lord Humphrey practically ground his teeth. "That obligation was never formally acknowledged by myself to Miss Ratcliffe," he said sharply. "According to the agreement made between my father and Lord Ratcliffe on the day of Augusta's birth, I was to offer for her hand when I reached five-and-twenty and thus further strengthen a long and dear friendship between my parents and my godparents."

"Idiots all," said Lady Cassandra without heat. She had heard the story once years before, when her daughter had conveyed the information in that maudlin sentimental way that always set up Lady Cassandra's back.

On that occasion, she recalled, she had reacted with such acerbity that the pretty tale had never been referred to again in her presence. Naturally, that accounted for the length of the explanation in the countess's letter to remind her of the circumstances behind the viscount's upcoming nuptials. But the viscount had put a firm oar of his own into the serene waters and that must roil the depths just a bit.

Lady Cassandra took note of her grandson's expression of astonishment. "Did you assume that I would condone such sentimental claptrap? How little you know of me, my boy." She reflected a moment. "And how little I know of you, I have discovered, and much to my chagrin." She shrugged. "But that is neither here nor there. What must be decided is how we shall go on."

"We, Grandmama?" asked Lord Humphrey, hardly daring to hope that he had found an ally, after all. He left the mantel and went to perch comfortably on the arm of a chair.

Lady Cassandra fixed him with a withering stare. "You are perhaps becoming deaf at your tender years, Edward?"

Lord Humphrey grinned. "No, Grandmama. I brought Joan to you in just such hopes of your understanding. I wish to spare her as much embarrassment as possible, despite the odd circumstances.''

Lady Cassandra nodded in satisfaction. She turned to her grandson's bride.

Joan had sat quietly by, her somber regard turning from one to the other of her companions as they spoke. Her gaze now fixed on Lady Cassandra's face as she waited to hear what the grand lady would say to it all. Her heart beat rather fast with her nervousness. She sternly reminded herself that she must bear whatever was decided, for with the viscount's ring and the exchange of vows between them, she had accepted as well whatever difficulties must arise.

''My dear, we must contrive a plausible story for you. I agree with Edward that scandal must be avoided at all costs. A runaway marriage is not at all the thing, even in more informal circles than ours. It will be best to cover up the very existence of the marriage,'' said Lady Cassandra.

Joan was completely taken aback by her ladyship's verdict. Though she had thought that she could expect resistance and even unfriendliness, she had never dreamed that Lady Cassandra would actually repudiate her. Casting an appalled glance at the viscount, she saw that he was equally stunned.

''What are you about, Grandmama?'' Lord Humphrey asked. His gray eyes had darkened. He said softly, ''I'll not deny my wife.''

Joan cast his lordship another swift, startled glance. The iron determination in his voice gave her a strange, fluttering feeling deep within her.

''I am not asking you to compromise your honor, Edward,'' said Lady Cassandra tartly. ''Exercise a bit of patience, I pray you. Joan, when you arrive at Dewesbury, you shall be engaged to my grandson.''

Joan looked at Lady Cassandra, struggling to make sense of her ladyship's convolutions. She shook her head in defeated bewilderment. ''Engaged, my lady? But why?''

''That is ridiculous. I cannot conceive how a bogus engagement will aid matters in the least," Lord Humphrey said impatiently.

"Can you not, Edward?" asked Lady Cassandra sardonically. As his lips parted, she threw up her hand in a commanding fashion. "No, allow me to finish before you leap forward with all sorts of objections. A runaway marriage cannot simply be swept under the rug, my dears, no matter with what amount of discretion it is handled. The announcement of your hole-in-the-wall marriage will cause quite an upset within the family, and the particulars must at some point involve public scandal. It is simply too delicious a story to be kept close in the bosom of one's family. I can easily bring to mind at least three relations who would spread the tale with all speed, though naturally with appropriate expression of horror and piety. It would be disastrous."

Lord Humphrey was brought up short by his grandmother's comprehensive observations. "Aye," he agreed gloomily.

Joan glanced fleetingly at him. She thought that he must already be regretting his noble impetuosity toward her and it was an unbearable thought. She owed his lordship so much already. "What then do you propose by this false engagement, my lady?" she asked quietly.

Lady Cassandra smiled at her approvingly, liking the young woman's practical air. "Why, only that you shall arrive at Dewesbury as the viscount's well-bred intended rather than his hurriedly acquired wife. I do not think that it would be wise to allow it to be believed that you married as a means to escape Miss Ratcliffe's pretty hands, Edward."

At that statement, the viscount gave a sardonic crack of laughter. "Devil a bit. That is not far off the mark," he said.

Joan lowered her eyes, gazing unseeingly at her folded hands. She was surprised at how jarringly the viscount's acknowledgment struck her. Suddenly she began to see the whole picture from a slightly different angle than before.

But surely his lordship had meant it when he had said that his honor demanded that he should shield her from scandal.

Surely she was seen by his lordship as more than a convenient excuse out of a distasteful alliance.

Surely her own motives were not so despicably mercenary as she now peceived them to be.

Thoughts of honor and cowardice swirled before her mind's eye—whether hers or the viscount's, she could not discern.

Lady Cassandra was speaking again. "We shall insert a modest announcement in the *Gazette* so that the engagement will have formal and public recognition, not easily to be ignored, you see. You, my erring grandson, will have the opportunity to smooth over matters between your parents and Lord and Lady Ratcliffe concerning the outdated agreement involving yourself and Miss Ratcliffe. And Joan shall have an opportunity to win over the family to herself without the hostile consternation that an immediate announcement of your marriage would visit upon her head. In a few months' time, there will be a proper wedding and the earl and my dear daughter need never know of the runaway match."

Lord Humphrey had listened first with skepticism but then with growing admiration and enthusiasm. "Ma'am, it is a brilliant scheme! Everything will seem to be aboveboard and quite respectable. The family shall take an engagement much easier than the dreadful draft that a runaway marriage would be to their consequence. We shall not have a whiff of scandal."

He did not say so, but he was greatly relieved. It had weighed more heavily on his conscience than he cared to admit that in order to do the honorable thing by Joan, he had to face the prospect of gravely wounding his parents and exposing them to the most distasteful of scandals.

But now he thought that with a little luck and a silver tongue he might come off better than he deserved. His godparents were fond of him, he knew, and he thought that he would be able to bring them around as well. Then all would be comfortable and his wife need not go through the crucifying that she must otherwise endure.

The image of Miss Ratcliffe's lovely face floated through his mind. Though he dreaded the scenes with his parents and godparents, he nevertheless was certain that he would vastly prefer to face their condemnations and protestations than those of his former intended. Miss Ratcliffe had a peculiar talent for flaying him alive, and in the past his only recourse had been to walk away. His position as her future spouse had left his hands tied in his dealings with her.

He quite suddenly realized that it no longer mattered what Miss Ratcliffe thought or desired. The fact of his marriage—his engagement, he amended to himself—changed matters dramatically. He was a free man at last. He grinned faintly to himself with an edge of anticipation.

"What is it that you find so amusing, Edward?"

Lord Humphrey looked up to find that his grandmother was regarding him with sharpened eyes. His smile broadened. "I fear that I am somewhat a villain at heart, Grandmama."

Lady Cassandra was on the point of pursuing the interesting point when Joan made a startling announcement.

"I am most sorry, my lady. But I do not think that I can be a party to this scheme, after all."

8

JOAN'S QUIET, strained voice fell into a well of silence as both Lord Humphrey and her ladyship stared uncomprehendingly at her.

"Heh? What are you saying, child," exclaimed Lady Cassandra in open astonishment. Whatever was the chit thinking of? She had concocted the perfect plan to scotch any scandal and enable the ungrateful girl to slip into the family circle with little opposition.

The fact that the scheme would also shake up Lady Cassandra's fine stuffy relations and throw a few mild fireworks into the midst of them was beside the point.

Her own amusements were secondary, Lady Cassandra thought piously. It was her grandson's future that she must preserve and protect. She would not have it, she thought with icy determination. The girl would do as she was bid and that would be the end of it.

Lord Humphrey caught his wife's dark eyes with his own steady gaze and held them. "What troubles you, my lady?" he asked quietly.

Lady Cassandra caught back the scathing question she would have uttered. She waited to hear how her grandson might fare in handling his bride, for it would be far better that the girl's recalcitrance be curbed by her lawful husband.

Joan had watched the cold imperiousness come over Lady Cassandra's face. It was with relief that she heard the viscount's reasonable tone. When she turned to him, she found the willingness to understand in his eyes. The thought fleeted through her mind that he had never really been impatient or cold toward her—an extraordinary thing, considering how they had been thrust together by circumstance.

"I can't but wonder what my dear papa would have said at such deception," she said. Without realizing that she neglected to do so, she did not make clear that the ambivalence of her feelings toward the viscount and her position as his wife were the crux of the matter, not the false engagement that had been proposed. She knew that as a minister her father would have deemed falsehood in a relationship of the gravest import. The marriage that she and his lordship had embarked upon in such a bizarre a fashion was surely a deception of the highest order on each of their parts.

Joan anxiously watched his lordship's face. "I wonder if perhaps it has all been a dreadful mistake. I should not have been so cowardly, nor succumbed so easily to temptation. I see that now. My lord, you should have a wife worthy of your position, and one whom you love." She faltered, then rallied. "But it is not too late. An annulment can be had, can it not?"

Joan glanced at Lady Cassandra, who sat regal and stiff in her chair. Silent temper snapped in her ladyship's eyes. Joan made an inadequate gesture. "I'm sorry, Lady Cassandra."

Lord Humphrey reached across the intervening space between himself and the woman he had made his wife scarce twelve hours before. He captured her hand and held it in the strength of his clasp. His gaze rested warm on her troubled face. "Your scruples continue to do you credit, Joan. I do not regret our marriage. I shall never do so, I promise you."

"I scarcely know what to say," Joan said, torn equally by her desires and her conviction that his lordship was due much more than she could ever provide to him.

"Good God, girl," exclaimed Lady Cassandra, exasperated.

"Say, then, that you will stay beside me," said Lord Humphrey.

She nodded slowly. "Very well, my lord."

He detected still a shade of doubt in her eyes and thought it was because of the proposed engagement. "If you cannot feel comfortable with the course as my grandmother has outlined it, then naturally we must make a clean breast of it all," he said quietly.

"Edward," exclaimed Lady Cassandra wrathfully.

Lord Humphrey ignored his grandmother's intervention. "Joan? It shall be just as you prefer."

Joan looked up at his lordship. She saw the sincerity in his eyes and she heard it in the determination of his voice. Her mouth softened into a faint smile. "You would do that, I think, even though it meant ever so much trouble."

He smiled and pressed her fingers. "I have told you that I shall shield you as much as it is in my power to do so. But I would not have you think ill of me or question my honor."

"I would never do so, my lord. You have been all that is honorable and more," Joan said, her eyes misting. She could feel the heavy signet ring on her finger and its weight was reassuring.

"Then I can only ask that you trust me in this, Joan. I swear that I will not take your confidence lightly," Lord Humphrey said.

It was an appeal that she could not stand against. The assaulting doubts faded. Joan smiled. "Very well, my lord. I still cannot quite like it all, but I accept the necessity. We shall become an engaged couple."

"Perhaps I should not ask, but curiosity has always been a failing of mine," Lady Cassandra said crossly. She was still upset that her carefully wrought entertainment had so narrowly missed its staging, but even so her quick ear was at work. She had not been behind in noting that Joan had spoken of her father in the past tense and it had come to her that she had all along taken for granted that the girl had no family to speak of or with which to acquaint of the present situation. "Who was your father, my dear?"

"Papa was vicar in a neighboring county, my lady. He was a truly generous and godly man. He passed away but eight months ago," Joan said. As she spoke, she felt the familiar blinding stab of grief and loneliness that had become a hovering companion to her spirits since that fateful day. She squared her shoulders against it. It was always worse when she was tired, and it had been a most arduous afternoon.

"I am sorry, my dear. It is most distressing to lose one who is well-loved," Lady Cassandra said sincerely. Even so, her agile mind quickly turned over the new piece of information to her advantage. "However, I cannot but think that this delay to announce the match between you and my grandson suits your own private needs very well. You are still in mourning. It would hardly be fitting to announce your marriage, with all the attendant hoopla and exclamation that it would entail, before you were completely out of black gloves."

"I had not thought of that," said Lord Humphrey, frowning. More than ever he was convinced of the rightness of his grandmother's advice on how to introduce his wife into his family. Joan should have her private period of mourning.

"Your mourning will also serve as a logical explanation for the quietness of the engagement, for certainly we must let it be assumed that the understanding between yourself and my grandson is of some duration," said Lady Cassandra.

"But it is not," Joan said. Disturbed, she recognized the beginning of a spiral of half-truths and fabrications.

"My dear, when first you entered this room on my grand-

son's arm, that is precisely what I assumed. I do not think
that you have suffered from it. On the contrary, I suspect
that if I had not tumbled to the matter of the special license
and had already known of the arranged betrothal, it would
have saved both yourself and my grandson several minutes
of embarrassment,'' said Lady Cassandra.

Joan could not deny it. She smiled, shaking her head.
"That is true, my lady."

Lady Cassandra said significantly, "I do not think that your
father would have wished you to suffer through scandal and
humiliation, my dear, especially at this sad time."

Joan was silent, reflecting that her father would have been
most shocked and distressed by the lack of support from his
parish for his only child. Indeed, the vicar would have been
incensed that she had been forced to the extremity of applying
for a post simply to keep a roof over her head.

Her thoughts graduated naturally to her prior concern. She
hoped that her father would not have been too disappointed
at her cowardice in acquiescing to the viscount's proposal.
It had seemed quite the best thing to do, and she did not think
that she would later regret it.

As she met the viscount's steady gaze, she felt her heart
lift. No, she would not regret it, she thought. "I am game
enough for it now, I think, my lord."

"Good girl," he said, smiling. He let go of her hand at
last and rose to his feet. "Shall you wish my company any
longer, Grandmama? For all that it is early still and incredibly
rag-mannered of me to own to it, I find that I am deuced
tired and in a few hours I shall wish only for my bed.
Therefore I beg that you ladies will accept my excuses and
allow me to get onto the road before I am completely done
in, as I must return to London at once."

Joan cast a startled glance up at the viscount, but she said
nothing to his unexpected announcement. However, she
could not still the sense of apprehension and abandonment
that swept through her. In the last several hours the viscount
had become a necessary anchor to her. She felt adrift at the

very thought of being left to her own devices in a world completely outside her experience.

"No, I think that will be all for the moment, Edward. I do think it would be wise to write at once to the earl and inform him that you will not be arriving quite so soon as expected," Lady Cassandra said, reaching for her bell and ringing it to alert her staff that the remains of the tea were to be cleared away. The drawing-room door opened at once to admit the butler.

Lord Humphrey grimaced. "You are right, of course. I shall do so as soon as I arrive in London," he said.

He held out his hand to his wife. Odd how easily he had come to think of her in that fashion, but she was a comfortable little thing. Not at all one to cut up a man's peace, he thought in a self-congratulatory manner as he compared what this moment might have been like if he had married Miss Ratcliffe instead. "Will you escort me to the door, my lady?"

"Of course," Joan said. Her voice was quite steady and betrayed none of the trepidation that she felt. She rose to her feet, and placing her hand in his, they walked from the drawing room.

Lady Cassandra delayed the butler in order to inform him that the young lady was Miss Joan Chadwick, the viscount's betrothed, and as such was to be accorded every courtesy of the house. Carruthers, though used to the rare starts of the gentry, was nevertheless surprised by her ladyship's revelation. His expression remained wooden, however, as he prepared to depart the drawing room and seek immediate refuge in the servants' hall, where he could impart the extraordinary news.

In the front hall, Lord Humphrey retrieved his beaver and greatcoat from the attendant footman. As he adjusted the beaver over his brows, he requested the footman to convey a message to the stables that he required his phaeton. The footman left on his errand and the couple was momentarily alone in the entry hall.

He said quietly, "You must not be anxious, Joan. No, do not attempt to deny it. You have the most speaking eyes, you know." There was the trace of a smile in his voice.

"To my continuing lamentation," retorted Joan with a touch of tartness.

The viscount laughed. He sobered quickly. He was very aware that the butler was emerging from out of the drawing room, and in an attempt to discourage possible listening ears, he lowered his voice. "I do not desert you at this late date."

"I never thought it, my lord," Joan said staunchly. "I shall do very well with her ladyship until your return."

The footman returned to inform the viscount that his carriage was at that moment being brought around. He opened the front door for his lordship.

Lord Humphrey thanked the man briefly. He drew Joan with him outside onto the portico. The viscount raised her hand to his lips. After the warm salute across her fingers, he said, "You do not ask me why I must leave."

"I am certain that if you wished me to know, you would inform me," Joan said.

"You are by far too trusting of me, my lady," said Lord Humphrey, shaking his head. "I return to London to place the advertisement of our engagement in the *Gazette* and also to procure a proper engagement ring for you."

Joan smiled at him. Her brown eyes suddenly twinkled. "I fancy *that* will be an onerous task for a confirmed bachelor."

He laughed. He saw that his phaeton was arriving at the curb and his team was stamping impatiently. "Farewell, my lady."

He bounded down the steps and climbed up into the phaeton. Taking up his whip, he nodded to the stable groom to let go the leaders and the team instantly started into motion. The phaeton rolled foward. The viscount touched his whip to his beaver and then the carriage swept past Joan.

Joan watched the phaeton progress away from her until the trees that shaded the graveled drive hid it from view.

She sighed and, turning to the door standing open behind her, walked back inside and into her new life.

The butler awaited her. "Miss Chadwick, her ladyship has suggested that you might wish a hot bath and to rest in your room before dinner," he said.

Joan flashed her warm smile. "Indeed I would," she agreed.

Carruthers permitted himself the flicker of a smile. "The footman will show you upstairs to your room, miss."

Joan followed the manservant. When she entered the bedroom and closed the door behind her, she found that the abigail she had acquired was busily tipping large copper pots of water into a brass hip bath. The bath was set between a roaring fire in the grate and a screen to discourage wayward drafts. "How lovely," said Joan in anticipation.

The abigail ducked her head in greeting. Her plump cheeks were pink from the steam rising from the water. "But let me finish, m'lady, and I'll give you a 'and with your buttons."

A few minutes later, Joan settled blissfully into the warmth of the water. She closed her eyes, enjoying the sensation. She hardly heard when the abigail announced that Lady Cassandra had sent in a clean gown for her to wear down to dinner.

Once she had bathed and had dressed in the borrowed gown, however, she started to laugh. "Look, Maisie, I am become a veritable beanstalk." Her wrists extended beyond the sleeve cuffs and the skirt ended somewhere up around her ankles, while the gown itself was a size too large around for her slender frame.

The abigail hid her grin behind one hand. "Oh, I don't know, m'lady. 'Tis a pretty gown, I'm thinking," she said stoutly.

Joan squared her posture, attempting to fill out the gown's drooping bodice. "I shall make a fine spectacle at the dinner table. I am glad his lordship is not here to see it, though," she said ruefully. She was struck by a thought and turned away from the mirror to look at the abigail. "Maisie, I do hope you have not said anything about his lordship and myself to anyone?"

"Now, what would I be saying, m'lady?"

"No one is to know just yet that his lordship and I are wed," said Joan. She felt heat rising into her face at the abigail's expression. She knew how odd it sounded. "Lady Cassandra believes it would be best to break the news gently to his lordship's family, so we are to pose as an engaged couple for a time."

"Oh, I'll not breathe a word to anyone, m'lady. Begging your pardon, *miss*," said the abigail.

"Thank you, Maisie."

Joan went downstairs to join Lady Cassandra for dinner.

Her ladyship eyed Joan's appearance critically and said, "I suspected you were a bit tall for that gown. You must write for your own things at once, my dear."

"Yes, my lady. I will be most happy to do so," Joan said.

Lady Cassandra shot a surprised look at her, then she chuckled. "Indeed! Well, my dear, it is just you and me this evening. We shall make it an early one, if you please. I am an old woman and this shocking situation has exhausted me. Mind you, I shall not sleep a wink for the worry of it all, but that is certainly none of your concern."

"No, my lady," Joan said. She thanked the footmen as they finished serving her and took up her fork.

"Aye, you've spirit enough, for all that meek tone. We shall begin on the morrow to see what else you are made of, my dear," said Lady Cassandra.

Joan cast a startled glance at her ladyship.

Lady Cassandra was seemingly oblivious to everything but her repast.

After a moment, Joan resumed eating her own dinner. She wondered, with the slightest *frisson* of apprehension, exactly what Lady Cassandra had meant.

9

DURING LORD HUMPHREY'S absence, Joan settled into her new role as his lordship's intended. Joan thought the intervening days until Lord Humphrey's return to Blackhedge Manor would be interminable and uncomfortable in the strange household, but such proved not to be the case. Lady Cassandra treated her civilly and even fondly, though she was a perfect tyrant otherwise.

Lady Cassandra saw to it Joan was kept busy with small tasks, such as running for her ladyship's shawl or slippers or viniagrette, a cushion for her ladyship's chair or her feet, or reading aloud to her. Joan swiftly learned that she was not the material of a hired companion or, as she acknowledged ruefully, that of a governess. She would not have wanted to be forever at some person's beck and call, even to one as stimulating as Lady Cassandra.

Joan suspected, and quite rightly, that Lady Cassandra did not want to allow her time for solitary reflection and it was to that end that the unceasing demands were made upon her good nature.

Lady Cassandra openly made known her determination that Joan was to be made over into the perfect lady of quality before the viscount presented her to the Earl and Countess of Dewesbury. "For I shall tell you directly, my dear, you'll have an easier time of it if you do not commit some silly faux pas or other that could be easily avoided with a little prior training," Lady Cassandra said.

"I am most willing to learn, my lady," Joan said.

"Good. I am glad to hear you say so," Lady Cassandra said with wicked relish. She began to initiate Joan into the finer graces of society, which ran the gamut from proper greeting of personages of varying degrees of importance to the question of her abigail.

"You shall have to rid yourself of that girl who arrived with you, of course," said Lady Cassandra. "I shall myself find a replacement, one who is more suitable for your station."

"I prefer to retain my present abigail, my lady. Oh, I know that she is not up to snuff as a proper lady's maid, but she learns very quickly and I am comfortable with her," Joan said.

"My dear, you must be guided by me in this. Believe me, it is quite dangerous to have that girl about. Did you not tell me that she actually witnessed the ceremony? All shall be lost if she so much as hints at what she knows," said Lady Cassandra. She delivered herself of a broad-brushed opinion. "Servants simply cannot be trusted with one's secrets."

"I shall speak to her myself, my lady," Joan said. She smiled, but there was an expression in her eyes that surprised Lady Cassandra considerably. "I shan't discuss it further, ma'am."

"Then we must hope for the best, of course," said Lady Cassandra, somewhat miffed. But she was also a good deal nonplussed. She had not before seen much evidence of the girl's strength of will, even though she had suspected Joan's quiet character cloaked much of interest.

Joan learned much about Lady Cassandra's character as well. She decided that for all Lady Cassandra's deliberately provoking ways, her ladyship was very likable. From the sometimes caustic comments that Lady Cassandra let drop, she also began to develop a hazy opinion of the viscount's relations. It was a large and sprawling family of uncles and aunts and nephews and nieces and cousins of several degrees.

"Worthless, most of them. But nevertheless, there are sharp minds among them, so you must always be on your guard. You cannot trust any one of them with the secret of your hole-in-the-wall marriage," said Lady Cassandra. She was quite aware that she sowed dismay in her recently acquired granddaughter, and seeing the expression of dread in Joan's eyes, she relented a little. She patted the young woman's arm. "You will do splendidly, my dear. I have every confidence in you."

"I hope so. Thank you, my lady," Joan said.

Joan also learned what would be expected of her in her role as Lord Humphrey's hostess. "You'll need all the poise and shrewd wit that God has granted you, my dear, if you are to survive the scrutiny of the most correct," Lady Cassandra said.

Joan had been used to commanding her father's household, so she was no stranger to accounts or to entertaining on a small scale—fortunately so, since Lady Cassandra ordered the manor housekeeper to take her in hand and discover what she knew. The housekeeper reported back to her ladyship that the miss's skills in these areas were suitable enough, which earned Joan a nod of approval from Lady Cassandra.

The old lady was in fact pleasantly surprised at how readily the vicar's daughter took to the more rarified life that she had been thrust into. Joan was gracious to a fault, her manner was kind and patient, her temper even despite the provocation Lady Cassandra provided by her incessant demands. Joan's conversation was knowledgeable and on occasion even erudite, reflecting an excellent education. If there was a spark of anger in her brown eyes at those times that her ladyship deliberately sought to overset her or drive her out of countenance, Lady Cassandra thought her the better for such show of spirit.

Joan wrote a note to the Percys requesting that her things

be packed up and put into the hands of the messenger who
carried her letter to them. Shortly thereafter, her clothes and
mementos were with her again. There was also a brief letter
from Mrs. Percy, expressing that lady's well wishes. Mrs.
Percy also managed to convey awe and rampant curiosity
within her short missive concerning Joan's unsuspected
connections with such a prestigious address.

Joan laughed when she read the arch phrases, for she knew
the good lady's love of gossip and intrigue. She promised
herself that she would one day return to visit the Percys and
satisfy their curiosity. But in the meantime, she thought, the
wiser course laid in the least said, the better.

Lady Cassandra covertly studied the clothing that Joan
wore through the succeeding days. She was satisfied by the
well-bred appearance that Joan always presented, but she
thought the girl's gowns were something lacking in dash.
When she commented upon it, Joan said in surprise, "But
I am in mourning, my lady."

"Yes, but one may be in mourning and still contrive a bit
of elegance. Perhaps a few ribbons for refurbishing, a second
muff," mused Lady Cassandra, a speculative light in her
eyes. She gave a decisive nod. "Yes, we must see about it."

Joan realized from the manner in which Lady Cassandra
was visually measuring her figure that her hostess planned
to go to an expense greater than the cost of a few new
ribbons. "Ma'am, truly I am in need of very little. I could
not possibly accept your largess, however gracious it is of
you to extend it."

"Nonsense! You are my granddaughter, so let there not
be another word about it, my dear. I shall have the dress-
maker in this very afternoon." Lady Cassandra smiled sooth-
ingly at her guest. "If it is the expense that has you in such
a pucker, pray put it out of your head. It pleases me to spoil
you, but if it should ease your conscience, I shall naturally
present the bills to your husband."

There was a wicked gleam in her cool gray eyes and Joan
flushed.

She thought she well knew what the lady was about, but yet she could not help the tingle of embarrassment that suffused her whenever she thought of the viscount in the role of her husband. She had recalled more than once the offhand comment that he had made while at the inn regarding "numerous progeny." She shied away from all the ramifications of that loaded statement.

"You are an incorrigible, my lady," she said, mildly scolding. "I suppose that I have little choice in the matter, do I?"

"None whatsoever." Lady Cassandra laughed. She stretched out her hand to the bellrope that hung beside her writing desk. In answer to her imperious tugging, a footman entered and Lady Cassandra issued the order to summon her personal needlewoman. The door closed again behind the footman's retreating figure.

Lady Cassandra turned her head to appraise her guest once more. She enjoyed the girl's frank manners and her lack of pretention. The refreshing qualities compared favorably against the solicitous cozenings of her own relations.

She was a wealthy woman, well-known for her perversity, who had often commented that there was scarcely a handful in the lot of her descendants who were worth their salt, and therefore were hardly suitable specimens to stand as her inheritors. As a consequence, she was much fawned over at any gathering of kinsmen and even the most outrageous of her opinions was given grave consideration.

"I liked you from the moment I met you, my dear. I hope that you will not lose that blend of gentleness and forthrightness that characterizes you," she said abruptly.

Joan looked at her ladyship, suspicious that she was being made game of again. But there was none of the taunting light in Lady Cassandra's eyes that she had quickly learned to associate with her ladyship's cutting and sardonic wit. She inclined her head, not daring to comment on her ladyship's unusual sentimentality.

Instead, she said, "I see that you have finished your

correspondence. Would you like me to give your letter into the footman's hands? I was just thinking that if you would not miss me, I would go for my shawl so that I could take a turn about the garden. I would gladly carry the letter out for posting as I went.''

The ladies were ensconced in the library. Joan had been reading a book of poetry beside the fire, occasionally commenting on various verses that took her fancy to Lady Cassandra, whom she had discovered shared her love of verse. Lady Cassandra had occupied herself at her writing desk, and Joan had seen that she had sealed the sheets with her own signet pressed into the wax.

"Thank you, my dear. And also convey my desire that a sherry be brought to me. I intend to move closer to the fire and enjoy the warmth of the flames with my wine," Lady Cassandra said.

Joan set aside the book and rose. As she took the letter from Lady Cassandra, she chanced to glance at the recipient's address. In Lady Cassandra's distinctive penning was the name of the Countess of Dewesbury. She felt herself pale.

Lady Cassandra noticed her expression. She said in an offhand manner, "I am inviting myself to Dewesbury in a few days' time. It has been too long since I availed myself of my daughter's hospitality and I have decided to seize the opportunity to take advantage of my grandson's escort whenever he should decide to travel in that direction himself. I hope that you will not mind it, my dear.''

Though it had gone hard against her inclinations, she had not penned a single word concerning the newly wedded couple to the earl and countess. Time enough for them all to learn of the vicar's daughter, she thought with rare anticipation.

The color returned to Joan's face. "Oh, no, not in the slightest, my lady. Of course I shall be delighted to continue our acquaintance." She could not deny her heartfelt sense of reprieve. When she had thought of traveling to Dewesbury, even with the assurance of the viscount's presence, she had felt apprehensive about facing his family. But if Lady Cassandra was also to go with them, she would feel herself much better able to carry it off.

Lady Cassandra smiled, well able to read the young woman's relief in her expressive brown eyes. "Go along with you, my dear. You will want to finish your walk before teatime, I expect."

Joan left the library, bearing the letter to be posted, and dutifully conveyed to the footman Lady Cassandra's wish for a glass of sherry. Then she went up to gather her shawl and returned downstairs to exit the manor through the back and thus into the garden.

She had quickly discovered the garden, and in the past several days she had managed to slip away in the afternoons to walk the overgrown paths. It was not the usual formal garden that one might expect of a noblewoman's abode; rather, it was a tangle of blooms and species that upon first discovery had strongly reminded Joan of her unconventional hostess.

Only one corner of the garden had any pretension to formality and it was highlighted by a charming arbor of climbing roses. As always, Joan avoided the path to the roses, preferring instead to wend her way among the rest of the garden.

Joan breathed the scented air, loving the feel of the breeze as it brushed her hair. She walked slowly, savoring the quiet as always. The peace that she had always felt among growing things had been a particular gift to her since her arrival at Blackhedge Manor.

Lady Cassandra had succeeded only to a point in diverting her attention for her circumstances. Joan was still nipped by doubts. There was so much unsettled about the future, so much that she could not easily discern. Joan sighed. She supposed that she would simply have to wait on events to show her whether she had made the wisest choice, after all.

The sun was slanting deep gold across the heads of the flowers. It was coming close to teatime, she thought. She turned her steps back in the direction of the manor.

10

AFTER JOAN had freshened up, she returned downstairs to the drawing room for afternoon tea. Lady Cassandra had apparently gone upstairs also and had not yet come down.

Joan amused herself while she waited for her ladyship by glancing through a lady's magazine. She was genuinely interested in the fashion plates, taking particular note of the small changes in waistline placement and hem lengths and the sort of trimmings depicted. She was used to making several of her own ensembles each year, her father's living having never stretched so far as to pay for a seamstress except for the occasional special gown.

Joan heard conversation in the entry hall, coming closer, and of a sudden she recognized the viscount's voice. She looked up quickly from her magazine. The next moment the drawing room door opened and the viscount entered with his characteristic quick step.

"My lord! I am glad to see you returned," she exclaimed, setting aside her magazine. She rose and went to him with her hands outstretched.

Lord Humphrey caught her hands, smiling in his turn. "How are you, my lady? But I hardly need to ask, for I can see that you are very well. My grandmother has not eaten you whole, after all. I am greatly relieved.''

Joan laughed merrily. She disengaged herself to gesture an invitation for him to join her on the settee before she sank down on the cushions. He seated himself beside her. "No, indeed. Lady Cassandra has been a most solicitous hostess. I have learned much from her ladyship. I am truly in her debt for any number of things.''

Lord Humphrey quirked a brow, his disbelief plain in his eyes. "Indeed! Dare I inquire in what way?''

Joan felt warmth start into her face and she put up her hands against her cheeks. She threw him a laughing look. "Oh! You have put me out of countenance—and without the least intention of doing so, I know. Lady Cassandra would have my head if she were to see me. She is forever drumming into me that I must maintain my poise whatever else may be happening about me.''

"That sounds a good deal more like her ladyship," Lord Humphrey said, laughing. He regarded her with curiosity. "But what should have embarrassed you in my question?''

Joan flashed a warm smile that invited him to share in her easy amusement. "Why, didn't you guess? Her ladyship is determined that I shall be the epitome of a *grande dame*, above reproach and unaccountable to lesser opinions. Indeed, I am to become so full of myself that I shall be able to deliver the most cutting of set-downs without the least effort.''

"Good Gad," said Lord Humphrey, taken aback. He eyed her in a considering way. She did not seem much changed, yet now that she had mentioned it, there was an air of easy confidence about her that had not been there before. There was surely something different about her hair as well, he thought, and her gown was more flattering than the one that he had seen her in previously.

He came to realize that he was staring at her when he saw that she was blushing again, even more vividly than before. For want of a better way to ease her self-consciousness, he said, "That is a particularly fetching gown.''

Joan inclined her head, suddenly to all appearances complete mistress of herself. "Thank you, Edward," she said in a throaty voice.

He was surprised, but obscurely pleased that she had called him by his Christian name. "You have gotten over your shyness of me, at least," he said.

"I am trying to do so," Joan admitted frankly. With a fleeting smile, she explained, "Lady Cassandra has told me it would be very odd in me to address you always in a formal manner, since we are to have been acquainted for some time. Her ladyship has impressed upon me that I must practice until it becomes quite natural to me."

Lord Humphrey laughed and she asked anxiously, "I hope that you are not offended?"

"No, of course not! Why should I be? If you recall, I requested the same of you several days past," Lord Humphrey said. He chose not to reveal to her that it was her earnestness that amused him. "I am glad that my grandmother is taking such a benevolent interest in you, Joan. I wondered whether . . . Well, one can never predict exactly how her ladyship might go on and at times she can be a frightful old dragon."

"Surely not! I have found Lady Cassandra to be exacting and decisively opinionated, perhaps, but never the least dragonish! She has been most kind to me, really," Joan said.

Lord Humphrey grinned. "She has had you fetching and carrying for her, has she? And perhaps reading to her as well? And requiring you to agree to all manner of things that are exactly counter to your own opinions?" He saw from her expression that he had hit uncomfortably close to the truth, and he laughed again. "I shall not ask you to admit it aloud, my lady. I can see that it would cause you a struggle to be so disloyal and ungracious as to do so."

Joan was relieved that she was to be let off so easily. "Yes, well, that at least I shall admit to."

Lord Humphrey laughed again, making it difficult to hide her own smile.

While they were still laughing, Lady Cassandra entered the drawing room. In her wake came Carruthers and a footman carrying the tea urn and a tray of cakes.

"What is this?" Lady Cassandra asked. "A party, and I have not been invited to it?"

The viscount leapt up and made an elegant leg. "On the contrary, Grandmama. You are most welcome to join us."

"Edward, my dear boy," Lady Cassandra bestowed her hand on him, feeling a surge of uncharacteristic affection. It made her voice warmer than usual as she said, "I am glad to see you."

Straightening, Lord Humphrey said, "I have just these few minutes past arrived. My lady has been regaling me with all that you have been putting her to during my absence."

Lady Cassandra threw a thoughtful glance at Joan's guilty face. "Indeed! I hope that I have not been cast into the role of tyrant, my dear."

Lord Humphrey realized that he had inadvertently exposed his lady to Lady Cassandra's possible displeasure. He rushed to Joan's defense. "Quite the contrary, ma'am. Joan would have it that you are not at all the dragon that I would paint you," he said daringly.

"Thank you, my dear Joan. You see with what lack of respect that I am treated by my own flesh-and-blood," Lady Cassandra said dryly. However, she did not seem in the least offended and in fact smiled at her grandson's newfound impudence. She seated herself and waved the viscount back to his place.

During the greetings, tea had been served and the servants left the drawing room.

Lady Cassandra arranged herself comfortably, giving a number of twitches to her skirt as she put her feet up onto the customary hassock. "Well, Edward, tell us what you have gotten up to since we last saw you," she said.

"I have submitted the notice of the engagement into the *Gazette*. It should be printed by the time that we go to Dewesbury Court. I have also apprised the earl and my mother by the post of my later arrival. I do not think that they will continue to speculate as to the cause behind my absence once they have the opportunity to read the next *Gazette,''* said Lord Humphrey. With a quick grin, he added, ''Lord, I am glad that I shan't be there.''

''Quite,'' said Lady Cassandra, at her dryest.

''I have also brought down my man with me this trip so that it will all seem quite respectable and thought out. There will not be a hint of unseemingly haste about the business,'' Lord Humphrey said, pleased with himself that he had thought of everything. He looked over at Joan. ''Have you that abigail still?''

''Yes. Lady Cassandra was concerned that the girl might gossip about the wedding, but I have spoken to her and she assures me that she will not do so,'' Joan said.

''That's all right, then,'' Lord Humphrey said, nodding. ''There will be all sorts of speculations running rife at Dewesbury, I shouldn't wonder, and you'll need a servant you can trust.''

Lady Cassandra sipped at her sweetened tea, then said, ''I am going to Dewesbury with you and Joan.''

Lord Humphrey looked startled. ''Are you, my lady?''

''Lady Cassandra goes to support me in my failing nerves,'' Joan said with a laugh.

''Nonsense, girl. I simply wish to see the expressions on the faces of my dutiful daughter and her most worthy husband when the viscount introduces his chosen fiancée. It will undoubtedly afford me much entertainment,'' said Lady Cassandra. Her tone was deliberately cool.

There was a short silence, during which Joan looked stricken, and Lord Humphrey surprised and angry. It was broken by the viscount.

''Grandmama, have I ever mentioned what a very wicked creature I think you?'' he asked quietly.

''Not before now, my dear,'' Lady Cassandra said serenely. She raised her brows as she regarded the subdued pair. Her eyes had turned rather hard. ''I am a capricious old woman. I care for very little and very few. Perhaps you would both be wise enough to keep that in mind.''

''Then why have you chosen to help us, my lady?'' Joan asked.

Lady Cassandra smiled slowly. ''It pleases me to do so, Miss Chadwick.'' She saw the start that the girl gave. ''Ah, does that form of address surprise you, my dear? Pray become comfortable with it, for you must be Miss Chadwick from this moment on.''

''I understand perfectly, my lady,'' Joan said, in a low trembling voice.

She turned her head so that she could look at the flickering flames, presenting her neat profile to Lady Cassandra. She was beginning to understand a great many painful things, she thought. She had believed that she and Lady Cassandra were becoming quite close. She had shared several confidences with her ladyship and in return Lady Cassandra had treated her as a well-liked young friend. However, her assumption of their mutual liking had just suffered a severe setback.

Joan recalled the several times in the last several days that Lady Cassandra had told her that she would not be able to trust anyone. She had simply brushed aside those hints, but Joan realized now that Lady Cassandra had also been speaking of herself.

Joan felt the rejection deeply. Lady Cassandra had encouraged her to talk of herself and her interests, of her father and her life with him. Lady Cassandra had been an exacting companion, but she had also appeared to be genuinely interested in her. But it had all been a dreadful sham. She had merely provided an amusement for Lady Cassandra, which was now done.

Satisfied that her cruel point had been taken, Lady Cassandra turned to her grandson. ''Edward, what date did you give to the earl and your mother for your arrival?'' she asked.

Lord Humphrey stared at her ladyship from under gathered

brows. He had not cared for the churlish manner in which
Lady Cassandra had spoken to Joan.

He threw a glance at Joan's averted face. He could not
see her expression, only the curving lines of her profile and
her slender neck. She had obviously taken the set-down to
heart, he thought. He discovered in himself an immense
dislike that his chosen lady had been treated with less than
respect. His reply to his grandmother reflected his anger and
was abbreviated almost to the point of discourtesy. "Two
days hence, my lady."

Lady Cassandra's fine-tuned ears caught the anger and
disapproval in her grandson's voice. She did not allow herself
to react in any way, but privately she thought it a satisfactory
sign. In the several days that Joan had been with her, she
had gotten the girl to reveal much of herself, and she had
come to some conclusions that might have surprised both
Joan and the viscount if they had been privy to her ladyship's
thoughts.

But Lady Cassandra was not one to tip her hand too soon.

"Good, good. There will be adequate time for the packing
and for the refurbishing of Miss Chadwick's gowns. She will
still look something of the dowd, but that cannot be helped
at this junction. I shall take my needlewoman with me so
that another gown or two may be finished at Dewesbury
Court," Lady Cassandra said.

She smiled faintly at her grandson's unfriendly expression.
She decided to throw him a bone. "You wish to eat me for
my callousness, do you not, Edward? But I shan't be the kind
of benefactress that you and Joan have grown accustomed
to once we leave Blackhedge Manor. It is better that you
adjust to the change now, so that you will not be caught
flatfooted with surprise at Dewesbury."

"So you do not actually go to lend us countenance, my
lady?" asked Lord Humphrey in a hard voice.

"Pray do not be ridiculous, Edward. You may naturally
count upon me to put in my oar. However, I shall seem to
blow hot and cold." Lady Cassandra's gray eyes were alight

with wicked irony. She asked softly, "Is that not what I am known for, my dear?"

"Indeed, my lady! You have earned a reputation for caprice, willfulness, and unpredictability," Lord Humphrey said shortly. However, his anger was beginning to slip away as he realized that his grandmother was baiting him.

Lady Cassandra laughed. She slid a sly glance in Joan's direction. "There you have it, Joan. I hope you are forewarned."

"I shall indeed be on my guard from this moment on, my lady," Joan promised. She had listened with surprise and even a lightening of spirit to Lady Cassandra's explanation. She had understood then that Lady Cassandra had not completely turned on her, after all. But certainly she would take a page from this unpleasant lesson to hereafter treat Lady Cassandra as more of an acquaintance than as the confidante she had made of her.

Lady Cassandra nodded in satisfaction. "Edward, my granddaughter has finished her tea. Might I suggest a walk about the garden?"

Lord Humphrey was surprised, but he rose to the occasion. "Of course." He thought it uncharacteristic for Lady Cassandra to encourage what would be considered conduct more becoming a wedded couple than one engaged, especially after her ladyship had just finished saying that they must all begin playing their roles. However, he was not at all averse to being alone with Joan. On the contrary, he had something of a private nature to say to her.

Joan did not remind Lady Cassandra that she had already been out in the garden earlier, but instead went up to retrieve her wrap. She did not know how it was, but she was looking forward to being alone again with Lord Humphrey.

When she returned downstairs, she and the viscount walked outside.

The evening was coming on softly by then. Insects had begun their nightly ritual of singing the sun down; the barest breeze stirred the flowers in their beds. The viscount and

Joan walked slowly, the silence between them borne out of a feeling of companionship.

Lord Humphrey steered Joan toward a stone bench. It was a pretty spot, the bench being set off by the blazing roses behind it. He thought it the perfect setting for what he wished to say.

He was astonished when his companion abruptly pulled free of his hand and stopped. He looked down at her, perplexed. "What is it, my lady?"

Joan stared at the bench and the roses. She glanced fleetingly up at his lordship. "You will think it nonsensical, but I would truly prefer to sit someplace else. I do not much care for roses, you see."

Lord Humphrey felt even greater astonishment. "Not care for roses? Why, I thought all females liked them. Dash it, I know they do, for once I spent hours combing all of London for a melon-colored bud for a particular lady. Melon-colored! I ask you, whoever heard of a melon-colored rose?"

"Is there such?" asked Joan, interested.

"No," Lord Humphrey said explosively. "At least, none that I could find. What's more, the particular lady-bird who desired it did not wait to see whether I found one or not. She—"

Joan's fine brown eyes held a fascinated expression and he realized that he was about to confide a rather scandalous tale to her genteel ears. "But that is neither here nor there," he said hurriedly. "Now see here! What's this about not liking roses? You do think they're pretty, do you not?"

"Oh, yes, they are perfectly lovely," Joan gestured in an apologetic way. "It is the scent, you see."

The viscount's countenance cleared. "I understand you, of course. I myself have always found the scent of roses to be cloyingly sweet. Come. I glimpsed another bench down the last walkway we passed. I have something of importance to say to you, you know."

At his lordship's words, Joan forgot about the roses. "Something of importance, my lord?"

But he refused to say anything more until they had reached their destination. Once Joan was seated, Lord Humphrey was ready to disclose his thoughts. "My lady, I realize that we have not known each other for very long, and certainly the manner of our meeting did not reflect well upon my own character—"

He saw that she was about to speak and he held up his hand. "Please, my lady. I have given much thought to this." She hesitated, then nodded her acquiescence and folded her hands in her lap.

"The vows between us were made in circumstances that I, for one, could have wished far different. I suspect that you have felt the same. That is why I wished you to know that I shall always attempt to uphold the true spirit of those sacred words," Lord Humphrey said.

"And I," Joan said quickly.

Lord Humphrey gave her a grave smile. He drew out of his coat pocket a small jeweler's box and placed it in her hands. "I shall not have another opportunity to express my gratitude to you. Nor do I have the words. I ask only that you accept this as a small token of my future devotion."

Joan opened the jeweler's box. She stared at the contents. "Oh, my word," she whispered.

"I hope that you like the set," Lord Humphrey said with a hint of anxiousness.

She looked up. Her brown eyes were like stars. "Oh, yes. I do, very much indeed."

He sat down beside her. "Allow me."

The viscount slid his signet ring from off her slender finger and placed it back onto his own finger. He removed the engagement ring from its velvet bed in the jeweler's box and slipped it on in the place of the too-large signet ring. "It looks well on you," he said quietly.

"It is perfectly lovely," breathed Joan. She flashed her warmest smile. Her face was radiant. "I do thank you, Edward."

Lord Humphrey blinked. The impact of her smile was

devastating. He felt rocked back on his heels. He had the most disconcerting urge to take her into his arms and thoroughly kiss her. He restrained the impulse, however, knowing instinctively that it would be wrong to the moment. His lady was not a sophisticated London miss who would take a stolen kiss in the light manner that it was intended.

Joan was very aware of a difference on the air. Suddenly a tension like no other she had ever experienced lay between her and Lord Humphrey. There was a strange look in the viscount's eyes, one that gave her the impression of a banked fire. She wondered why ever that particular simile crossed her mind.

"I shall return the wedding band to you for safekeeping," she said breathlessly, holding out the jeweler's box.

The odd moment vanished as swiftly as it had come. Lord Humphrey looked down thoughtfully at the gold band still reposing in the box. He closed the box and gently curled her fingers about it. "No, it is yours by all rights."

Joan looked up into his earnest expression, and after a moment she gave a hesitant nod. She slipped the jeweler's box into the pocket of her gown. "I shall wear it on a gold chain tucked inside my dress," she said.

The viscount glanced fleetingly at the lace-trimmed edge of her bodice, envisioning the gold band resting between the soft swell of her breasts. He cleared his throat hastily. "Shall we return to the house, ma'am?" he asked.

Joan rose at once from the bench. "Of course. Lady Cassandra will be wondering what is keeping us."

"Somehow I very much doubt it," murmured Lord Humphrey.

Joan cast a glance at his face. She saw his twisted smile. She was on the point of asking the viscount what he was thinking about when something in his expression recalled to her the odd breathlessness that she had felt only moments before.

She did not ask his lordship what he had meant, after all.

11

THREE CARRIAGES drew up to the front of the sprawling
country house commonly known as Dewesbury Court. The
arrival was apparently expected because the front door flew
open and revealed a handful of footmen. The footmen pulled
down the iron step to each of the carriages and unlatched
their doors.

Lady Cassandra and Joan had traveled in the lead carriage.
The second carriage had carried their abigails and most of
Lady Cassandra's baggage. The third carriage carried Bates,
Lady Cassandra's favorite cook, whom she always insisted
accompany her wherever she went, and the needlewoman
whom Lady Cassandra had brought to remedy Joan's meager
wardrobe. The rest of the baggage, including the viscount's
trunks and the few trunks that were Joan's, were also in the
third carriage.

Beside the lead carriage was an outrider astride a fine gray
gelding. The gentleman dismounted and negligently tossed
the reins to one of the footmen. "Take him about to the
stables. Mind, tell the head groom that the gelding is to have
no grain for an hour. I'll not have him foundered."

"Yes, my lord." The footman turned about, resigned. It
was not his duty nor his inclination to deal with big brutes

like the viscount's gelding. He had not taken two steps before
he was accosted by one of the grooms, who indignantly took
exception to having his own duties usurped.

"Aye, ye can have the nasty brute, and welcome to him,"
assured the footman. "And mind, no grain for an hour!"

The groom threw him a look of contempt and clicked his
tongue at the gelding as he led it off.

Lord Humphrey turned to give his hand to Joan. She placed
her gloved fingers in his strong clasp, meeting his gaze with
an anxious expression in her brown eyes. He smiled reassuringly. "There is naught to be frightened of, I promise you,"
he said softly. "The dragons were all slain generations ago."

Joan allowed herself to be helped down to the graveled
drive. She looked up at the mansion that overshadowed them.
"It is not mythical reptiles that I am afraid of," she
murmured.

Lord Humphrey laughed. His glance was at once warm
and conspiratorial. "I appoint myself knight protector, my
lady."

"It is Miss Chadwick, my lord," Joan said in a warning
whisper. They had ascended the steps and were entering the
front hall, where she could see that a small party awaited
them. Joan felt herself tensing and she was but half-aware
that she was clutching the viscount's elbow with uncomfortable force.

"Of course. I quite see your point," Lord Humphrey said
in a normal voice. He laid his hand reassuringly over her
fingers.

Lady Cassandra was speaking to a well-dressed woman
who appeared to Joan to be much like her ladyship in face
and stature. Joan thought that this must be Lady Dewesbury,
and she looked across at her curiously. The countess's brows
were puckered into an anxious frown and she replied to Lady
Cassandra in a voluble and rapid style.

At the sound of the viscount's voice, Lady Cassandra
turned. Her gray eyes were alight with what Joan suspected
was anticipation, but her ladyship's voice betrayed only

urbanity. "Ah, here is Edward now. And of course Miss Chadwick as well."

Lady Dewesbury's expression lightened. She came swiftly across the marble tiles. "Edward!" She literally fell into his arms, forcing him to give up his polite escort of the lady who stood beside him.

Lord Humphrey supported her. "Here, Mama, what's this?" he inquired in a rallying tone. He had decided to force the issue, reflecting philosophically that it was best to have the worst done with. "You've not had bad news, I hope?"

Beside him, Joan stood rigid, disbelieving that she had heard his lordship correctly. Her alarmed senses were acutely attuned. She saw the fleeting look of surprise that crossed Lady Cassandra's face, and the outrage that entered the faces of the gentleman and the lady who had thus far stood silently by. Joan knew without a word being said that the silent pair were Lord and Lady Ratcliffe. Their affront was too apparent and too violently felt to belong to objective bystanders.

As for the countess, she instantly drew herself erect, spurning the viscount's supporting hands. "Edward, I do not find that in the least amusing," she said sharply. The anxious air had returned to her and she cut a comprehensive glance at the young lady standing a little apart from her son.

Lady Dewesbury was surprised by her first impression of Miss Chadwick. Since reading the unbelievable announcement in the *Gazette* of her son's engagement, she had vacillated between doubting the actual existence of the woman and the horrid conviction that the woman was a painted hussy of the worst sort who had entrapped her darling with hideous wiles. Miss Chadwick at least did not fit the vulgar woman of her imagination. She was dressed as a lady and her bearing was that of a lady, thought Lady Dewesbury with a thankful sense of relief.

On the other hand, Miss Chadwick did undeniably exist.

"Nor do I find it amusing," said the other lady. Her voice was like cut glass. She was taller than the Countess of Dewesbury by half a head and was possessed of classical

features and a broad patient brow. The overall impression
of wisdom and serenity was belied by the unfriendly
expression in her cold blue eyes as she slowly stared Joan
up and down.

The gentleman put up his eyeglass and also stared in Joan's
direction. His magnified blue orb appeared monstrous.
"Perhaps it is all a ghastly mistake," he said ponderously.

Lady Dewesbury threw a harried glance over her shoulder.
She lowered her voice. "Edward, this is the most dreadful
thing—"

Lady Cassandra decided it was time for her to take a hand.
She disliked the notion of standing about at any time, but
especially in a drafty front hall where any number of servants
were going about their duties in a suspiciously creeping
manner, their attention obviously directed more onto their
betters instead of their work.

"Daughter, could we not continue these pleasantries in the
drawing room? I am of an age that demands the comforts
of cushions and hassocks and warm sherry," Lady Cassandra
said.

The Countess of Dewesbury, recalled thus brusquely to
her duties, gathered her tattered dignity about herself like
a mantle. "Of course, Mama. I do not know what I was
thinking of, I am sure." The polite phrases that came so
readily to her lips served to impart some balance to her.
"Pray do come into the drawing room. You must all be
yearning for a cup of tea or perhaps wine. Yes, yes, wine
it shall be. See to it, Hudgens." She flapped her hands in
ineffectual movements to urge them all into the drawing
room.

"I think not," Lady Ratcliffe said in freezing accents, still
staring at Joan. She turned away her gaze at last, only to
fix the same chilly stare on the viscount. "We shall talk later,
my lord."

"I think we shall go in now, Aurelia," Lord Ratcliffe said
in a thoughtful manner.

"Sir!" Lady Ratcliffe turned her disbelieving and outraged

countenance onto her spouse. "You cannot be serious."

"I am perfectly serious, Aurelia. If you cannot see the forest for the trees, I can," Lord Ratcliffe said obscurely.

"Whatever can you mean?" demanded Lady Ratcliffe.

Lord Ratcliffe firmly slipped her hand into the crook of his elbow and gestured for her to accompany him across the hall. "Mere curiosity alone must surely persuade you, Aurelia."

Lady Cassandra seized the initiative and took hold of Joan's arm. "Come, my dear. You shall aid me to my chair, if you please. I am taking you away before proper introductions are made, but then I am rude to a fault when I so wish it." So saying, she made Joan accompany her into the drawing room.

The viscount followed with his mother while the Ratcliffes brought up the rear.

The butler brought the wine and served it in silence. Lady Cassandra settled herself next to the fire, her feet comfortably perched on a hassock. Joan seated herself in a wing-back chair opposite her ladyship. Lord Humphrey wandered over to the mantel and stared thoughtfully into the yellow flames. Lady Dewesbury and Lord and Lady Ratcliffe took their places roughly opposite the young woman whom they all seemed unable to take their respective gazes from.

Joan very much wished herself somewhere else. The antagonism aimed in her direction was palpable. She was amazed that she had ever thought she could brazen out the displeasure of the viscount's family and acquaintances, when already within a very few minutes she was quite willing to run away as fast as she was able. She turned the ring on her finger over and over.

The nervous movement inexorably drew Lady Dewesbury's gaze. Her eyes snapped then to the viscount's face in shock and disbelief. "It is true, then! That infamous announcement in the *Gazette* is true," she gasped.

"Of course it is true. Why should it not be?" Lady

Cassandra asked. She impatiently waved the lingering servants out of the drawing room.

"But . . . Oh, Edward, how could you?" wailed the countess, covering her face with one trembling hand.

Lord Humphrey swiftly knelt beside the overwrought countess. He took her free hand between his own. "Mama, pray—"

Lady Dewesbury dropped her hand from her face, revealing suddenly flashing eyes. She pulled free of her son's grasp with a show of revulsion. "How dared you, Edward? I demand that you apologize at once. At once, do you hear?"

A nerve jumped in the viscount's jaw. "Indeed, Mama? For taking my destiny into my own hands at the ninth hour?" He rose to his feet. As he looked down into his mother's face, he gave a twisted smile. Softly, he said, "I have been the dutiful son and heir. I have done all that has ever been asked of me. Neither you nor my father has ever had cause to be disappointed in me. Perhaps I made a grave error in never giving you such cause." He turned on his heel and aligned himself beside Joan's chair. So close together, she seated gracefully in her chair with his lordship standing beside her and his hand laid on the back of the chair, they presented a picture of complete unity.

Lady Dewesbury stared speechlessly at her son, as much stricken by what he had said as his obvious determination to support the usurping Miss Chadwick.

At Lord Humphrey's declaration, Lord Ratcliffe's heavy brows rose in astonished comprehension. He stared hard at the viscount, as though seeing him for the first time, and a long-buried thought turned over in his mind. He said something under his breath.

"Rubbish," snapped Lady Ratcliffe. She shook off her husband's warning hand. Trembling, she said, "Fine talk, my lord! No, I shall *not* be quiet! Someone must speak for our poor daughter. You, sir. You have betrayed my innocent's hopes and expectations. When the announcement was discovered in this morning's edition, she was positively shattered. She could not be brought to believe it.''

"Did the girl fall into the fits?" Lady Cassandra asked with polite interest.

Lady Ratcliffe glared at her ladyship. Lord Ratcliffe looked meditatively at the ceiling. "She drummed her heels on the floor, actually," he murmured.

"Gad, I am glad I was not here to hear it," Lord Humphrey said fervently.

Lady Cassandra gave a cackling crow of amusement.

Lady Ratcliffe rounded on her husband, raining a furious fusillade of words upon his head. Lord Ratcliffe merely shrugged. "Facts are facts, my dear heart," he told his lady.

She was not mollified, but jumped to her feet and with barely controlled venom, she said, "I shall not remain another moment in the same room with those who are completely abhorrent in my sight. Between the pair of them, they have made my baby miserable. I shall never forgive any of you, but most particularly you, my lord, never!" She ran from the drawing room.

Lord Ratcliffe was slow to follow his wife. He looked shrewdly at the viscount, who met his reflective gaze with an air of stiff defiance. "I have thought for years that Augusta was too heavy-handed with you." With that surprising comment, he, too, left the drawing room.

"Just see what you have done by your churlishness, Edward," exclaimed Lady Dewesbury. "There is dear Aurelia completely overset. Oh, I do not know what is to be done now. Poor Augusta was calmed only after a liberal dose of laudanum. Such a fragile girl—I had no notion! And now there is Aurelia! The Ratcliffes are fixed here for weeks. I do not know how I shall be able to bear the mortification.''

"Put a damper on it, daughter," Lady Cassandra said crushingly. "I do not think I have ever seen a Cheltenham tragedy acted better."

The countess turned an outraged gaze on Lady Cassandra.

"How can you berate me so, Mama? I can see that it pleases you to champion Edward's cause, though how even you could be so unfeeling, so utterly insensible, I cannot fathom."

She had gotten to her feet as she spoke and now she whisked herself about to the door. She glanced over her shoulder at her son, who had stationed himself behind his fiancée's chair and now rested a hand upon the unknown girl's rigid shoulder. "You may as well know, Edward: your father has gone out for birds." With that triumphant shot, she exited the drawing room, letting the door fall shut behind her with a loud bang.

"Birds?" Lady Cassandra repeated, intrigued. She cocked an inquiring brow in the viscount's direction.

Lord Humphrey smiled grimly. "My father detests shooting birds. According to him, they are puling sport and not worth the effort. Actually, of course, it is because he is such an abominable shot. He only takes out his fowling piece when he is in an ungovernable temper. It is the worst sign."

"How utterly charming," Lady Cassandra said. "I actually had no notion."

"I think that I shall be ill," Joan whispered, still tingling from the explosive scene. She had never been exposed to such shoking uproar before, and she was shaking in reaction.

"Don't be missish, Miss Chadwick. Edward, make her drink that wine at once. It will settle her nerves," said Lady Cassandra. She watched while the viscount solicitously bent over the white-faced girl with a half-filled glass.

Joan shook her head quickly, but after a moment of listening to Lord Humphrey's persuasions, she dared to sip at the wine. The color began returning slowly to her face. She smiled fleetingly at the viscount. "I am better. Thank you, my lord. It was just all so horrible!"

Lady Cassandra nodded in satisfaction. "Good. I have rarely seen a good wine fail. Miss Chadwick, you are obviously suffering under a misapprehension. Contrary to what you may believe, and considering everything, the first hurdle has been gotten over surprisingly well.''

Joan stared at her ladyship in open disbelief. ''My lady, you cannot be serious. Everyone was at daggers' points. As for my own reception . . . why, I would scarcely have lasted five seconds alive saving the viscount's and your own presence.''

''Joan, my grandmother is right. It went somewhat better than I expected. After all, Miss Ratcliffe was not present to contribute full-blown hysterics,'' Lord Humphrey said. He smiled down at her appalled expression. ''You may breathe more freely now. I suspect the worst to be over, my lady.''

''Do you indeed? How young you are still, Edward,'' Lady Cassandra said cheerfully. She lifted her wineglass and drained it with relish.

Joan felt a sinking feeling. ''Just what are you saying, my lady?''

''Only that I'd wager that there will be a few more uncomfortable moments to be gotten through,'' Lady Cassandra said. ''You have yet to meet Lord Dewesbury, as well as the score of others that I would have expected Lady Dewesbury would have invited in honor of the wonderful news of my grandson's nuptials.''

''Oh, Lord,'' groaned Lord Humphrey. ''I had not thought. Mama undoubtedly invited a houseful of family and friends who were to have celebrated the happy ties between myself and Miss Ratcliffe. It was the reason I originally meant to come down only for the weekend. I had no desire to play the proud fiancé for a crowd of mistaken well-wishers.''

''My daughter has always been an excellent and meticulous hostess. It is one of her few redeeming qualities,'' Lady Cassandra said musingly.

Joan paid not the least bit of attention to her ladyship. The picture conjured up by the viscount's words was too horrible to contemplate. "I do not think that I can go through with it," she said with a shudder.

"Nor I. I'd as lief be gone within the hour," Lord Humphrey said. "Joan will you come with me?"

"Gladly, my lord," Joan said fervently.

"Pudding hearts, the both of you," said Lady Cassandra roundly.

"I beg your pardon," the viscount said stiffly.

"What will you do once you leave?" asked Lady Cassandra, ignoring her grandson's affront. "There is still the matter of your hasty marriage, or have you forgotten, Edward? You shall have to make a full confession. Or will you play the coward and leave the earl and your poor mother to suffer under the painful delusion that you have taken Miss Chadwick away to her ruin?"

"It is all one and the same at this juncture, my lady," Joan said with a spurt of temper. "The situation is intolerable as it stands."

Lady Cassandra smiled slightly. "Is it, my dear? I suspect that my grandson realizes differently."

12

JOAN LOOKED UP quickly at the gentleman standing beside her chair. Lord Humphrey was scowling. "My lord?" she questioned.

He looked at her, the expression in his frowning eyes inscrutable. When he spoke, it was grimly, reluctantly. "She is right, dash it! We shall have to go on with it. We've gone too far now to cry craven."

"Indeed, I rather think that running away now would make matters even more difficult later," Lady Cassandra said. She added delicately, "Especially if you were to wait until you were forced to impart the news of an impending event."

Lord Humphrey glanced sharply at his grandmother. He had not given thought to that particular possibility before, and the implications stunned him. It was going to be uphill work to introduce into the family a betrothed who was not Miss Ratcliffe. His mind fairly boggled at the notion of presenting a wife, who had never been accepted, with a babe in arms. No, decidedly he would not wish to go through that.

The initial responsibility that he had shouldered for an unknown young woman's reputation was now assuming such proportions that he felt he carried a massive weight.

Joan was wrapped in her own unhappy reflections and she did not gather the import of what had been said. "I had prepared myself for opposition and discomfort. I never dreamed it would be so perfectly ghastly."

Lord Humphrey felt suddenly suffocated. He forcefully slapped his palm against the top of the wing chair. "It is a damnable business! I wish that I had never embarked upon it."

His outburst touched spark to Joan's own insecurities. She shot out of the chair, startling him.

She was trembling when she faced him, and her hands were clenched into fists at her sides. "And I also! Do you think that I actually enjoyed that horrid scene? And when I think that I am expected to sit through more of the same, I positively shiver with dread and revulsion. I wish you had simply left me in that ditch, my lord. It would have been infinitely preferable."

His expression was shocked. "Joan—"

She suddenly could not bear to look at his face for a second longer and she turned her back on him. "There is still the alternative of annulment."

Lady Cassandra's crisp voice rasped raw against Joan's stretched nerves. She raised her head, her eyes closing tight for the brief instant that it took for her to draw a shuddering breath. It was all she could do not to round on the insensitive woman.

Lord Humphrey crossed the distance to his wife. It was strange how he thought of her that way. Nothing had ever passed between them but the exchange of vows, and he could not fathom what there was in that to place her in his thoughts so firmly. He placed his hands on her shoulders and under them felt her violent start of surprise. "I do not wish an annulment. I pledged my vows in all sincerity and honor."

Joan turned under his hands and looked up to search his face.

Lord Humphrey said quietly, "I told you this once before, my lady. I shall not regret taking you for my wife." Their eyes locked and an unnamable expression flitted across the viscount's face.

Joan felt the most curious sensation. She held herself very still. His hands tightened on her shoulders.

"Very prettily said, Edward."

Lady Cassandra's acid tone recalled the couple unpleasantly to their surroundings. The viscount dropped his hands from Joan's shoulders. He turned toward his grandmother, and as much for Lady Cassandra's benefit as for his lady, he said, "I apologize for my hasty words. They were borne out of frustration. I could only wish an easier time of it for Joan's sake."

Lady Cassandra shrugged in a bored fashion. "You have made your bed between you. It is a pity that the sheets are not smooth enough for your mistress's taste."

Hot color surged into Joan's face.

The viscount exclaimed angrily, "You shall not speak in that fashion to my wife!"

"Your wife, Edward!" Lady Cassandra's voice dripped ice. Her eyes were equally cold as she stared at her grandson. "Pray recall that you have entered upon a delicate masquerade. *Miss Chadwick* is your betrothed, Edward. And *Miss Chadwick* should be prepared for just such talk, though not again from myself." She made a gesture of contempt. "I grow weary with this farce. I shall leave you alone to digest what I have said. I hope that you may come to a reasonable acceptance of the reality that you have created, but after your poor performance just now I do not place any confidence in it. I doubt that you shall be able to attain the happy outcome that you desire, Edward."

Lady Cassandra left the drawing room.

There was a long silence while the viscount and Joan stared at each other. The temper in his eyes was not for her, she knew. She lifted her hand in an inadequate gesture. "I was mistaken, my lord. Lady Cassandra can indeed be a dragon," she said.

"Yes, and one with a razor-edged tongue," said Lord Humphrey, still smarting from his grandmother's scathing disparagement.

"Yet, I do believe that she has your best interests at heart."

"She has a damnable way of showing it," Lord Humphrey said.

"But nevertheless her ladyship is correct in her estimation. We are fools, the both of us, for believing that we might spare your family some measure of suffering," Joan said. She made a short turn about the room, pausing to touch a figurine here, a vase there.

Lord Humphrey watched her. He was aware of her distress, but he was powerless to remedy the situation, and that angered him further. "What would you have me do, my lady? I am not a wizard that I might magically set all aright. I have done as my honor has led me. Am I to be condemned for that, and by you? You forget yourself, my lady. *I* do not forget that it is you who stands to profit the most by this rotten coil."

Joan rounded on him then, her own eyes snapping in anger. "I do not expect magic, Edward. As for profit, if it was not for me or some other poor idiot, you would be firmly leg-shackled to a lady whom you hold in utter revulsion."

Lord Humphrey's smile twisted unpleasantly. His gray eyes were wintery. "One leg-shackle is much like another, my dear."

Joan whitened. She appeared stricken as she stared across the room at him. Then her face altered, taking on a distant expression that he had never seen before.

"There is nothing more to be said, my lord." She swept around and pulled open the drawing-room door. Blindly, for the tears had already started to her eyes, she fled.

Lord Humphrey stood irresolute, at once angered and ashamed. He did not know why he had cut up so harshly at her. He felt impelled to go after her, but his pride held him in check.

Joan had no goal in mind except to flee the viscount's presence. She scarcely saw the lady approaching the drawing room until she had precipitously collided with her.

"Miss Chadwick!" Lady Dewesbury was scandalized by

the young woman's ill manners. Then she saw that the girl was in grave distress, fighting back tears and making quick, ineffectual wipes at her eyes. The countess's natural compassion asserted itself and softened her voice. "My dear! Whatever has upset you so?"

"Forgive me, my lady. I—"

"Joan!"

At the viscount's harsh voice, Joan's head snapped around. Her eyes went wide with dismay when she saw that his lordship had come through the door of the drawing room after her. She would not talk to him then, she thought, she simply could not! She would almost certainly humiliate herself by bursting into inexplicable tears.

Lady Dewesbury was astonished at the look almost of panic on the young woman's face. She threw a forbidding glance in her son's direction as she firmly took the girl's arm. "Come, Miss Chadwick. You are fatigued, and little wonder. I was just coming to tell you and Lord Humphrey that we dine late this evening, so that if you wish to do so you may indulge in a little rest after tea. Allow me to show you up to your bedroom. Your trunks have already been carried up, of course."

Lady Dewesbury spirited away the viscount's prey, for she was not a stupid woman and she had instantly perceived that her son was in a freakish temper. That his displeasure had something to do with Miss Chadwick, she also knew, and she was resolved to discover the root of it.

The countess led her uninvited guest upstairs and opened the door to a charming bedroom. She ushered Miss Chadwick in, keeping up a prattle to cover up her interest in the young woman. "Here we are, my dear. I hope that you will be comfortable. As I told you, here are your trunks. Ah, this must be your abigail. How do you do? I am Lady Dewesbury. I trust that you are finding everything to your mistress's satisfaction?"

The abigail was astonished to find herself so addressed. She bobbed a quick curtsy. "Yes, my lady." She folded her hands over her apron, waiting uncertainly for what would next be required of her.

Lady Dewesbury did not waste a moment. "I should like to visit with your mistress alone for a few moments."

Joan had stepped away from the countess as though to admire the room, but in reality it was to enable herself to wipe away the remaining evidence of her stupid tears. At the countess's words, however, she turned back. Alarm and dismay were writ openly on her countenance. She thought wildly how she could possibly clue her abigail that she did not want to be left to the countess's tender mercies. Joan tried to catch the abigail's eyes, but to no avail.

The abigail understood the countess instantly and perfectly. She bobbed another curtsy. "I shall just be in the closet room when you might require me, miss," she said, withdrawing at once.

Lady Dewesbury regarded her guest somberly. "Miss Chadwick, you are overwrought. I saw it at once. I hope that you will not consider me prying, but I must ask. What has my son done?"

Joan swallowed before attempting to smile. "Done, my lady?"

The countess reached out and took her hand. She drew the unwilling young woman toward the settee that was situated under the room's large bay window. "You shall confide in me, I insist."

Joan realized that Lady Dewesbury had little intention of leaving until her curiosity was satisfied. Nevertheless, she made an appeal. "My lady, pray do not. It is nothing that must concern you."

"Miss Chadwick, when you became betrothed to my son, everything about you must concern me," Lady Dewesbury said forcefully. She saw that the young woman had averted her face as though struck, and she gentled her tone. "My dear, what is it?"

Joan rose hastily from the settee and took a quick step away. "I should not confide in you, of all people. Lady

Cassandra . . .'' She broke off, realizing instantly that she had erred. It was a measure of her agitation that she had so easily betrayed herself. She turned back to face her hostess and tried to regain her ground. ''Lady Dewesbury, I am most sorry to put you through such unpleasantness. I would undo it if I could, really I would. But it is such a tangle, I do not think that I would be able to take up my old life now.''

Lady Dewesbury received several impressions at once. The revelation that her mother was somehow involved was filed away for later contemplation. She was more concerned with Miss Chadwick's obvious sincerity and what little that she had revealed. On the basis of a suspicion that suddenly reared its ugly head with her unwelcome guest's words, Lady Dewesbury probed a little deeper. ''I suppose that my son has much to do with your inability to, as you say, take up your old life?''

Miss Chadwick's expression gave credence to the countess's suspicion. Lady Dewesbury's lips tightened briefly as she thought what questions she would like to put to a particular young gentleman. ''Miss Chadwick, when I came up to you the viscount was pursuing you, obviously to take up a conversation that had been abruptly suspended. You were in tears—yes, I saw them, my dear. His lordship had been ill-tempered with you, hadn't he?''

Joan tried to laugh, but the sound caught in her throat. ''His lordship had never been so before, you see. Stupid of me, really. It was just that it came so swiftly after—'' She brought herself up short. She did smile at the countess then, tremulously and politely. ''Forgive me, my lady. I am not usually one to wear my thoughts on my sleeve. As you said, it has been a most fatiguing day.''

Lady Dewesbury saw that the young woman had at last gotten herself well in hand. She was not disappointed, however. What she thought she had gleaned had set her mind seething with further conjecture and strengthened suspicions. ''I shall not disturb you further, then, Miss Chadwick. I shall see you again at tea, of course.''

Joan murmured assent and it was with relief that she saw her inquisitive hostess out of the bedroom.

With the sound of the outer door being shut, the door to the closet room opened and the abigail put her head around it. Her eyes were wide and held a conspiratorial expression. "Is it safe, miss?" she whispered *sotto voce*.

Joan laughed shakily. She dashed her hand across her eyes for the last time. "Yes, of course it is, Maisie."

The abigail left her hiding place and came into the room. "I heard everything, miss. Begging your pardon and all, miss, but it is a proper turnabout, isn't it? I heard ever so much from the upstairs maid, who was dusting the room when I came up with the trunks, and this Miss Ratcliffe is a regular tartar. She'll not make it simple for you, I'll warrant."

Joan sighed. "It's none of it simple, Maisie. It was perfectly ghastly this afternoon, and it can only become worse. Oh, Maisie! Whatever shall I do? I almost wish that I had never met his lordship."

"No point in wishing that, miss," said the abigail. She began to help Joan undress so that she could put on a fresh gown for tea. "You can't go back, and especially after what has passed between you and his lordship."

"No," Joan agreed dismally.

Neither she nor the abigail realized that, behind them, the bedroom door was being softly closed.

Lady Dewesbury went along to her own rooms, very much shocked.

She had turned back to Miss Chadwick's room, recalling that she had not given her guest the hour that dinner would be served. She had turned the knob and started to hail her guest, but she paused on hearing the abigail's repeating of the servants' gossip. Then she had been captured by Miss Chadwick's reply and she had listened for a moment longer.

It was reprehensible of her to have eavesdropped. She knew that, and she was heartily mortified by her uncharacteristic action. But she was glad, too, that she had heard what she had, for it made some sense out of her son's unprecedented departure from obedient duty.

However, the thoughts that had been set in motion in her mind were disturbing ones, and Lady Dewesbury was not at all certain that she wanted to learn more about what was behind the strange engagement between her son and Miss Chadwick.

As it was, the household was in an uproar.

Her husband was out murdering innocent birds. She could never become used to that, even if one could later justify it by serving fowl at table.

Her dearest and best friend was furious and would probably shake the dust of Dewesbury Court from her heels, never more to be heard from. She could scarcely blame Aurelia, but it was so utterly unfair that their friendship was threatened, and through no fault of her own.

The rest did not bear thinking of. She would much rather shut her door and wait for everything to be resolved without her. However, she could hardly avoid the situation when everyone must meet again at tea.

13

TEA WAS ALMOST as uncomfortable as the initial meeting.

Joan knew herself to be ill-at-ease, but she made a gallant attempt not to appear so. She had chosen to wear one of her most flattering day gowns in hopes of giving herself courage. The long-sleeved gown was a pale-lavender muslin and was tied close under the bosom with gray satin ribbons. She knew that she appeared at her best and therefore she was able to meet the gazes of those already in the drawing room with an air of quiet confidence. She paused on the threshold.

Lord Humphrey crossed the room at once to lead her in. His gray eyes appeared shuttered and his expression was distant when he glanced down into her face, but nevertheless Joan derived some comfort from his presence. "Miss Chadwick, I am glad that you have joined us," he said.

"It is my pleasure, my lord," Joan murmured.

He looked at her sharply, suspecting her of sarcasm, but there was nothing in her expression to point to it. "You know my grandmother, Lady Cassandra, of course."

"My dear Miss Chadwick. I hope that you have found everything to your taste?" asked Lady Cassandra, amusement tingeing her voice.

Brief annoyance flashed in Joan's eyes. "I am not at all disappointed, Lady Cassandra. Quite the reverse, in fact," she said. Her reply was just pointed enough to convey something of her feelings.

Lady Cassandra laughed.

While Lady Cassandra still chortled, Lord Humphrey hurriedly turned Joan toward his mother and the gentleman who stood beside her. "I was remiss earlier in not making proper introductions. This is my mother, Lady Dewesbury, and my godfather, Lord Ratcliffe. Miss Joan Chadwick."

"How do you do, my lady, my lord," said Joan, offering her hand to each in turn. Though Lady Dewesbury and Lord Ratcliffe acknowledged her with cool reserve, their greetings also reflected proper civility.

Joan's worst fears loosened their hold on her. She had been prepared for more outbursts or at the very least patent hostility. Apparently, the countess and Lord Ratcliffe had at some time between this and the last meeting concluded that the matter should be handled with more decorum.

Joan was surprised when Lady Dewesbury went so far as to compliment her on her appearance. "Thank you, my lady."

Lady Dewesbury knitted her brows as she surveyed Joan's gown once more. She looked as though she wished to pose a question, but she apparently thought better of it. Instead, she inquired of Joan how she preferred her tea.

Joan indicated that she liked her tea sweetened, with milk. She took the cup from her hostess's hands, thanking her ladyship for the courtesy.

"Have you been long in this part of the country, Miss Chadwick?" Lady Dewesbury asked with her best hostess smile. She could not help noticing certain things about Miss Chadwick, most particularly the young lady's well-bred manners. The girl was obviously quite used to taking tea in company.

Miss Chadwick was not a stunningly beautiful young woman, but Lady Dewesbury thought she was beginning to

see what must have attracted Lord Humphrey to her. She
had a certain dignified air about her. Her short dark curls
provided a frame for her expressive brown eyes and her
pleasant-featured face. She was well-turned-out, her gown
the work of an obviously superior needlewoman, but Lady
Dewesbury thought the choice of color too subdued. She
presented an overall picture of quiet gentility that was
reinforced whenever she spoke in her well-modulated voice.

"No, my lady. I think it is a very beautiful county,
however, what I have seen of it in the last few weeks," said
Joan.

"Have you friends in the area, then?" asked Lady
Dewesbury.

"Miss Chadwick has been staying with me for the last few
days," Lady Cassandra said, an edge of challenge in her
tone.

"Indeed," said Lady Dewesbury. It was another piece of
the puzzle and it was almost irresistible, but she hoped that
she was intelligent enough to see what her mother was about.
She did not take up the gauntlet that her mother had so
blatantly flung down, but instead turned again to her
unheralded guest and set herself to engage Miss Chadwick
into conversation.

Joan rose nobly to the occasion. She was used to the tone
of such conversation, which was gently probing yet polite.
As the vicar's daughter, she had been the object of a good
many well-meaning dames who had stirred themselves to an
interest in her. It was old stuff to parry Lady Dewesbury's
veiled inquisitiveness, yet she did so in such a fashion as
would not offend her ladyship by volunteering small
impersonal tidbits about herself that would satisfy the lady's
curiosity for the moment.

"Yes, my lady, I quite enjoy drawing and music and other
such gentle pastimes. One can find much enjoyment in
expressing oneself creatively," she said.

"Oh, yes," agreed Lady Dewesbury. She was herself too

clumsy to enjoy painting and she was so tone-deaf that music did not particularly appeal to her. However, such ladylike accomplishments proved nothing about Miss Chadwick's background. Miss Chadwick looked and acted the part of a lady, but Lady Dewesbury wanted to know who her family was and their connections.

As he watched Joan, Lord Humphrey found himself reluctantly admiring her. He was still angry, both with himself and with Joan, but as he stood by in the presence of her quiet courage, he found himself wishing that circumstances were different. He would have liked to go over to her and make light conversation, as he would have done with any young lady whom he found attractive. But instead he was forced to make himself agreeable to his mother and to Lord Ratcliffe, with an eye to persuading them to accept his wife's—or Miss Chadwick's—presence.

For his mother's benefit, he had decided almost immediately that his best present course was not to seem too protective or possessive of his betrothed. It would give Lady Dewesbury the time she needed to adjust to Joan and to learn a little about her without the irritant of his own interference, he thought. He was well aware that he was in deep disgrace and quite unforgiven. That had been made perfectly clear to him by the countess.

Lord Humphrey had been greeted upon his entrance into the drawing room by a reproachful look from his mother. She had said nothing untoward to him, nor later to Joan, but the expression in her eyes had spoken volumes, he thought with a sigh. He suspected it would take some exertion on his part to convince her of the rightness of his actions. At least she had not cut up publicly again or given the cold shoulder to Joan. Indeed, he was astonished that his mother treated Joan with so little antagonism after that first disastrous meeting.

He was also pleasantly surprised by his own reception at Lord Ratcliffe's hands. Though there had remained a degree of affront in the continued stiffness of Lord Ratcliffe's manner, that gentleman had unbent enough to greet the viscount with a degree of warmth that earlier had been missing. Lord Humphrey felt his confidence go up a notch regarding his ability to bring around at least one of his godparents.

Lady Ratcliffe was an entirely different matter, however. She would naturally feel the insult sharper, having so obviously taken to herself her daughter's indignation.

The viscount was unsurprised when Lady Ratcliffe did not come down for tea. Lord Ratcliffe had made her excuses gracefully, but the lady's absence was still felt keenly by the gathered company as a measure of her disapprobation.

Lady Ratcliffe was not the only defector. Her daughter, Miss Augusta Ratcliffe, also did not put in an appearance. Lord Humphrey thought rather grimly that he was only too glad that Augusta had chosen to remain abovestairs. He was certain that when at last his erstwhile intended did decide to come down, they would all be treated to a rare show. He was not at all put out by Miss Ratcliffe's absence.

However, Lord Humphrey was worried about the earl's absence. He asked quietly of his mother, "Is his lordship returned?" Lady Dewesbury shook her head, an anxious pucker between her own brows.

Lady Cassandra heard the quiet question and she turned her eagle regard upon her daughter and grandson. "The earl is still behaving like a schoolboy, is he? I would not have thought it of him. I am surprised—yes, surprised that so worthy a gentleman indulges in such frightful tantrums."

Lord Ratcliffe, seated in the wing-back chair beside Lady Cassandra, had full view of her ladyship's expression. His heavy brows climbed into his hairline.

Lady Dewesbury pinned a determined smile to her face. "Do you wish more tea, Mama? I shall be happy to pour for you."

Lady Cassandra showed her teeth in a wicked smile, but she did not make the acid reply that all thought she might.

Instead, she merely proffered her cup to Lady Dewesbury.

Truth to tell, Lady Cassandra was feeling oddly off-balance. She had come down to tea prepared to defend Miss Chadwick from a vicious attack, but the attack had never materialized. It was not as though the betrothal had suddenly become accepted, but there were such strange undercurrents emanating from Lady Dewesbury and Lord Ratcliffe.

Lady Cassandra could not quite put her finger on the elusive change in atmosphere that she sensed, and it annoyed her. After a single sip of her freshened tea, she sat down her cup with force. "Pah! The tea has grown cold."

Lady Dewesbury knew that to be untrue, but nevertheless she felt bound to turn her attention to smoothing over Lady Cassandra's ill temper. She rose from her place beside Miss Chadwick on the settee and crossed over to bend solicitously over her mother.

Lord Humphrey seized the opportunity to exchange a few words with Joan. He leaned over the back of the settee. "You appear very fine this afternoon, my lady," he said quietly.

Joan glanced around at him, coolness in her eyes. "A pretty compliment, my lord. To what should I attribute it?" Despite the challenge of her reply, she was sitting stiffly, proof that she was uncomfortable at his proximity.

Lord Humphrey grinned faintly to himself. The expression in his eyes rivaled the devilish glint that so often appeared in his grandmother's. He allowed himself the liberty of lightly brushing his fingers across the back of her neck as he folded his arms on the edge of the settee.

His touch electrified her, making her start. Joan gave an inarticulate gasp. "My lord! Pray do not!" She was acutely aware of him, only measuredly less so of the others in the room. Lord Ratcliffe had some minutes before quietly excused himself from the conversation and taken up the day's papers, but he was still within hearing distance and so were the countess and Lady Cassandra.

"What, my dearest Joan? I have spoken for you, after all," he said teasingly.

She very nearly turned on him then, the insult that he had flung at her quite vivid in her mind. But she caught herself back in time, having seen that Lord Ratcliffe's eye had left his paper and now rested thoughtfully on them.

"You will have the goodness to move away, my lord. Or I shall," she said in a furious whisper.

Lord Humphrey realized that he had set up her back and he abandoned his teasing. He lowered his quiet voice even further. "I wished only to apologize, my lady. What I said earlier was both cruel and inaccurate. You are not in the least like that other lady. I spoke from hasty temper and I regret it."

There was a short silence.

"I shall accept that, my lord. What choice have I, after all? We are irrevocably bound together in this strange alliance," Joan said. She slid a glance from under her lashes at the viscount.

It was his turn for silence. "As you say, my lady." He straightened and walked away.

Joan watched his lordship as he left her, not particularly unhappy that she had struck him such a foul blow. It was time he learned that her acquiescence was not to be taken for granted, and nor was it without cost. She had agreed to everything that he had wished, and because of it he had obviously never considered that she might question her role or, more to the point, his.

Her hurt and anger at Lord Humphrey's unfair observation earlier that day had given her cause for unpleasant reflection, and she had come to see matters from an angle that did not allow for sentimentality. It was wrong of her, but she resented what had happened to her. Her life had been turned on its head, and though she had agreed to accept the change in her fortune, she could yet visit scathing thoughts on the viscount.

Joan had decided that Lord Humphrey had not often thought deeply about the feelings of others. Nothing in their relationship thus far had given to her the impression that he thought further than the moment, or perhaps the next moment.

He had treated her with a kindness and a gallantry that she had thought a reflection of a fine sensitive nature. But since he had returned to Blackhedge Manor, and more particularly since they both had come to Dewesbury Court, she was beginning to wonder whether she had divined him truly.

He was not the same gentleman who had behaved so protectively of her at the inn or had so defiantly introduced her to his grandmother. She found him more distant, more complex, in his manner.

He had married her out of hand in order to protect her reputation, but by doing so, he had also saved himself from a despised entanglement. He had leapt at the notion of hoodwinking his family with his false engagement in order to spare the earl and countess and the Ratcliffes some of the shock, but thus he had also avoided part of the censure that would have been his if he had instead presented to them a wife.

Joan could not but wonder what the viscount would say or how he would act toward Miss Ratcliffe. Alone of all the company, she wished that Miss Ratcliffe had come down for tea, if only so that she could observe Lord Humphrey in the lady's company.

As for her own conduct in all of this, Joan was beginning to despise herself. It did not matter that she thought the viscount quite the handsomest gentleman she had ever seen, nor that her heart started beating a little more quickly whenever he was near her. She knew that their relationship was based strictly upon convenience, both hers and his. What existed between them had nothing to do with the finer qualities that she had observed in her own parents' marriage before her mother's untimely death.

But here Joan's thoughts faltered. She turned the ring upon her finger, at the same time aware that under her bodice lay the warm touch of the band of gold against her breast.

Like gold, honor was of sterling quality. She had had proof enough that Lord Humphrey possessed it in full measure. His lordship had wedded her, whatever the deeper of his motives might have been. Moreover, he had pledged himself to her a second time. Not with love, but surely with the respect and honor that any woman might expect once she had accepted his name.

14

JOAN SIGHED SOFTLY. She looked up and her eyes traveled to the viscount, who stood a short distance away at the mantel. She rose and went to him. She touched his sleeve. Lord Humphrey looked down at her expressionlessly. Before her courage failed her, Joan said, "I believe it is now my turn to apologize, my lord. I was abominable."

"You have a deuced temper," he said, as though in discovery.

"Yes," she admitted. Her eyes began to gleam. "But I suspect that I shall need it at times when dealing with your lordship."

Lord Humphrey grinned reluctantly. He lifted her hand to his lips. "I do not deny it, my lady."

Their interchange had not gone unnoticed. The others present, though they could not hear what had led up to it, had observed the apparent tiff between the viscount and Miss Chadwick and the subsequent patching of relations.

Lady Cassandra gave a short cackle. "There you have it, daughter. A most worthy pair of cooing doves."

"Pray, Mama!" Lady Dewesbury cast an apologetic glance in Lord Ratcliffe's direction, whom she was certain was not at all edified by the sight of his erstwhile future son-in-law making up to an unknown girl. But she was surprised, for, instead of the stiff affronted expression that she had expected to find on Lord Ratcliffe's face, there was the faintest suggestion of a smile.

"The viscount cuts quite a dash with the lady," he said imperturbably.

Lord Ratcliffe caught Lady Dewesbury's glance, and his smile came out into the open. "Why so surprised, Charlotte? Some time ago it occurred to me to suspect that your fine young son was not one to come tamely to the cart that had been prepared for him, not when my daughter showed him at every turn that she thought she held the reins. But I was foolish enough to set aside the thought, believing that I was most likely mistaken. After all, Aurelia never saw it, and apparently neither did anyone else."

"I am truly astonished, John," faltered Lady Dewesbury. "I would have thought you, of us all, would be thrown quite into the boughs."

Lord Ratcliffe shrugged. "I admit to feeling a certain outrage and insult, and I still do. But what is done is done, and I am not one to hold a grudge, especially against my own godson."

Lady Cassandra reached across the intervening space between their chairs and cracked her fan against Lord Ratcliffe's arm. "I like you, my lord. You accept the inevitable and go on from there. You will live longer with that attitude, I promise you."

Lord Ratcliffe sketched a bow to the elderly lady. "I am most appreciative of your approval, Lady Cassandra. It is my understanding that few earn it."

"Few deserve it," Lady Cassandra responded promptly.

Lady Dewesbury threw up her hands in defeat. It was all beyond her. She didn't understand any of it. Her mother was behaving uncharacteristically benevolent toward an interloper in their midst, while Lord Ratcliffe, who was just as prideful as her own spouse, had virtually given his blessing to the surprising betrothal.

"I suppose I should be grateful for your forbearance, my lord," said Lady Dewesbury.

"Indeed you should, daughter," Lady Cassandra said dryly.

"I shall be most interested in learning what your private opinion on all of this is, Mama," said Lady Dewesbury.

Lady Cassandra's eyes narrowed. Abruptly she rapped her fan against the arm of her chair. "Here, Miss Chadwick! I see that you have done with your tea. I wish you to come up to my room with me now and read to me. It will put me in the proper mood to rest before dinner," she said belligerently.

"Really, Mama! How can you impose upon Miss Chadwick's good nature in such a manner?" asked Lady Dewesbury. She was desirous of a few words with her mother in private and she suspected that Lady Cassandra was only too aware of it and so that lady had dreamed up this outrageous tactic to avoid her.

"It is quite all right, my lady. During my stay with Lady Cassandra I came to enjoy reading aloud to her ladyship," Joan said hurriedly, hoping to fend off the conflict that she saw looming. She was also recalling how the countess had invited herself up to her bedroom earlier.

The command performance at Lady Cassandra's bidding was not without its drawbacks, but at least it offered a graceful way to extricate herself from the possibility of additional intimate conversation with the countess. She would rather keep her first acquaintance with Lord Humphrey's family on a general footing as long as possible, which meant avoiding such uncomfortable *tête-à-têtes* in future.

Lady Cassandra smiled, her eyes snapping with unholy satisfaction. "There, you see? Not everyone is so unaccommodating as you believe, daughter."

Lady Dewesbury took her defeat gracefully, but she was more than ever determined to take her mother to task and learn what Lady Cassandra could tell her about Miss Chadwick. Obviously Miss Chadwick was on good terms with her mother. That was extraordinary enough in itself, so there must be something about this business that appealed to Lady Cassandra's deplorable sense of humor, thought the countess with most unfilial feelings as Lady Cassandra left the drawing room on Miss Chadwick's arm.

"My lord, I feel fortunate this afternoon. Can I interest you in a game of billiards?" asked Lord Humphrey of his godfather.

Lord Ratcliffe regarded the viscount with a shrewd expression in his eyes. "I have no objection to it, my boy," he said in his ponderous fashion, with just the merest thread of irony.

Lord Humphrey flushed slightly. He knew that Lord Ratcliffe had tumbled to his intention to get off alone with him so that they could speak in private.

"Thank you, sir," he said quietly.

Lord Ratcliffe's mildness augered well for him. The viscount hoped that over the green baize table he might discover exactly what his godfather thought and felt about the surprising betrothal. It was an opportunity to press his case in convivial surroundings.

The gentlemen made their excuses to the countess and went off to the game room.

Lady Dewesbury herself left the drawing room to inquire of her butler if there had been anything seen of the earl. Hudgens regretfully had to say that his lordship had not been seen to return to the house.

Lady Dewesbury sighed. "You do know what that means, Hudgens."

"Indeed, my lady," he said. "Shall I send Cook to you, my lady?"

"No, I shall go down to the kitchens myself and prepare her for it all," said Lady Dewesbury gloomily.

The countess descended into the bowels of the servants' stronghold, the kitchen, to inform her devoted cook of the coming deluge of fowl that the earl would almost certainly bring in that evening. Perhaps more than anyone else, the cook deplored the earl's habit of shooting everything at wing when he was in one of his black moods. "For how many ways can one dress and cook a bird, my lady?" she asked.

It had become Lady Dewesbury's unenviable task on these occasions to smooth over the cook's acerbated feelings and assure the woman that no one questioned her abilities, nor was it some sort of hellish test of her loyalty. Always at the last the cook would tearfully offer her resignation and always the countess would graciously decline to accept it, and that would be the end of the matter until the next time that the earl set out with his fowling piece.

The situation was even more taxing than usual, for the cook was already resentful that Lady Cassandra's personal chef had commandeered much of her domain. Lady Dewesbury found it difficult to hang on to her flagging temper, and by the time that the cook got around to offering her resignation, she was quite willing to accept it. But the countess's good sense prevailed and she managed to decline the resignation once more. Excellent cooks were difficult to find, and once found, one must be prepared to go to ludicrous lengths to keep these indispensable worthies content with their lot.

When at last the impending domestic crisis seemed to be averted and Lady Dewesbury felt able to get away, she was so exhausted that she went immediately upstairs to her rooms to rest. She did not rise until her maid came into the room to waken her in order to start dressing for dinner.

An hour later, Lady Dewesbury dismissed her maid. She was dressed for the evening except for the last touches to her appearance, which she preferred to add herself in privacy.

She sat down in front of her vanity to begin the task of adding a little artifice to her face. She had set aside her long-held bias against cosmetics upon the discovery that a touch of rouge, discreetly applied under her face powder, enabled her to retain the illusion of the natural color in her face that had begun to fade with the years.

The countess felt herself more than justified when she had set down her rouge pot and her hare's foot and looked into the mirror. She was still a pretty woman, and that assurance particularly pleased her when she thought of all that awaited her that evening.

The countess did not like conflict, but especially under her own roof. She prided herself on her hospitality and her table, and it had always distressed her on those few occasions when some of her guests did not enjoy themselves. Lady Dewesbury was quite certain that this evening would be the first of many uncomfortable evenings, and she was not at all happy about it.

Her bedroom door suddenly swung open. A large gentleman strode in and closed the door behind him with a snap. She was unsurprised by the heavy frown that still lengthened his face. The earl had left the manor in a thunderous temper and it was not to be expected that his recent vigorous activity would do more than take the edge off it.

She saw from his attire that he must have just returned to the house. "Have you bagged every bird on the place?" she asked brightly.

The Earl of Dewesbury stared down at her from his great height. He wore a long frock coat over buckskins and there was mud on his boots. He was generally accorded to be still quite a handsome gentleman. His red hair was grizzled and his heavy frame had thickened a bit around the middle, but his strength was undiminished and so was his forceful personality.

"My word, Charlotte! How can you sit there so calmly making ready for dinner when at this very moment our scapegrace son and that scheming minx that he had the audacity to bring with him resides in our home. Yes, I know all about her. I spoke to Hudgens just moments ago, and very astonished I was to hear that Edward is so far gone as to actually have introduced his doxy under this very roof," exclaimed the earl. He ground his teeth. "I shall have something to say to him presently, never fear."

"I wish you wouldn't," said Lady Dewesbury. She saw

that her husband was turning a rich puce and she hurriedly clarified herself. "At least, not right away. You were not present when they arrived, Greville. Aurelia positively flew out of the room, renouncing us all. It was horrid. *I* was horrid! My behavior was not at all what I am accustomed to expect of myself. One wishes to conduct one's duties with grace and dignity. Instead, I attacked Edward and I actually turned upon my mother. I was never more mortified in myself, Greville."

"I remain unmoved, my dear. In fact, I perceive that you acted just right," said Lord Dewesbury. A glint entered his eyes. "Turned on your mother, heh? I should have liked to have heard that."

"Really, Greville! You act as though you do not even like Mama," Lady Dewesbury said. She realized that was perhaps not the most efficious tact to take and immediately she dropped it and picked another. "In any event, I do not want a repeat of that grisly scene over dinner. Be a dear, Greville, and speak to Edward in the privacy of your study. Can you not do that for me? Promise me, Greville."

"Very well," he said grudgingly. He had never been able to deny her anything that she had earnestly set her heart upon. "But you do not know what you ask of me, Charlotte, you really do not."

"Of course I do, dearest Greville." Lady Dewesbury reached up to briefly, gently, lay her fingers against his cheek.

He caught her fingers and turned his lips into her palm.

She smiled at him. It was on the point of her tongue to divulge her base suspicions, if only to be reassured that she must be mistaken, but she thought better of it. Time enough when she knew more, she decided, and wondered if she was not a something of a coward.

Lord Dewesbury was removed from her by his own thoughts. He suddenly swore. "Charlotte! We were to introduce Augusta as Edward's betrothed at that house party you planned for next week. We cannot have it take place now, not with this mess on our hands. You must write everyone at once to cancel,'' he said.

"It wouldn't do a bit of good, Greville.''

"What nonsense is this, Charlotte? Pray, do you realize what we will have on our hands? It will be a circus, I tell you. The whole place will be buzzing and there will be the Ratcliffe's, trapped, unable to escape until those repairs and renovations at the manor house are completed. Can you imagine their feelings, my dear? Or mine, for that matter,'' exclaimed the earl.

"But, really, my dear, I don't see what we can do about it. Everyone is either already on their way, or if they meant not to come, they will certainly do so now after seeing that notice in the *Gazette*,'' Lady Dewesbury said on a sigh.

The earl looked grim. He said heavily, "I suppose you are right, my dear. We shall just have to make the best of a bad situation. It will be deuced uncomfortable, however.''

"I think that the finest understatement of the age, Greville,'' said Lady Dewesbury with a flash of uncharacteristic tartness.

"I shall not allow Neville to come home, nor Margaret. They can be spared the humiliation, at least,'' said Lord Dewesbury.

"I do not agree with you, Greville. I do not think it right that our youngest children must be deprived of their holiday because of Edward's situation. They should not have their hopes dashed in such a fashion,'' Lady Dewesbury said.

"There is something in what you say,'' said the earl, frowning. "Edward must be made to realize that his actions do not influence only himself and us, but his siblings as well. Perhaps once he sees this woman in the midst of his family, he will come to realize what a ghastly mistake he has made in disappointing us all.''

Lord Dewesbury's lips tightened. "As for this interloper, she will be brought to realize how far out of her ken she aspires. Perhaps it may even cause her to rethink her position and then she can be persuaded to withdrew her claims upon our son.''

There was something in Lady Dewesbury's eyes that made him think for an instant that she meant to relay something of importance, but she said only, ''Dress for dinner, my lord. The bell will soon ring.''

15

JOAN WAS NOT able to escape from Lady Cassandra until nearly time to change for dinner. She hurried back to her bedroom, where her abigail was impatiently awaiting her.

"There you are, miss. I was beginning to suspect foul play," said the abigail. She swiftly undid the buttons down her mistress's back.

Joan laughed. It was good to be able to do so, she realized. On impulse, she turned and hugged the abigail. "You are my sanity, Maisie," she said affectionately.

The abigail flushed to the roots of her brassy gold hair. "Get along with you, miss. Now hop out of that crumpled gown, do. I've a nice bath waiting for you, but you needs must hurry or keep everyone belowstairs waiting on you."

"You are a true dear," Joan said gratefully, slipping out of her clothes and dropping them to the floor. She stepped expectantly into the hip bath, and sank into tepid water. Shivering, she said, "It's a bit cold, Maisie."

"Now, what were you expecting when you delayed so long in coming?" asked the abigail severely, hurrying to get out fresh undergarments and set out her mistress's dress. She had heard an earful from the other servants, among whom she was fast forming friendships, and she knew that this evening was an important one for her mistress.

All of the Ratcliffes would be at table, including Lord Humphrey's former lady. She was shrewd enough to realize that her mistress had to look her positive best if she was to come out of the evening with her pride intact. In listening to the other abigails, she had gathered a fair notion of what the other ladies would be wearing, and that had guided her choice for her own mistress.

Maisie looked critically at the gray satin gown that she had readied. It was well enough, but the color was too drab. She shook her head. A pity that her mistress was in half-mourning, but there it was.

Joan got out of the bath and dried herself. She dressed in her undergarments. The abigail threw the gown over her head and pulled it down into place. While the abigail did up the buttons in the back, Joan stared critically at herself in the mirror. She asked slowly, "Maisie, why this particular gown? It is quite the most elegant that I possess."

The abigail shot a look at her face, meeting her eyes in the mirror. "Miss Ratcliffe will be coming down to dinner, so I've heard."

Joan digested the information. Her mouth curved in a small smile. "I see. Thank you for your concern, Maisie."

The abigail finished the buttons. She was surprised by her mistress's calm reaction. She would have expected at least a hint of agitation. "Will there be anything else, my lady?"

"I don't know what else you could possibly do to make it any easier, Maisie," Joan said on a short laugh. She shook her head at her abigail's anxious expression. "Don't you understand, Maisie? It shall be a relief simply to have it done and over with." She turned away from the mirror, as ready as she would ever be to go downstairs and face the hostility that would of a certainty be her main fare that night.

Joan met Lord Humphrey on the stairs. They greeted each other and she accepted his proffered arm.

He shot a keen glance at her pensive expression. "Nervous, my lady?" he asked sympathetically.

Joan looked up quickly, meeting his eyes. She gave a little laugh. "Yes, I admit it. I am quailing inside. Is it so obvious?"

"One would never know it," he assured her.

They had reached the bottom of the stairs and now slowly traversed the entry hall toward the drawing room. Naturally the entire household would congregate before removing to the dining room. Joan could hear the low buzz of conversation. She set her eyes on the door, dreading the moment when she would become the focus of all eyes.

The viscount paused just before entering the drawing room. He drew a deep breath, then opened the door. Surprised, Joan glanced up at his aquiline profile. She had not realized before that his lordship must also feel a touch of nerves at this debut, but his steadying of himself had been obvious. She was glad to know that Lord Humphrey found the moment difficult. It made her own nervousness seem less pressing.

Since Joan was not thinking about herself when she entered on the viscount's arm, she missed the combined attentions of those already gathered in the drawing room. Her poise remained intact despite the hostile gazes pinned on her. The worst moment was over by the time that Joan looked away from the viscount, for Lady Dewesbury was already moving forward to greet her.

"Edward, my dear! Miss Chadwick, how delightful you look," she said, casting an approving and yet wondering glance over Joan's gown.

Joan murmured an appropriate reply. Her eyes strayed past the countess. She met the hostile stares of Lady Ratcliffe and a heretofore-unknown young lady.

Joan thought quite honestly that she had never seen a more dazzlingly beautiful girl.

Miss Ratcliffe was perfect of feature and figure. She was the possessor of masses of guinea gold hair, large indigo-blue eyes, and a delectably bowed mouth. At the moment there was a hard expression in her eyes and her full underlip was caught between her teeth, lending her a petulant expression, but Joan could forgive her those unangelic inconsistencies. Without those traces of human failings, Miss Ratcliffe would have been simply too perfect to bear looking at.

Lady Dewesbury was determined to make things go in as civil a manner as possible. She therefore made an effort to introduce Miss Chadwick with a bright voice. "Miss Chadwick, you have met Lord and Lady Ratcliffe, of course. And this, naturally, is Miss Augusta Ratcliffe."

"Miss Chadwick." Lord Ratcliffe bowed to Joan and she was surprised when he actually smiled briefly at her. However, Lady Ratcliffe vouchsafed only a freezing stare and the barest of nods.

As for their daughter, Miss Ratcliffe slowly stared Joan up and down before dismissing her very existence. She turned to the viscount, who was one step behind Joan, and held out her hand to him. The hard look disappeared from her brightening eyes and her pretty mouth softened into a beguiling smile. "Edward, come sit beside me."

"Yes, my lord. We have not seen much of you these past weeks. You must tell us how you found London when you left," Lady Ratcliffe said.

The viscount had stiffened at Miss Ratcliffe's unmistakable command. He was on the point of making an excuse, but Lady Ratcliffe's added joiner put him on the spot. He did not want to further antagonize his godmother when it was so important to him that she be brought to understand his position. He knew that Lady Ratcliffe was his mother's dearest friend, and for that reason more than any other he hoped to soften Lady Ratcliffe's ire against him.

"I will be happy to tell you all that I know," he said. He seated himself, but not beside Miss Ratcliffe, choosing instead to position himself in a chair opposite the two ladies.

Miss Ratcliffe's nostrils quivered in brief temper, but she did not challenge the viscount on his careful maneuvering.

She shot a swift daggerlike glance at the back of Miss Chadwick's head as that lady was being led off by the countess.

Lady Dewesbury took Joan up to the Earl of Dewesbury. The earl had maintained his ground separated from the rest of the company, where he stood beside the mantel. The firelight cast ruddy shadows over the planes of his stern face. His hands were clasped behind his back and he stared down from his greater height with an uncompromising set to his mouth.

"My dear, this is Miss Joan Chadwick, whom you have already heard so much about. The Earl of Dewesbury, my husband," said Lady Dewesbury. The anxious air rested prominently upon her features.

"My lord." Joan inclined her head. She did not offer her hand, being quite certain that it would not be accepted. There was such a look of heavy disdain and actual dislike in the earl's eyes that she felt herself oppressed just by the flick of his glance.

"Miss Chadwick." Lord Dewesbury's voice was flat, expressionless. After another moment of staring at her, he turned his gaze onto his flustered wife. "I should like to go into dinner now."

Lady Dewesbury fluttered her hands, consternated both by her lord's arctic behavior and by his abrupt demand. "But Mama is not yet down!"

"You need not worry your peabrain over me, Charlotte," came Lady Cassandra's voice. "I am quite certain that Greville does not." With all eyes turning upon her, Lady Cassandra swept into the drawing room with the aid of a footman.

After an astonished second, while he digested his mother-in-law's unexpected insult, the earl began to flush an interesting shade of red.

Lady Cassandra watched his lordship's transformation sardonically. "I am an old crow, Greville, but you are not yet up to properly training your fowling piece in *my* direction," she said.

Lord Dewesbury restrained himself with difficulty. He bowed stiffly in Lady Cassandra's direction. "As you say, Lady Cassandra," he said. He offered his arm to his wife and Lady Dewesbury placed her fingers on his arm. The earl and countess proceeded to lead the way into the dining room.

Lady Cassandra got in a parting shot. "A most worthy pair, indeed!"

The earl missed a step and half-turned. Lady Dewesbury's agitated whisper was perfectly audible to everyone. "Greville, please! You gave me your solemn word." The earl's snarling reply was lost in the flurry of forming up for the trek to the dining room.

Joan found the viscount at her side. She smiled gratefully to him for his proffered escort. "Thank you, my lord."

Lord Humphrey nodded to her and spoke over her head to Lady Cassandra. "Grandmama, I have a second arm if you will do me the honor."

Lady Cassandra smiled, twin points of wicked light snapping in her cool gray eyes. "Of course, my boy. I would not so insult you by denying you the privilege of acting as my escort."

Lord Humphrey broke into a wide grin. He found himself for once thankful for his grandmother's pricking wit. Given Lady Cassandra's irascible mood, she would undoubtedly detract some of the disapprobation from himself and Joan. He could not think of anything that could please him more.

It had pained Lord Humphrey to observe his father's stiff reaction to Joan, but even more to the point, he had felt the singular lack of greeting that he had himself been granted by the earl. He had always enjoyed an extremely cordial relationship with his father, and the earl's pointed omission had wounded him deeply. Perhaps with Lady Cassandra presenting herself as a target, the earl would unbend enough to toss a grudging word or two in his own direction.

With Joan on one side and Lady Cassandra on the other, Lord Humphrey followed his parents into the dining room.

The Ratcliffes brought up the rear, Lord Ratcliffe resignedly partnering his two seething ladies.

The earl presided at the head of the table and Lady
Dewesbury at its end. Joan was seated between Lady
Dewesbury and the viscount and beyond Lord Humphrey was
Lady Ratcliffe's place. Opposite the viscount was seated Miss
Ratcliffe. Lady Cassandra took her place beside the earl,
throwing a mildly malicious glance in his lordship's direction.
The last chair awaited Lord Ratcliffe between his daughter
and Lady Dewesbury.

Lord Ratcliffe was not greatly surprised by the seating
arrangements, but apparently his wife was not of similar
mind.

"The gall," hissed Lady Ratcliffe in her lord's ear as he
seated her. Her eyes were narrowed on the tableau farther
down the table. "To place that nobody's claims ahead of
those of my dearest Augusta."

"Recall that the young lady is Lord Humphrey's betrothed.
Naturally she is seated beside the viscount. You cannot fault
Charlotte for that," Lord Ratcliffe said quietly.

"Of course I may," exclaimed Lady Ratcliffe. The
glimmer of tears appeared in her blue eyes. "When I recall
what good friends we once were, it positively overpowers
me."

Her voice had risen to its normal level and all those at the
table overheard her. Lady Dewesbury visibly winced. Joan,
having noted her reluctant hostess's distress, lowered her
eyes. At that moment she did not have the courage to meet
the various and swift glances that were angled in her
direction.

Without comment, Lord Dewesbury solicitously offered
his own linen handkerchief to his distressed dinner partner.
Lady Ratcliffe snatched it, mumbling an inarticulate word
of gratitude.

Lord Ratcliffe made good his escape and went around the
table to his own place. As he settled into his chair, he glanced
about and met the bright anger in his daughter's lovely eyes.

He decided that it was going to be a very long evening. Lord Ratcliffe signaled the footman to fill his wineglass.

The first course consisted of a nice barley soup removed by small quail in aspic and baked doves.

Miss Ratcliffe addressed the viscount in a playful manner from across the table. "I have missed you. Naughty, naughty Edward."

The viscount pretended not to hear. He had no intention of allowing himself to be drawn into just the sort of dialogue that he particularly despised. Instead, he attempted to divide his attention equally between his dinner partners on either side of him. Lady Ratcliffe gave him the cold shoulder and twice cut him dead with a contemptous look before she turned in an obvious fashion to address the earl.

Lord Humphrey gave a philosophical shrug and thereafter felt himself free to devote himself to Joan. "I hope that you have a taste for fowl," he said quietly.

Joan slanted a brief, interested glance at his lordship. She had done full justice to the quail in aspic. "I do, as it happens. But why do you inquire, my lord?"

Lord Humphrey grinned. "I think that you shall soon gather my meaning, ma'am."

Lady Cassandra picked with her fork at the dove on her plate. "I've never cared for skinny birds," she observed.

Upon hearing her ladyship's pointed comment, the earl's mouth tightened. Lord Dewesbury requested the hovering footman to bring out a particular bottle of wine. He called down the table, "My dear John, you must try this next vintage. It was a gift from one whom I consider a true connoisseur."

"Bring it on, Greville," said Lord Ratcliffe. He was more than ready to indulge himself.

The second course featured fresh asparagus, peas, and scallops, several enticing meat pies, and three braised ducks served with herb dressing on the side. Joan eyed the ducks. It was the third offering of fowl. She was beginning to understand what Lord Humphrey had alluded to.

Miss Ratcliffe smiled across the table at Lord Humphrey. Her indigo-blue eyes were bright. "I expected you to arrive several days ago, my lord." She spoke loud enough so that there was no mistaking her determination to have an answer. Everyone at the table paused for a scarce second, their forks suspended. Their gazes traveled between Miss Ratcliffe and Lord Humphrey.

The viscount could not ignore this time the challenge in Miss Ratcliffe's voice. "There were matters to attend to," he said shortly.

"Oh, so I gathered," said Miss Ratcliffe, sliding a glittering glance in Joan's direction. "But I dare to opine that my claim on you was of greater moment."

Lord Humphrey seemed about to deliver himself of a hasty set-down. Lady Dewesbury hurried to intervene. She said hurriedly, "The Spanish onions are particularly delectable this evening, do you not think, Edward?"

"Yes. Of course," said Lord Humphrey.

Lady Cassandra snorted, whether in laughter or not was anyone's guess. She speared a piece of dark meat and held it up to eye level. "I detest duck. The meat is so very greasy," she said meditatively.

Lord Dewesbury growled somewhere deep in his throat. He turned determinedly to Lady Ratcliffe. "Aurelia, are you in need of anything? Another serving of potatoes, perhaps?"

"No, nothing." Lady Ratcliffe managed a wan smile for the earl. "I am sorry, Greville. The food is sticking in my throat now. I am sure I do not know why."

"Perhaps you should try some of this excellent wine," suggested Lord Ratcliffe helpfully.

Lady Ratcliffe sent him an evil look.

The third-course entrée was a large goose, roasted and swimming in its own gravy.

Lady Dewesbury's eyes widened at sight of the domestic bird. "A goose?" she murmured. She threw a reproachful look down the table at the Earl of Dewesbury. He appeared supremely unconscious of the countess's glance, but he could be seen to be reddening.

Miss Ratcliffe shrugged her slim shoulders in an elegant fashion that called attention to her shapely bosom. "Really, Edward, I am most annoyed with you. You have somehow contrived to entangle yourself in a most displeasing situation. But I do not doubt that with a little thought it may yet be worked out to our satisfaction."

Lord Humphrey gave his twisted smile. His gray eyes held a hard light. "I am not at all displeased with my situation, Miss Ratcliffe," he grated. "On the contrary! I do not know when I have felt more in control of my own affairs."

Lord Dewesbury muttered angrily under his breath. He stared at his plate with palpable reserve.

"What was that, Greville? Something about the goose, I feel almost certain. I do not blame you in the least. There is something so peculiarly unsettling in having a Christmas goose served in June," said Lady Cassandra.

The earl suddenly seemed on the verge of apoplexy.

Lady Dewesbury flung down her napkin and hurriedly rose from the table. "I, for one, am quite finished. Greville! Greville, I think that I shall take the ladies off. Hudgens, we shall have the desserts later with our coffee, if you please." By her stern example, Lady Dewesbury forced the other ladies to rise also. The ladies murmured their excuses to the gentlemen and left them to the private enjoyment of their wine.

16

THE LADIES WITHDREW to the drawing room and settled themselves comfortably. Almost at once, Joan found herself the target of Miss Ratcliffe's unwelcome attention. That young lady had picked up a lady's magazine and flipped through it until a certain page caught her eyes.

"Why, Miss Chadwick! I do believe that I have found that very same gown you are wearing," she said. She turned the magazine so that they could all view the fashion plate.

Miss Ratcliffe smiled, saying with a shade of malice, "My compliments to your seamstress, Miss Chadwick. She managed to capture quite the essence, if not the superiority, of the design."

"I prefer Miss Chadwick's version myself," Lady Cassandra said unhesitantly. "All that trim and frippery pictured on the plate crosses the line into gauchery."

Miss Ratcliffe inclined her head in pretty deference for the elder lady's opinion. "Perhaps it is the color of your gown that does not do it proper justice, then. Gray is so dreary, is it not? I prefer scarlet for you—yes, scarlet, I think. Some quite famous characters are said to have worn scarlet. Jezebel, for instance."

"My dear Augusta," murmured Lady Ratcliffe in mild reproof. It was not a strenuous rebuke, however.

"I am fond of red," Joan said, ignoring Miss Ratcliffe's deliberate and insulting allusion. She continued with the quietest of set-downs. "However, since I am in half-mourning, Miss Ratcliffe, such a vivid color would hardly have been appropriate."

Miss Ratcliffe was momentarily silenced, as even she recognized the boundaries that could not be crossed.

"Mourning, my dear?" Lady Dewesbury asked, startled. She was at once reminded of her own inner questions concerning the hues of Miss Chadwick's chosen wardrobe. "I do hope not a close family member?"

"My beloved father, my lady, eight months ago."

"I am sorry, Miss Chadwick," Lady Dewesbury said with ready sympathy.

"Indeed, a grievous loss," agreed Lady Ratcliffe grudgingly.

"It is a harsh thing to be cast upon the world, suddenly and without family," said Lady Cassandra.

Joan was seated beside her ladyship on the settee and Lady Cassandra patted the young woman's arm. "But Miss Chadwick is more fortunate than many, for we are now to become her family."

Lady Ratcliffe stiffened in her chair, her eyes flashing, all of her sparse sympathy at an end. Miss Ratcliffe's expression froze, her face a beautiful mask to offset her glittering eyes. She caught her full underlip between her teeth in an excess of impotent temper.

Lady Dewesbury closed her eyes briefly. She wished heartily for the horrible evening to be done with. It had been so trying, and matters certainly had not been aided by her mother's several unfortunate observations. It was almost beyond Lady Dewesbury's considerable capabilities as a hostess to continue on in the face of her guests' determined ill will toward one another, but she made the effort.

"Aurelia, you have not told me how Princess Esterhazy's ball came off. If you recall, I had already left London then," she said brightly. With slowly gathering success, the countess engaged Lady Ratcliffe into conversation about the just-ended London Season. Miss Ratcliffe had a natural interest in the reminiscences, since many concerned her own social triumphs, and she abandoned her baiting of Miss Chadwick.

"Well, my dear? How are your spirits holding up?" asked Lady Cassandra, the shade of a smile on her face.

Joan gave a small laugh. "I survive, my lady."

"I am glad to hear it."

It was not many minutes later that Lord Ratcliffe came into the drawing room. He was alone and he shut the door behind him.

Lady Dewesbury's gaze went from the closed door to Lord Ratcliffe's face. A worried expression entered her eyes.

"Are not the earl and Lord Humphrey joining us?" asked Lady Cassandra.

Lord Ratcliffe shook his head in a thoughtful way. "I believe that Lord Dewesbury had something of import that he wished to convey to the viscount," he said. As he finished speaking, raised voices began to be heard through the walls.

"Oh, no," Lady Dewesbury said, faintly.

"Oh, yes," snapped Lady Cassandra.

Lady Dewesbury wrung her hands. "I had hoped it would not come to this!"

"Pray do not be such a clunch, Charlotte. Of course it had to come!" Lady Cassandra snorted her contempt. She grasped Joan's arm. "Help me up, girl. I'm going to my room. I'm of no mind to sit around with a bunch of huddling hens, straining to hear what I may. I'll hear all about it on the morrow when it's done with."

In the resulting silence, Joan walked with Lady Cassandra to the door. Lady Cassandra opened it and shook off Joan's hand as she called for a footman. She looked at Joan. "I shall now leave you to face the wolves alone, my dear. Good night!"

Joan had no choice but to return to the drawing room, where she was at once attacked by Miss Ratcliffe.

"It is all your fault. You have no business here at all."

"Augusta." Lord Ratcliffe's warning tone was not attended, as Lady Ratcliffe also rounded on the interloper.

"Who are you, Miss Chadwick? I do not recall ever seeing you in London during the Season." Lady Ratcliffe's voice was not as blatantly hostile as her daughter's, but nevertheless its cold undercurrent was just as antagonistic.

Joan returned to the settee and seated herself, folding her hands gracefully in her lap. "I am not surprised. I have never been up to London for Season, Lady Ratcliffe," she said quietly.

"Indeed! However then did you meet Lord Humphrey?" asked Lady Ratcliffe grimly.

"It was a chance meeting, my lady," Joan said shortly, not liking her ladyship's tone. She was beginning to be quite angered by the arrogance with which Lady Ratcliffe and her jealous daughter treated her.

Miss Ratcliffe trilled a pretty laugh. Her eyes were bright with anger. "Oh, *that* I am certain to be the truth. Come, Miss Chadwick. You cannot sit there and expect any of us to believe that you did not positively *toil* to bring yourself to the viscount's attention."

"That will be enough, Augusta," Lord Ratcliffe said explosively.

Miss Ratcliffe tossed her head, but she was silenced.

Lady Ratcliffe started to open her lips. Lord Ratcliffe caught his wife's eyes and held them by sheer force of will. "That will be quite enough all around." Lady Ratcliffe sniffed resentfully, but she also subsided.

The drawing-room door opened. Lady Dewesbury jumped nearly out of her skin, but it was only the coffee and desserts being brought in.

"Hudgens," she exclaimed with relief. She heard an enraged bellow emanating from the direction of the dining room and she paled.

At the butler's soft query, she said, "No, that will be all. We can manage ourselves. Thank you!" She rose from her chair and hurried the butler out with a whispered command and urgent gestures. After shutting the door against the distant voices still raised in conflict, she returned to her chair. "Coffee, anyone?" she asked with determined hospitality. "Or perhaps a tart. Cook always turns out such superb pastries."

Lady Ratcliffe rose abruptly. "Not for me tonight, Charlotte. I discover in myself a touch of indigestion. I shall retire now, I think."

Miss Ratcliffe leapt to her feet. "I shall go with you, Mama."

"That is probably best, pet," said Lord Ratcliffe quietly.

Miss Ratcliffe rather pointedly ignored her father as she prepared to follow her mother. She threw a haughty look at Joan as she passed her.

"Oh! Well, I do hope that you will feel more the thing in the morning," said Lady Dewesbury lamely.

She accompanied her friend toward the drawing-room door, not a word more being spoken between them. Miss Ratcliffe trailed them. Just as the ladies reached the door, it was flung open. They started back in surprise, until they saw that the viscount stood on the threshold. "My dear! How you startled us," exclaimed Lady Dewesbury.

Lord Humphrey's gray eyes glittered above his stony expression. His lean cheekbones were flushed and he was breathing rather quickly. "My pardon, ladies," he said shortly. "Hudgens reminded me that I was neglecting my duties."

"Your father?" faltered Lady Dewesbury. She looked quickly past her son's shoulder to meet the glance of the hovering butler. Hudgens spread out his hands helplessly.

The viscount spoke through his teeth. "His lordship will not be disturbed from his port, my lady."

Impervious to the viscount's temper, Miss Ratcliffe smiled prettily and edged past her mother and Lady Dewesbury so as to be nearer his lordship. She placed her hand gently upon his sleeve. "I did not think that you would be coming in, Edward. I was about to go with Mother, but—"

Lord Humphrey stepped back, pushing the door wide. "Pray do not let me keep you then, Augusta."

Miss Ratcliffe sucked in her breath. Her eyes flashed. "How dare you," she whispered, trembling.

Lady Ratcliffe perceived the moment to be quite wrong for any recriminations to be lodged against the viscount. Lord Humphrey looked to be capable of saying anything and she knew her own daughter's temper. She took hold of her daughter's arm. "Come, darling. You must not let this unfortunate evening upset you. We are all of us rather testy. Lord Humphrey will be much more himself in the morning, I promise you."

Lady Dewesbury threw a wild look up at her son's face, torn between her familial duty and her duty as a proper hostess. "I shall walk up with you, Aurelia."

"Pray do not bother, Charlotte. I am certain that Augusta and I am quite able to find our rooms," said Lady Ratcliffe loftily.

Lady Dewesbury turned back into the drawing room. She saw that Miss Chadwick had retreated to the window and had drawn back the drape so that she could look out on the night. Lord Ratcliffe sat in a wing-back chair. He had served himself coffee and was meditatively sipping at the hot brew, the expression in his eyes distant.

The countess felt her son's hand on her arm and she glanced up quickly. He still looked very angry, but there was regret, also, in his eyes. "I am sorry, Mama," he said quietly.

"Are you, Edward? I am heartily glad to hear it," she said with unusual bitterness. The viscount jerked as though he had been slapped and Lady Dewesbury hurried away from him. "John, I see that you have served yourself. Forgive me, I have been remiss in my duties. Miss Chadwick, would you like coffee or dessert?"

Joan turned away from the window, allowing the drape to fall back into place. "No, my lady, thank you," she said quietly. "I rather think that I shall also retire. It has been a long day for me."

"Of course, my dear. I hope that you sleep well," said Lady Dewesbury courteously.

Joan murmured good night to Lord Ratcliffe and crossed the drawing room.

Lord Humphrey awaited her at the door. He detained her a moment with his hand. "Shall I walk up with you, Joan?" he said softly.

She shook her head swiftly. "No!" Realizing that she had been unpardonably abrupt, she drew her breath in slowly before she turned her expressive eyes full on him. Her gaze reflected her own perturbation over the events of the evening. "I think it would be best if you did not."

The viscount's mouth tightened. "Very well."

He bowed her out of the drawing room and watched as she went swiftly up the stairs. He could not recall ever having had a worse evening in his life, and all of it was due to the young woman who was now racing away from him.

"Edward, you have not said one way or the other. Would you like coffee?"

Lord Humphrey turned his head. He regarded his mother's anxious expression. Suddenly, wearily, he smiled. "Thank you, I would." He let the drawing-room door swing closed behind him.

The viscount knew that his mother was anxious to know what had been said between himself and the earl, but he could not bring himself to speak of it. For one thing, Lord Ratcliffe was in the room, and even though his lordship was an intimate acquaintance of the family, the viscount felt extremely reluctant to air his differences with the earl before him. In addition, Lord Humphrey knew himself still too furious to swallow with patience his mother's inevitable words of counsel. So, instead, he made the effort to appear as unaffected as possible and idle the time away with quiet conversation.

Lord Humphrey's attitude was clue enough that he had no wish to discuss the subject. Lady Dewesbury was wise enough to accept for the moment her son's wishes. She resigned herself to the desultory conversation, but she waited tensely for her husband's appearance. Lord Dewesbury never came to the drawing room, however, an unusual breach of etiquette for the earl.

After coffee was finished and the two gentlemen had gone their separate ways for the evening, Lady Dewesbury inquired of Hudgens if he knew the earl's whereabouts. She was informed that his lordship was still keeping company with his port. Lady Dewesbury nodded and quietly thanked the butler before she climbed the stairs to the first floor. She knew that it would be some time before the earl came upstairs. His lordship rarely drank himself silly; rather, brooding came easier to the earl when he held a wineglass between his fingers.

Lady Dewesbury went along the hall to her mother's suite. She knocked and was immediately admitted by Lady Cassandra's starched-up personal abigail. The abigail quietly left so that the ladies could be alone.

17

THE COUNTESS SAW that Lady Cassandra was settling herself comfortably, and not just for the night, but as though for a lengthy stay. The furniture had been rearranged to suit Lady Cassandra's taste and there were a number of emptied trunks and pormanteaus on the floor.

That Lady Cassandra meant to remain for more than a day or two was in itself surprising. Lady Dewesbury knew quite well that despite her sincere efforts to make her mother's visits as pleasant as possible, Lady Cassandra was never truly comfortable at Dewesbury Court. Lady Cassandra always hared off back to Blackhedge Manor, after imparting her usual pithy shot about cloying hospitality.

Lady Dewesbury did not question her ladyship about her plans, however. She knew better than to do that. In any event, the duration of Lady Cassandra's visit was of minor importance to her at the moment. She had come to find out about Miss Chadwick. But naturally she would have to lead up gradually to her main interest.

"I came to be certain that you have everything you require, Mama," said Lady Dewesbury.

"I require nothing, Charlotte, at least for the moment. I was about to enjoy my evening sherry," said Lady

Cassandra, gesturing at the tray on the bedside table. She was attired in her dressing gown and had on comfortable slippers. On her head was a muslin and lace sleeping cap.

She shot a penetrating glance at the countess. "I was disappointed not to have served to me at dinner any of those dishes that I am partial to. I hope that my cook has been given proper run of the kitchen?"

Lady Dewesbury sighed. Turmoil in the kitchen was one of the crosses she bore whenever Lady Cassandra chose to descend upon her well-ordered household. She had long since given up the attempt to persuade her mother that her own cook was just as able as Lady Cassandra's. "Of course, Mama. Everything will be just as you wish it, as always. The cook will be able to see to those dishes that you particularly like and mine will allow him to do so."

"You have very properly satisfied yourself as to my creature comforts. Is there anything else that you wish to discuss, daughter?" Lady Cassandra asked. She smiled when she saw the denial forming on her daughter's lips. "Pray do not dissemble, Charlotte. I have always been able to discern when you have your mind fixed upon something."

"Very well, Mama. Let us have plain speaking," Lady Dewesbury said, feeling a prick of annoyance. Really, her mother had the most irritating habit of reducing her to the status of a child. "I wish to know about Miss Chadwick."

Lady Cassandra pretended to yawn, but it was a smile that she hid behind her hand. She had had every expectation of this visit. It did faintly surprise her, however, that Lady Dewesbury had come to her so quickly. She had assumed that the countess would be occupied for some time in her efforts to smooth down the rift between the earl and Lord Humphrey. The strength of the countess's familial instinct was one for which Lady Cassandra had always held a reluctant admiration, though at times it was of considerable annoyance to herself. "Miss Chadwick? Why, I believe she is a very worthy young woman. Is that what you wish to hear?"

Lady Dewesbury gestured impatiently. "You know very well what I mean, Mama. I wrote to you not a fortnight since of Edward's fixed betrothal to Miss Ratcliffe."

"Yes, a most worthy young lady," murmured Lady Cassandra sardonically. "Miss Ratcliffe was most persistent in presenting herself as the rightful owner of my grandson's allegiance. I am surprised that we were not treated to a genteel spasm in the course of things."

Lady Dewesbury decided that she would let that provocation pass. She had not been behind in noticing that her mother had taken an instant dislike to Miss Ratcliffe, and really, it was no wonder when the girl had behaved as she had. She herself had resented Miss Ratcliffe's attempts to bear-lead the viscount. She was about to say so when she caught herself up.

The countess was irritated that she had allowed her thoughts to be diverted by even so much as a hairbreadth. She had not sought out her mother to compare notes on Miss Ratcliffe, though she suspected that Lady Cassandra would enter into such an exercise both willingly and gleefully.

Lady Dewesbury said with dignity, "It was a nasty shock to read that brief, inexplicable notice in the *Gazette* that Edward had engaged himself to an entirely different young lady. Naturally I wish to learn all that I can about my son's unknown inamorata, and I believe that you can enlighten me. She did arrive in your company, after all."

Not for worlds would Lady Dewesbury ever reveal that she had actually heard Lady Cassandra's name from Miss Chadwick's own lips. She could make a shrewd guess how Lady Cassandra would react to that, though, she thought with another flash of irritation, she did not know how her mother could make judgmental statements when her ladyship was herself a meddlesome incorrigible.

"I can actually tell you very little, not being intimately acquainted with the girl or her family. I know of her father, of course. He was the vicar of a neighboring parish and, as I have heard, a very good man," said Lady Cassandra.

"A vicar," repeated Lady Dewesbury blankly. Miss Chadwick was the daughter of a vicar. Without noticing that she had done so, she sat down weakly in the wing-back chair that had been situated in front of the fire.

Lady Cassandra did notice, and her brows rose, but she did not bring the matter to her daughter's attention. It was a measure of the countess's obvious dismay that she should so forget herself as to take Lady Cassandra's own seat.

Lady Cassandra settled herself gingerly on the edge of the bed. "Yes. A rather learned man, actually. As I understand it, Reverend Chadwick published a small number of very well-received treatises. It is quite possible that I may even have a copy or two in my own collection at Blackhedge."

Lady Dewesbury felt gray depression gathering about her with every word. "Miss Chadwick comes of decent family, then."

"If you are fishing about for some hint of a vulgar past, you may put away your line, Charlotte," Lady Cassandra said roundly. "When I met her in my grandson's company, I naturally wondered the same. But since then I have had occasion to speak with the girl at some length on a great number of topics. I can say truthfully that Miss Chadwick is everything that she appears to be: educated, genteel, and possessing of no vices that I could discover. A rather dull girl, by my standards."

Lady Dewesbury sighed. It was all much as she had begun to suspect and to fear. She glanced up at her mother. "Do you happen to know how Miss Chadwick chanced to meet Edward?"

"He ran her down with his phaeton and then took it into his head to abduct her," Lady Cassandra said baldly. She awaited with lively interest the countess's reaction.

Lady Dewesbury did not disappoint her ladyship. She emitted a small howl and pressed her hands against her bosom. Though she had begun to wonder whether her golden son had led a life hidden away from his parents' eyes, one that was not as exemplary as it had always seemed, it was still a shock to hear her base suspicions put into words.

"No, no! I cannot possibly believe it! *Edward?*" she gasped. "Why, he has always been a model of propriety. Surely Miss Chadwick exaggerated the thing to you. I am not saying that Miss Chadwick lied, precisely, but a well-bred girl can be misled by her perceptions of a gentleman's solicitousness."

"I did not have the story from Miss Chadwick," Lady Cassandra said pointedly. She was rather enjoying herself. She was deliberately laying the stage for such misconception that must certainly prejudice the correct countess in favor of the viscount's chosen lady. It was quite heady to be able to affect the outcome of the delicious situation.

"Edward told you this?" asked Lady Dewesbury, quite appalled.

Lady Cassandra inclined her head. "At the same time, he informed me that he had done the honorable thing by the girl." She paused. "I am most sorry that I could not forewarn you, Charlotte."

Lady Dewesbury waved her hand in dismissal, her thoughts on quite different tracks. The situation was even worse than she had conjectured. Abduction and seduction! It was no wonder at all that Miss Chadwick did not feel able to return to her old life. Already in mourning for her parent and thus deeply vulnerable, she had been torn out of her known sphere and made prey to all manner of humiliation. At least her son had been sensible to the damage he had done her. He had paid heed to the family honor, and for that much at least she could be grateful for.

It was but small comfort, however, in the face of the disillusion that Lady Dewesbury had suffered. Her son, her own beloved Edward, was a careless libertine and the callous seducer of a vicar's daughter. Lady Dewesbury shuddered. It was a thought scarcely to be borne.

"Charlotte? Are you quite all right?" Lady Cassandra asked. She was vaguely concerned, for the countess had accepted without a blink of an eye what she had said. She would have expected Lady Dewesbury, who was vastly fond of all her children, to have at least made a show of protest or tried to excuse her most favored son.

Lady Cassandra had been poised with a ready barb for puncturing Lady Dewesbury's defenses, but it did not seem to be needed. On the contrary, Lady Dewesbury had turned white and there was an unusual tightness about her eyes that Lady Cassandra could not like. "Charlotte, my dear?"

Lady Dewesbury shook herself free of her careening thoughts. She passed a shaking hand across her eyes. "I am sorry, Mama. I was woolgathering. I shall leave you now, I think. The hour is getting on and I suspect that I have outstayed my welcome." Without another glance or word for her mother, the countess left the bedroom.

Lady Cassandra was left baffled and angry. She did not like the odd acceptance that Lady Dewesbury had exhibited. It was uncharacteristic of what she knew of her daughter's character. Lady Cassandra had expected something quite different, and she did not care for the suspicion that she had played her hand rather more ineptly than she had any notion of doing.

Lady Dewesbury went along to her own rooms. Her brows were knit in concentration and she returned her abigail's greeting in a vague manner. The inattention was uncharacteristic of her, for she believed it important for her servants to feel themselves personally recognized.

Lady Dewesbury felt that she was on the brink of a momentous decision, one that could very well put her into direct conflict with her lord the earl.

But she could not yet accept all that she had heard, for to do so would mean that she must go counter to an understanding that had withstood two decades. It would also mean that she must forever revise her opinion of her son, and that was indeed a difficult thing to face. She must be absolutely certain of her facts, she thought.

She thought about her dilemma while she allowed her maid to ready her for bed. She did not see how she could go about learning what she felt she needed to know. She could not very well ask her questions outright of Miss Chadwick or her son. That would be both embarrassing and very bad *ton*. Reluctant as she was to contemplate such, she saw no recourse but to stoop to despicable means that she would have had no hesitation in condemning in another.

At last coming to a decision, Lady Dewesbury sent her maid to request that Miss Chadwick's abigail visit her after the girl had settled her mistress for the night.

18

LADY DEWESBURY WAITED impatiently for the abigail's knock. When the young maid came into her bedroom at last, she smiled and beckoned the girl forward. With an autocratic gesture that, if she had but known it, was quite in Lady Cassandra's style, Lady Dewesbury dismissed her own maid and turned to the fearful abigail. "My dear, what are you called?"

"Maisie, my lady."

"Maisie, I have asked you here because I am somewhat curious about your mistress."

The abigail was instantly on the alert. She had concientiously kept her mistress's secret as she had been bidden, and she felt instinctively any inquiry must threaten the trust that had been bestowed upon her. "Yes, my lady?"

The servant's air of wariness did not register with Lady Dewesbury, who was discovering it was more difficult than she had assumed it would be to pry into her guest's concerns. It was one thing to ask Lady Cassandra, but to attempt to pump another's servant went hard against her nature. As hard as eavesdropping, inquired one part of her mind sarcastically. The countess stiffened her resolve. "Maisie, have you been long with your mistress?"

The abigail thought about that. She did not wish to lie precisely, but neither did she want to tell more than she should. "One might say that I have been with miss long enough to know things that perhaps I shouldn't," she said cautiously.

Lady Dewesbury sighed in satisfaction. The girl was a reliable source, then. She leaned forward. "Did you have opportunity to observe your mistress in the company of Lord Humphrey?"

"Yes, my lady," said the abigail. She smiled to herself. She did not think that she would ever forget the first time that she had seen her lady together with his lordship. It had been such a romantic sight, listening as they pledged themselves to each other, and so proud she had been to put her own hand as witness to the marriage papers. But naturally she could not tell her ladyship of that.

Lady Dewesbury was stumped as how to proceed. She could not openly ask what she wanted to know; it simply went against every fiber of her being. However, she must know if she was to make up her mind about what she should do.

The countess rose from her chair and paced restlessly about the room. The abigail watched her, wondering what was to come next. She would never betray her mistress's trust in her, she thought determinedly. It would not come from her lips that her lady had secretly wed his lordship.

Lady Dewesbury finally turned. She said diffidently, "I am not certain how best to proceed. But you appear an intelligent girl, Maisie, and so perhaps you might well read my meaning. You must tell me if I am not making myself clear, however."

"Yes, my lady."

"What was your mistress's manner when she was in his lordship's company?" Lady Dewesbury asked delicately.

The abigail turned the question over in her mind, examining it for trickery. At last she decided that it was forthright enough, being as how it could easily be answered without betraying her mistress.

"Miss was proper shy with him, as I recall," said the abigail. She had always thought it a rum way to spend one's wedding night, apart from the groom and all, but she had thought at the time that her ladyship was an unworldly sort and perhaps his lordship had not wanted to press her. At the time Maisie had shrugged in uncomprehending acceptance. For herself, she would have preferred a bed warmed by a lively tumble. But the gentry were known to have some odd notions.

Lady Dewesbury expelled her breath. "Thank you, Maisie. That will be all."

The abigail was startled, but she was relieved as well. She bobbed a curtsy, silently congratulating herself on a task well done. She had managed to answer all of her ladyship's questions without once betraying the great secret that she had been entrusted with. Maisie left the countess's rooms with a light step.

Lady Dewesbury was not so lighthearted.

She sat down limply in front of her vanity to begin the task of removing the rouge and powder from her face. She was always careful to clean her skin of the muck as soon as she was able, convinced that to leave it must imprint greater age upon her face. She had observed that raddled complexions came to those who indulged too heavily in artifice. She hoped that cleanliness and a liberal application of lotion would preserve her own countenance.

As she worked, she thought over all that she had heard that day. All of her worst suspicions and conjectures had been justified. Miss Chadwick was hardly to blame for the mess that things had become, she thought with extreme weariness.

Abduction, seduction, and the quite probable advent of a child had forced Miss Chadwick out of her own comfortable sphere.

A child. A grandchild, in fact.

Her hand froze in midmotion as Lady Dewesbury blinked at the novel thought. It would be her sixth grandchild. A tiny smile curved her lips. An infant in the house once more! How truly delightful that would be. She never tired of the family additions presented with regularity by her two married daughters.

The countess's smile vanished. She abruptly set down the pot of lotion. Yes, and if there was a child in the offing, it would be most scandalously early if the mother was not soon wed.

"Drat that boy," she exclaimed, furious with her son. He had done the honorable thing by resigning himself to his duty, but he could hardly have given the matter proper thought. Everyone could add and subtract, and it was a matter of common knowledge that nine months were required for an infant's triumphant advent into the world.

Lady Dewesbury thought that she would far rather have been required to deal with a runaway marriage than this hole-in-the-wall betrothal and the subsequent marriage, all perhaps to be followed by a suspiciously early birth. The scandal would be infinitely greater and would always be remembered by the ungenerous, who would have no compunction in visiting the sins of the parents upon the head of an innocent child.

"Edward shall marry that girl of his, and as soon as is possible," she said grimly to her reflection in the glass.

Behind her, a deep voice bellowed, "Have you gone stark raving mad!"

Lady Dewesbury swiveled quickly. "Hullo, darling. I did not hear you come in," she said with a smile. She did not realize that with the lotion still streaked across her face the effect was not quite as salubrious as she could have wished.

The Earl of Dewesbury's blue eyes pierced his wife. "Do not think to turn me from the point, Charlotte. I heard what you mumbled to yourself. You need not deny it to me."

Lady Dewesbury turned around and reached for a towel. "What a perfectly frightful thing to say! I have no intention of denying anything, Greville, so you may simply pull in your horns.''

Lord Dewesbury was thus robbed of an anticipated squabble, which only served to infuriate him further. ''Really, Charlotte! I am not some testy old bull . . . But that is not the issue here. What did you mean that Edward should marry that female? What do we know of her? Yes, and what of the Ratcliffes, I should like to know? What are we to do there?''

Lady Dewesbury calmly finished cleaning off her face. ''Edward has behaved disgracefully toward 'that female,' as you so disdainfully call her. He quite rightly offered her the protection of his name.''

Lord Dewesbury regarded his wife with the beginnings of alarm. ''My dearest Charlotte, this whole thing has obviously overset you. You do not realize what you are saying.''

''I am in my full faculties, Greville.''

He shook his head. ''I beg to differ, wife. You cannot be when you do not recall the humiliation—the anguish—that Edward's wanton conduct has catapulted all of us into. I have never seen Lord Ratcliffe so affected; no, nor our dear Aurelia. Even in the extremity of my own disbelief, I felt for them. As for poor little Augusta—well, enough said! Mind, I do not hold with hysterics as a rule—frightful to behold and all that—but in this instance, I must admit that the provocation was intolerable.''

''I shall admit that I was just as affected, and I believed the same as you, darling. Edward simply had no right to cast aside our honor in such a cavelier fashion,'' said Lady Dewesbury.

The earl nodded in satisfaction. ''There, you see it exactly right. Why, the agreement is of such long standing that to renounce it now would be unthinkable. The only proper thing to do is to have that female sent away and the notice retracted as a ghastly error.''

''No, I do not think that the proper course at all,'' said

Lady Dewesbury. She rose from the vanity and faced her husband, whom she was well aware could be formidable in his convictions. But in this instance she would not give way. "I am sorry for the Ratcliffes. Why, how can I be otherwise, for they are our oldest and our dearest friends. Nevertheless, Edward must go through with this engagement that he has so precipitously entered into with Miss Chadwick."

Lord Dewesbury was rendered speechless. His neck and face turned slowly red with his emotions, but he managed to retain enough control over himself so that he did not blast away with unforgivable forcefulness. "I must assume that you have good reason for this unconscionable opinion?" he asked hoarsely.

Lady Dewesbury regarded her husband anxiously. She could see that he was in a towering rage. Perhaps it was best if he heard it whole and unadulterated. "Our son abducted and seduced her."

The earl was caught broadside. His mouth opened, and closed. Lady Dewesbury watched his struggles with interest. She could not recall any time previous that she had so shaken him, except perhaps years before when she had demonstrated her acceptance of his proposal by throwing her arms about his neck.

The memory curved her lips in a small smile. She felt just the same about his lordship now as she did then, she thought, and she wondered whether this night was to be one during which the earl would be sharing her bed. When the earl came to her room so late, it generally meant just that.

Lord Dewesbury finally rallied. "I do not believe it," he said flatly. "Edward would never do such a thing. No, if there was even a whiff of such dishonorable conduct involved, it was undoubtedly on that woman's part. Somehow she has managed to so hoodwink our son of her innocence that he completely lost sight of his clear duty. She lied to you, m'dear, depend upon it."

"I did not hear it from Miss Chadwick," said Lady Dewesbury.

Regretfully, she put aside all thoughts of connubial pleasures. She doubted very much that her dear obstinate husband would be in the proper frame of mind after this particular discussion was completed.

"Then from whom, Charlotte?" Lord Dewesbury saw that his wife hesitated to answer and he asked sarcastically, "Am I not then to be trusted with the source of these marvelous confidences?"

Lady Dewesbury had hesitated to lay the whole before her husband because it would also mean that she would have to reveal how she had stooped to eavesdropping and to spying upon another through that person's servant. The earl was a stickler of the highest form. He would be gravely shocked and disapproving of her nefarious action. Lady Dewesbury really could not bring herself to allow him to see her as less than she had always been to him.

"Do forgive me, Greville. But I cannot say without exposing someone quite close to you to unbearable censure," she said in all truth.

Lord Dewesbury was not mollified. Far from it, in fact. He breathed heavily while he regarded his wife from under lowered brows. "What you are telling me with your avoidance, my lady, is that I am surrounded by perfidy and untruths among the members of my own family. I shall not have it, Charlotte. I shall not allow anyone, and least of all you, to whom I long since pledged my love and my life, to cast suspicions upon the tradition of honor that I hold so dear."

"Oh, my dear!" Lady Dewesbury understood that she had deeply wounded him by her reluctance to speak freely to him. But still, better that than her own tumble from grace were she to do so. She touched his face gently, sadly.

The earl glowered at her a moment longer, then swung around and stomped from her bedroom. He slammed the connecting door between their bedrooms with resounding force.

Really, thought Lady Dewesbury with understandable bitterness, the viscount had much to answer for.

19

THE WEEKEND SETTLED into a state of uneasy truce. It had become obvious that Dewesbury Court was firmly divided into two camps. Ranged upon one side were the Earl of Dewesbury, Lady Ratcliffe, and Miss Ratcliffe; upon the other, Lady Dewesbury and Lord Ratcliffe.

The turnaround of the countess and Lord Ratcliffe was completely unexpected and inexplicable to the others. Explanations were demanded and spurned, in some instances rather loudly. Indeed, it was whispered about by the servants that there had been shouting heard outside the Ratcliffe's suite and certainly something must also have transpired between the earl and the countess, for when they met at the breakfast table, they were very cool to each other.

Lady Cassandra was not looked upon as a reliable ally by either side. She visited her corrosive observations equally and without bias upon everyone's heads.

The atmosphere in the house was deadly. Tempers were short, civility was delivered with cold precision. Worsening matters, the weather had turned unseasonably gloomy. Heavy gray clouds masked the summer sun, but the threatened rain had not materialized when Joan escaped from the house into the gardens.

Dewesbury Court had large formal gardens. The stone-flagged pathways were bordered by yew hedges and led the casual stroller from vista to pleasant vista. As usual, Joan avoided the beds of roses, preferring the old-fashioned pinks and sweet williams and other Elizabethan favorites.

As she bent to sniff one of the pinks, Joan recalled that Lord Humphrey had once told her that Dewesbury Court had a resident ghost dating from the Tudor period. She straightened and surveyed the back of the house. When she looked, she could actually pick out the original Tudor mansion, built with stone of a heavier cut and massive timbers. It was readily discernible where builders through the generations had tacked on their own proud additions, until Dewesbury Court had become a gallant example all its own of fine proud architecture. Joan thought it might be rather interesting to tour the older part of the house, despite its colorful ghost. She was smiling when she made her way through the herb garden and came to the maze.

Joan was entranced at once by the maze. She had never had occasion to enter one, and she spent a delightful hour simply exploring its corridors. The dark-green hedges were higher than her head so that she could not peek over and check her progress. She failed to reach the center, but that did not particularly dismay her. The exercise in itself was what she found to be intriguing.

Finally she sat down on one of the benches provided in the depths of the maze. It was heavenly simply to relax and not be concerned that some other veiled or hostile comment was coming her way to be countered or otherwise dealt with. Joan sighed. The past several days had been very difficult. She glanced up at the leaden sky and discovered an answering recognition in her own spirits. She honestly could not see a hint of sun, either in the sky or in the situation that she had pitchforked herself into. The only redeeming factor in all of it was her strange friendship with Lord Humphrey, who was at once a mere acquaintance and something much more intimate.

The viscount found her there in the maze. Joan glanced up at him, greatly surprised by his unexpected presence. She had been thinking of him and thus it was startling that he should suddenly appear.

He sat down beside her and answered her unspoken question. "I chanced to glance out of my window and saw you. I hope you do not mind that I join you."

"No, I do not mind in the least," Joan said.

Her original dismay over her harsh reception had lessened with a few days' reflection, and the last few moments had helped her to further gain her equilibrium. She thought she had finally accepted her lot and that she was beginning to adjust to it. After all, there was still to be gained those things that she had initially hoped for out of the bizarre marriage proposal. Naturally all of her hopes hinged upon the continued growth of her relationship with the viscount, and so she was not at all averse to have a few moments alone with him. "I was enjoying the calm."

Lord Humphrey laughed. "As in the eye of the storm?"

Joan smiled. Her eyes twinkled. "Precisely."

"You are a gallant lady," he said sincerely.

"Nonsense. I am a grasping upstart, a deceiving seductress, and an impertinent baggage," Joan said cheerfully.

Lord Humphrey flushed with anger. "Who has said so?" he asked roughly.

"Really, Edward! It has not been put into so many words, but I think that is an accurate summation of how my presence is regarded," said Joan. She touched his arm. "I do not regard it, not anymore. I was warned by both yourself and Lady Cassandra, after all."

"Yes." The viscount frowned in a brooding fashion. He said, "I did not actually expect it to be quite so difficult, you know." He looked at her, his smile twisting. "I was caught flat-footed, my dear. I expected resistance and disapproval, of course, but not . . ." He gestured wordlessly.

"The earl still has not directly spoken to you since that night?" Joan asked.

Lord Humphrey gave a short unamused laugh. "Oh, he vouchsafes me a grudging word now and then, when he must. Usually at my mother's urging, of course." He hesitated. "I have not told anyone what was said between us. It still pains me. But I shall tell you this much. My father threatened to cut me off if I did not set you aside and marry Augusta."

Joan gasped. "My lord! Surely his lordship was not serious." She saw from his expression that he was perfectly convinced of his father's sincerity. "But what shall we do? Indeed, what can you do? You are finely caught, are you not?" She shook her head. "I cannot allow you to make such a sacrifice, Edward. I shall myself apply for an annulment."

"Joan, do not be a peagoose. His lordship's threat does not affect other than my pride. Yes, and my sensibilities. The wound was deep, I will grant you," said Lord Humphrey, a shade grimly. He shrugged. "But as for the rest, it was an empty threat. The earl knew it and I saw that he regretted it almost the instant the words left his mouth because he realized it could serve no real purpose. I am not dependent upon my father's purse strings. Since I reached my majority, I have gained control of a trust that was established on my behalf by my late grandfather." He slid a sly grin in her direction. "So you must not think that you shall be forced to live in penury, my lady."

"As if I would think of that," exclaimed Joan. "You know little enough of my character if you believe me so shallow, my lord."

"No, I do not think you shallow, Joan. Quite the contrary. How else could you have put up so patiently with such abuse as you have suffered since coming here?" Lord Humphrey said somberly.

"That will be quite enough of that, Edward," Joan said decidedly. "I'll not be put on a pedestal or anything of that sort. I shall take leave to inform you, my lord, that I have harbored quite uncharitable thoughts regarding some of those under your ancestral roof.''

"Including myself, I have little doubt," he said with a grin.

Joan flushed. "We shall not discuss that, if you please. I am still most ashamed that I doubted you at all. You have been placed in a very difficult position and it is only natural that you should sometimes lose your composure or—or strike out.''

"I should not have done so with you, however. I should have reserved my churlishness for those who most deserve it," said Lord Humphrey. He fetched a quiet sigh, his eyes turning away from her so that he stared at the yew hedge in a contemplative fashion.

Joan was all sympathy. "It is hardly to be wondered at that your determination to have things seen in a particular light serves to set your family and friends on edge. Indeed, I can feel their reproach whenever I enter a room, and I am but a stranger. It must be twice as difficult for you, a beloved member of the intimate circle.''

"I cannot imagine that it could have been any worse if we had simply announced that we had married," Lord Humphrey said.

Joan hesitated, then she said, "That thought has occurred to me also.''

"My grandmother thrives on this sort of flap," said Lord Humphrey meditatively.

"Yes."

Joan and Lord Humphrey looked at each other for a long moment. He suddenly swore. "Her ladyship has used us finely for her entertainment, has she not?''

"Indeed, I cannot but suspect that to be the case," Joan admitted. "I do like Lady Cassandra, I truly do, but there are times that—''

"That her ladyship could use a thorough hiding," Lord Humphrey said shortly.

"My lord!" Joan choked on a laugh. "That isn't precisely

what I had intended to say. Oh, it is true, but can you honestly imagine such a thing?''

He gave a reluctant grin. ''The vision fairly defies the imagination,'' he admitted. His smile faded. ''I have made a rare muddle of it, haven't I?''

''Never mind. What is done is done. Now we must simply forge on and hope for the best,'' Joan said.

''Admirable, my lady,'' said Lord Humphrey dryly. ''And what strategy do you suggest?''

Joan flashed a half-ashamed glance at him. ''Actually, I should like to teach Lady Cassandra a well-deserved lesson. It is a rather unworthy ambition, I realize, but such a satisfying one to contemplate.''

''I, too, have not much cared for the notion that I have been a regular cat's-paw,'' Lord Humphrey said. ''Lord! What a ripe pigeon I made for her ladyship. I haven't been so gulled since my first trip up to the metropolis and I was persuaded to drop all my blunt on a three-legged donkey race. Mine lost; it was bellows-to-mend for me, I can tell you. My father did not at all see the humor.''

''A three-legged donkey?'' repeated Joan, who looked at him with wide wondering eyes.

''It wasn't actually three-legged, of course, but . . .'' Lord Humphrey broke off, feeling himself incapable of explaining how a four-legged animal could possibly be construed as anything else. ''Look here, I've an idea. Let's put an end to Lady Cassandra's little entertainment. We shall make a proper clean breast of the thing, which we should have done to begin with, and endure the consequences. At least it will all be over and we shall not be caught up in this farce for the Lord only knows how long.''

''I do like the sound of that,'' Joan admitted.

The viscount's eyes kindled. He caught her hand in an excess of exuberance. ''Then that is what we shall do. Now, this minute! We shall go inside and make an announcement to everyone. That will put a crimp into my grandmother's fiendish orchestration.''

"Oh, no! No, we couldn't possibly do it that way," Joan said, shaking her head.

"What do you mean? I thought we were agreed," said Lord Humphrey, taken aback.

"But think, Edward! It will be so humiliating to your god-parents in any event. If we simply bray it out, it will be ever so much worse."

Lord Humphrey's brows came together in a frown. "Yes, you are right again, Joan. I could not do that to them. My fondness for Lord and Lady Ratcliffe is sincere, and though I do not give tuppence for Augusta's pride, I would not like to be the author of a grievous wound to her sensibilities, such as they are."

"Perhaps a private interview with Lord and Lady Dewesbury would be best," Joan suggested.

"Yes, it would be kinder. My parents will be shocked as well, but I think the news would come better from them to the Ratcliffes," said Lord Humphrey. His smile twisted in self-derogation. "They could all then commiserate with one another over my defection and loss of wit."

"Thank you very much, sir," Joan said, pretending miff.

Lord Humphrey burst out laughing. He lifted her fingers to his lips. "You are good for me, Joan Chadwick. I have never felt my natural arrogance so well-checked."

"Really, my lord? I am most happy that I have gained even a particle of influence over your waywardness since our original meeting," Joan said swiftly, her smile quick.

He laughed again. Rising from the bench, he drew her up to stand beside him. He slipped her hand through his elbow. "I suspect that you shall keep me properly upon my toes," he admitted.

"No more three-legged donkey races to be lost, my lord?" inquired Joan, her eyes twinkling up at him.

"On my honor," said Lord Humphrey.

There was a crack of thunder and wind whirled through the yew corridor. The viscount and Joan as though on cue turned their faces to the sky with startled expressions.

"We shall have to hurry or we'll be drenched," Joan said.

"Yes." At another warning rumble, Lord Humphrey pulled her after him. He moved quickly and unerringly in a direction that Joan was positive that she had not traversed before in her explorations of the maze.

"Edward, do you know precisely where you are going?" Joan asked breathlessly, clutching her skirts up in her free hand as she hurried after him.

He shot a mirthful glance at her. "Not precisely, no. But close enough, I hope."

Joan felt the first drop hit her cheek. She cast an alarmed look up at the darkening clouds. "So do I!"

20

JOAN AND LORD HUMPHREY emerged from the maze and returned to the house with the rain chasing them at every step. Gaining the safety of the older part of the house, they laughed breathlessly at each other. Joan shook out her skirt and regarded herself in an old cracked mirror. She ran her fingers through her curls, attempting to tame the effects of the damp wind. "I look a fright," she exclaimed.

"I do not find you so," said the viscount, coming up from behind. There was something quite suddenly sober in his voice that at once made Joan's heart begin to pound. Meeting her startled eyes in the mirror, he laid his hands tentatively upon her shoulders. "Joan."

A servant wench appeared from around the corner of the narrow hall. She stopped dead at the sight of them. "Ow! My lord, miss! What a fright you gave me. I wasn't expecting anyone about."

The viscount's hands dropped away and Joan felt her face burning. Lord Humphrey stepped in front of her to shield her from the girl's interested gaze. "I was explaining to Miss Chadwick about the family ghost," he said.

" 'Tis a creepy story, indeed!" The girl gave an exaggerated shudder. But she quickly turned to the source of her surprise. "All the others be in the entry hall, my lord, what with the coming of guests. Excuse me, my lord, but I must be off. I was told to bring fresh chamomile for Lady Cassandra's tea quicklike."

"It is raining," warned Joan.

But the girl was already gone, the heavy door banging behind her.

Lord Humphrey extended his hand to Joan. "I believe you are about to meet some of my mother's numerous acquaintances," he said.

Joan regarded his lordship with dismay. "Surely not!"

"My mother is a hostess of considerable renown," he said with a slight grin.

"But I must change. Pull a comb through my hair, at the least."

The viscount shook his head. "There won't be time, depend upon it." He smiled at her. "Besides, you look charming. You've roses in your cheeks from the wind, did you know?"

His voice vibrated and Joan colored once more. "I shall remember that when I am called on the carpet for my appearance," she said with dignity.

The viscount laughed. "No such thing! No one will even notice in the flurry. You shall make an excuse at the first opportunity and I shall contrive to draw everyone's attention to myself."

"Very well, my lord. I shall hold you to that," Joan said. She had noticed that they traversed narrow halls with low ceilings and massive beams. "Is this part of the original house?"

"It is. I shall bring you back for a proper tour one day and show you the gallery that my headless ancestor so mournfully haunts," said Lord Humphrey.

"Thank you ever so much," Joan said.

Her doubtful appreciation came through her words and the viscount laughed at her. "One more doorway and we shall be in our own time," he assured her.

Immediately upon turning the last corner and entering through the door that the viscount had promised her, the sounds of raised voices and the commotion of activity impinged on their ears. They looked at each other and, as one, followed the sounds.

The front hall was a scene of considerable chaos. Trunks and portmanteaus and bandboxes were scattered everywhere, and through the front door the drenched footmen were bringing in more of the same. Several other personages milled about, including two valets and a superior lady's maid. A nursemaid comforted a toddler who had fallen and was vocally venting his loud outrage at his own clumsiness. Two very lively little boys dodged about in a game of tag, shouting shrilly above the raised voices of the adults engaged in lively conversation.

Lady Dewesbury was talking to a young matron, who was stripping off her gloves as she animatedly answered. The earl was shaking hands with a portly gentleman of amiable demeanor. Lord Ratcliffe guffawed at something the newly arrived gentleman uttered. Lady Ratcliffe and Miss Ratcliffe formed a receiving party to the arrivals. Another gentleman bowed negligently over their hands, his attitude one of worldly boredom.

On the threshold of the drawing room stood Lady Cassandra, from whence she regarded the tableau with an expression of mild interest. It was she who first espied Joan and Lord Humphrey. "Ah, there you are! As you see, the house party begins in a most rollicking manner."

"Athene," exclaimed Lord Humphrey.

The young matron stopped in midsentence and turned her head. Her face lighted up and she started forward, completely uncaring that one of the boys now clung to her skirts while the other skirmished with him behind her back. "Edward! How glad I am to see you! It has been forever. Or, no, more precisely it has been three months. What have you been up to? But I must not ask. My good Thomas has solemnly impressed upon me the need for tact and I quite see, what with

Augusta here and all . . . Really, I had no notion it would be such an awkward thing. But how are you, Edward, really?'' So saying, she raised up on her toes and kissed him soundly on the cheek.

The viscount was laughing. He scooped her up in a hug that lifted her free of the floor and made her squeal. Setting her down again, he asked affectionately, ''Athene, will you never change?''

Rendered breathless by his lordship's familiarity, the young matron attempted to smooth her gown. ''Who is it who never changes? I should like to know,'' she retorted. ''I haven't screeched like that in ages. But the instant that I am in the same room with you, it is like we were back in the school-room all over again.''

Lord Humphrey turned to Joan. ''Joan, this is my sister, Lady Athene Harrington, an incorrigible rattlepate if ever there was one. That gentleman there is her long-suffering husband, Sir Thomas Harrington. Sir Thomas, Athene, I would like you to meet my—''

''Your betrothed, of course! It must be. Miss Chadwick, I am delighted,'' exclaimed the viscount's sister.

Sir Thomas made a most proper bow. ''Most happy,'' he uttered.

Lady Athene was not so few of words. She caught at Joan's hands, her gaze at once curious and friendly. ''My dear Miss Chadwick! You have no notion how I have positively longed to meet you. Ever since my Thomas brought that notice to my attention, why, I—''

Sir Thomas gave the slightest cough and Lady Athene threw her husband a knowing glance. ''But I am warned that I run on. We shall talk later.''

She gave Joan's hands another squeeze and turned then to Lady Ratcliffe. She saw at once that her forthrightness toward Miss Chadwick had put Lady Ratcliffe out of curl, and she set herself to cajole her ladyship into a better humor. ''Lady Ratcliffe, it is truly a pleasure to see you again. Mama always has such kind things to say about you. And Augusta!

You are always in such amazing good looks. I cannot begin to tell you how envious I am of you. What an absolutely dazzling toilet. You must impart to me the name of your modiste. She is a genius, truly.''

Lady Athene drew the Ratcliffe ladies toward the drawing room, on the way pausing to pay her respects to her grandmother. "Grandmama! Why, I did not perceive you before. But of course you would be here. Where else, indeed?'' She cast a knowing glance backward at the viscount and Joan.

Lady Cassandra gave her impudent granddaughter short shrift. "You are a menace, Athene.''

Lady Athene only laughed as at a grand joke and continued on in her usual style. "Oh, Thomas will agree with you, my lady. Will you not, my dear?''

"Indisputably,'' murmured Sir Thomas with unimpaired good nature. He signaled the nursemaid and his valet to collect his wayward children. The older boys went protesting loudly until the nursemaid promised to have a sticky treat brought to the nursery for them all.

Lady Dewesbury bestowed a kiss on the toddler, who earnestly informed her that he was to have a treat, too, and a hug on each of the older boys. She waved them upstairs before she turned to her adult guests. "Let us all go into the drawing room. Hudgens will have had refreshments sent in. I know that you must all be parched,'' she said gayly. She was always happiest when the house was full and her talents as a hostess could be given wide rein.

There was a general slow exodus in the direction of the drawing room, the earl drawing Lord Ratcliffe and Sir Thomas with him with bluff goodwill. Lord Humphrey and Joan did not immediately join the others.

"Shall I make good my escape, my lord?'' Joan whispered.

"It's as good a time as any,'' said Lord Humphrey, smiling. He lifted her hand to his lips. "I shall make your excuses, but I warn you I shall not remain long unscathed without you to ward off some of my sister's frank curiosity.''

Joan laughed. "I shall return as soon as I may," she promised. She turned to the stairs then, but her progress was impeded.

The other gentleman, after making his bows to the Ratcliffe ladies, had stood looking on with a cynical glint in his eyes. Now he stepped directly into Joan's path. As he did so, he threw an amused look at the viscount. His lean face bore the lines of dissipation about his eyes and mouth and his manners were careless to the extreme. "Do I not also rank an introduction to your betrothed, cousin?"

Lord Humphrey regarded the gentleman with a singular lack of warmth. "Joan, this is Mr. Vincent Dewesbury, my cousin."

"How do you do, sir," said Joan politely. She was quite cognizant of the viscount's patent dislike of his cousin, and so she was wary of displaying too much warmth. There was something, too, that instantly set her on the alert against the gentleman. Instinctively she knew that she had finally met one of the wolves that young maidens were always warned about.

Mr. Dewesbury raised Joan's hand and brushed his lips across her fingers lightly. Still retaining her hand, he looked directly into her eyes. His clear green eyes were disconcertingly penetrating. "Believe me, the pleasure is entirely mine," he said deliberately.

Joan colored slightly. She recovered possession of her hand. "You are kind, sir."

Mr. Dewesbury's smile widened. His white teeth flashed briefly. There was a satirical look in his eyes. "Kind? No, I am not kind. You may ask Humphrey."

"Come, Joan. We are set to join the rest of the company," said Lord Humphrey, tight-lipped. He took her arm and bore her off to the drawing room. Joan threw a despairing glance up at his face and resigned herself to the fact that she was not going to have the opportunity to remedy her windblown appearance, after all.

Without comment, Mr. Dewesbury sauntered after them. Upon crossing the threshold, he was instantly hailed by Lady Cassandra.

"Ah, Vincent! Sit beside me, my dear sir. I always derive huge enjoyment from your peculiar brand of humor," she said.

"I am happy to oblige, as ever," said Mr. Dewesbury, with a tinge of sarcasm edging his acceptance. Lady Cassandra chuckled, completely armored against such as him. Mr. Dewesbury gave a half-shrug and seated himself on the settee beside the peppery old woman. She commanded him to procure a cup of chamomile tea for her from the tray, which he did with nonchalant elegance, never allowing his irritation to be seen that he was forced to rise again so quickly.

Lord Humphrey handed Joan to a wing-back chair near the grate and stationed himself close beside her, leaning his shoulders against the mantel. The butler offered refreshment to Joan and the viscount, both of whom refused.

Lady Athene was as usual talking and she shifted slightly to include her brother and his betrothed in her conversation. "I was just telling Mama that Bethany cannot be here, Edward. Her confinement is upon her at last and naturally Robert and the other children remain close by until she is delivered."

"Thank God for small favors," said Lord Humphrey fervently.

Lady Dewesbury scolded him over the general laughter. "Really, Edward, one would think that you were not at all fond of your eldest sister and her family."

"Of course I am fond of Bethany and Robert and the girls. But I am fonder of them all at a distance. Admit it, Mama! My nieces are perfect little monsters," Lord Humphrey said, pretending to shudder.

Lord Dewesbury gave a hearty laugh. Joan regarded the earl in open astonishment. It was the first time that she had ever seen other than a forbidding expression upon his face.

She thought that his lordship was really quite a handsome gentleman when he was not going about looking so dour.

The earl was not aware of her regard as he said, "Edward has you there, Charlotte. Robert disclosed to me their last visit to us that they have seen four governesses in as many months. When those girls are old enough to leave the schoolroom, Bethany will have the devil of a time getting them taken off her hands."

"I dearly love my granddaughters," Lady Dewesbury said with dignity, sipping her tea. "They are perhaps a bit spoiled and headstrong, but I am certain those qualities must be tempered with time."

"Robert hopes for another girl," Sir Thomas murmured, his eyes fixed contemplatively on the ceiling.

Lady Dewesbury's expression altered radically at his revelation, causing another burst of laughter. She gathered herself, a small smile teasing at her own lips. "Laugh at my expense if you will. I still maintain that my granddaughters are as perfect as can be."

"Of course they are," said Lady Ratcliffe. She met Lady Dewesbury's swift astonished glance. "We are all of us quite certain that our own progeny and their children, too, are deserved of accolades. That is why we always stoutly defend them and their interests."

Lady Dewesbury flushed. She turned her shoulder on Lady Ratcliffe. "I have been thinking for some minutes about it. Perhaps I should go to Bethany and remain with her for a week or so."

"Oh, decidedly not," exclaimed Lady Athene. "Bethany charged me strictly to persuade you not to come. You know that she never has the least trouble, Mama, and besides, we agreed between us that you are needed more here at Dewesbury. I do not recall there ever being such a strange turnabout in the family, but there it is. One could never have foreseen such a thing, could one? Edward, you shall tell me later every detail of your little romance with Miss Chadwick. I am agog with curiosity."

An odd, muffled sound emanated from Miss Ratcliffe. All eyes turned on her, with varying degrees of sharpening interest or dread, depending upon the owner's character. But Miss Ratcliffe thoroughly disappointed those who anticipated at least a minor tantrum. She only rose to her feet, carefully setting aside her unfinished tea and biscuit. "I fear that I am developing the headache, Lady Dewesbury. I hope that you will excuse me."

"Of course, dear child," said Lady Dewesbury, hiding her sense of relief that there was not to be a reoccurrence of the hysteria that they had all been treated to some days before.

"Poor darling! I shall go up with you, Augusta, and see you made comfortable," said Lady Ratcliffe, also putting down her teacup.

"Thank you, Mama. But I had hoped that I might prevail upon one of the gentlemen to escort me," said Miss Ratcliffe. Her lovely eyes lifted, to come to rest commandingly upon the viscount's face.

Joan felt herself stiffen and she tried hard not to allow her disapproval, her outrage, show in her expression. She thought Miss Ratcliffe's tactics quite unashamedly forward, especially when she directed them at a gentleman who was announced to be betrothed. She turned her head, waiting to see how the viscount would handle this newest of Miss Ratcliffe's importunities.

21

LORD HUMPHREY was to all appearances absorbed by the small fire in the grate and he was slow to react, even to the small pool of silence that had fallen about the company.

Miss Ratcliffe was heard to give a smothered exclamation. The earl cleared his throat, but Lady Dewesbury shot such a bright forbidding glance at him that he subsided farther into his chair. His face took on all the expression of stone. Sir Thomas looked at the ceiling, by his example hoping to hold his wife's tongue in check. Lord Ratcliffe's hand fell onto his wife's arm. She looked around at him, then irritably turned her shoulder. Lady Cassandra regarded all of them with unholy amusement lightening her gray eyes.

Vincent Dewesbury was the first to break the uncomfortable silence. "I hold myself completely at your service, Miss Ratcliffe," he said suavely, rising and covering the distance between them. He held out his hand.

Miss Ratcliffe was caught in the coils of her own trap. Her eyes glittered, but her obvious temper was not evident in her sweet voice. "Why, thank you, Mr. Dewesbury. It is a pleasure to associate with a true gentleman." With that rather clumsy shot in the viscount's direction, she placed her fingers delicately upon Mr. Dewesbury's arm.

He firmly drew her hand through his elbow so that they were in nearer proximity. She glanced up at him quickly, then away when she met his cynical gaze. His expression was bland as he walked with her out the door.

Lady Ratcliffe watched her daughter's exit with a small frown marring her broad brow. "Perhaps I shall just go along to see Augusta safely into her room," she said. She hurried after her daughter and Mr. Dewesbury.

When the door had closed behind his wife, Lord Ratcliffe snorted. "I do not know what Aurelia expects Dewesbury to be able to accomplish between here and the upstairs. In a house full of servants, too."

"I suspect that if my rascally nephew were to try to steal a kiss or two, Augusta would be quite able to put him firmly into his place without the least difficulty," Lord Dewesbury said with heavy humor.

Lord Humphrey was set to contribute his own opinion regarding Miss Ratcliffe's powers of survival, but he swallowed back the biting words. Considering the situation, his opinion would hardly be well-received by either his father or Lord Ratcliffe.

"Really, Greville! What an odd way to speak of dear Augusta," said Lady Dewesbury reprovingly.

"Oh, but how utterly true! Why, when I recall how Augusta was used to cut up at poor Vincent when we were all children together, I wonder that he dares to say a word in her presence," Lady Athene said, making her third choice from the array of cakes and biscuits that had been provided along with tea.

"Vincent is no longer a sensitive child," said Lady Dewesbury.

Lord Dewesbury coughed. "No, he is not that," he agreed.

Lady Dewesbury threw the earl a look of exasperation. A pucker formed between her brows. "I don't know why Vincent is here. He is always welcome, naturally, but he visits so rarely these days. I wonder what has brought him at this particular time? Athene, have you any notion?''

"I haven't the least clue, Mama. He did not come with us, you may be assured. A young family is not the sort of company that my cousin keeps," Lady Athene said on a laugh. She popped the remains of a biscuit into her mouth.

"Curiosity," uttered Sir Thomas. He bowed in Lord Ratcliffe's direction. "Begging your pardon, my lord."

Lord Ratcliffe waved aside the simple apology. "Oh, don't think to insult my pride, Sir Thomas. It has taken quite a battering, but I have found it almost liberating."

Lady Cassandra ignored Lord Ratcliffe's levity. "Vincent comes to do mischief, mark my words. Miss Chadwick, you would do well to watch your back. You are just the sort of delectable morsel to appeal to one of Mr. Dewesbury's cut."

Joan spluttered on a disbelieving laugh. "Come, ma'am! I am hardly one likely to interest such a worldly gentleman as Mr. Dewesbury seems to be."

"Oh, come, Grandmama! Vincent is what is known as a 'bad man' and all of that, but you cannot accuse him of anything worse than being a libertine and I have never yet heard that he preys on the innocent or the respectable," Lady Athene said. She smoothed her sleeve. "Still, I do think he holds a certain fascination."

Sir Thomas shot up his brows. "Does he, indeed!"

Lord Humphrey was frowning. He had not liked his grandmother's advice to Joan, bringing up as it did quite an unpleasant possibility. "I have never liked Vincent above half."

"Lord, why should you?" retorted Lady Athene. "The feeling has been mutual since you were both boys, vying over Augusta's pretty golden head. When I recall how many times Vincent drew your claret and played such mean tricks upon you and . . . Well, it just shows one, does it not? We are all set in our roles as children. There is no hope for it at all, for just look at Edward and Vincent, still at loggerheads whenever they chance to meet, circling each other like stiff-legged hounds."

"I have never vied for one single hair belonging to Augusta," Lord Humphrey said from between his teeth.

"Oh, no, of course not. I do beg your pardon. How silly of me, to be sure," Lady Athene said, rolling her eyes heavenward. She rose from her place, shaking out the skirt of her pelisse. "I am still quite deplorably damp. I am certain that Nurse must have taken proper care of the children and made sure that they were dry, but I am always such a worrier. I shall just run up to the nursery before going to rest before I must change for dinner. It is just family here, so I know that I may make my excuses without giving offense. Thomas?"

"Quite," said Sir Thomas, also rising. He lingered to take a polite exit from the earl and the others.

Lady Dewesbury also rose, to walk with her daughter to the drawing-room door. "We dine at the usual hour, Athene, so do not think that you must hurry."

"Still keeping town hours, Mama? How utterly fatiguing. I shall be half asleep before ever we are through the first course," said Lady Athene cheerfully. Her voice dropped, but not enough to prevent those behind from hearing her next words. "It is such a turnabout, is it not? So unlike Edward! Has Papa been out with his fowling piece? I do so like fowl of all sorts. One's figure suffers from beef, you know."

The Earl of Dewesbury reddened at his daughter's words. He growled something unintelligible.

Throwing his father-in-law an apologetic glance, Sir Thomas hurried to take his wife's arm. "Come, my dear Athene."

"Have I disgraced myself again, Thomas? Ah, well. When I reach Grandmama's age and continue to speak my mind as she does, everyone will think me an eccentric as well," said Lady Athene.

Lord Humphrey had the audacity to laugh. He saluted his sister with a brief gesture of one hand to his brow. "Bravo, Athene!"

His sister threw him a puzzled glance over her plump

shoulder as Sir Thomas escorted her out of the room.

Lady Cassandra glared at the viscount before her glance swept the others in the room. She discerned amusement in all their faces. "An entire generation without respect for their elders," she snapped.

"Come, Mama. What do you expect? You have often said how like yourself Athene is," said Lady Dewesbury in a reasonable tone, returning to her chair.

"I do not recall ever making such an error in judgment, daughter," said Lady Cassandra at her haughtiest.

Joan stood up, judging that her own chance to exit had come at last. "Lady Dewesbury, pray excuse me as well. I was walking in the garden earlier and I, too, am a bit worse for the turn in weather."

"Of course, Miss Chadwick."

Lord Humphrey at once offered his arm to Joan and walked with her out of the drawing room. He escorted her to the bottom of the stairs and there lingered a moment. "I apologize for thwarting your escape earlier," he said.

"No matter, my lord. I was quite interested in all that was said. I am learning a great deal about your family," said Joan.

Lord Humphrey grinned. "You are learning more than you ever bargained for, I'll wager."

Joan laughed and shook her head. "No, but—"

What she would have said was forever lost, for the front door crashed open. On a flurry of wind and rain, two slim figures dashed inside. The young male turned swiftly and slammed the door closed, cutting off the blowing rain.

The young lady attempted to shake off her soaked pelisse. Her straw bonnet hung bedraggled and sad about her face. "Really, Neville! What a perfectly ghastly notion! Trust you to think of something so corkbrained. Only look at my bonnet!"

"Corkbrained, was it? Then why didn't you just stay with the carriage until someone had been sent for you? *I* shall tell you why! You couldn't bear that I would be having a small adventure all to myself," retorted the young man.

"Adventure! Why, what is so grand about running through a summer storm and trouncing through nasty puddles? I should like to know," demanded the young lady.

Lord Humphrey laughed. The two skirmishers left off battle and looked around, their expressions reflecting profound astonishment. At the same time, the occupants of the drawing room spilled out into the hall.

"Neville! Margaret!" exclaimed Lady Dewesbury. She hurried forward. She hugged both swiftly, then released them in gathering dismay. "Whatever are you doing here so early? Look at the both of you! You are soaked to the bone! Go up at once and soak in a hot tub before you catch your deaths!"

"Mama! Papa!" squealed the young lady. Deserting her mother, she threw herself into the earl's arms. She placed a resounding kiss upon his cheek. "Oh, it is so good to be home!"

The young gentleman was not far behind in greetings, but he was much more circumspect, offering his hand to his father and Lord Ratcliffe. But when he came to Lord Humphrey, he grinned and feinted a punch at the viscount's forearm.

"Well, brat? Have you been given the sack again?" asked Lord Humphrey, grinning, as he warded off the mock blow.

"No such thing! I am on holiday, I shall have you know! Yes, and so is Margaret. It is the jolliest treat! We are to be home a full month," said the young gentleman.

The young lady turned again to her mother. She was trying unsuccessfully to undo the sodden satin bow of her ruined bonnet. "Mama, pray—!" Lady Dewesbury went at once to work on the knot and the young lady slewed her bright eyes round on the viscount. "Edward! You shall never guess! The new music teacher says that I dance quite divinely. And you once called me a clumsy ox, only for mashing a few of your worthless toes!"

Lord Humphrey turned to Joan. "If you have not already guessed it, this is my younger brother. Neville, make your leg to Miss Joan Chadwick, my betrothed. And that pert baggage is our sister, Miss Margaret Dewesbury.''

"Betrothed?" squeaked Margaret. Her large gray eyes widened to their full extent. She did not even notice that her mother had lifted away the disgraceful bonnet. "But I thought that Miss Ratcliffe was—"

Lady Dewesbury hurried to interrupt her youngest daughter. She threw a comprehensive glance at Lord Dewesbury's descending glower. "You shall be told all about it in due course, Margaret. But for now you must go upstairs and get out of those clothes. You, too, Neville. No, Margaret! Not another word! Now come along, the both of you!''

Lady Dewesbury firmly marched her two slack-jawed progeny up the stairs. As they passed Joan, they stared hard at her with burning curiosity.

Joan nodded in a pleasant way and she smiled faintly. There seemed to be no end to the people to whom she was to become known as the viscount's betrothed. The farce had grown to ludicrous proportions and was still gaining momentum. It only needed the neighborhood gossips to drop in for a chat with Lady Dewesbury, she thought with resignation.

At the turn of the stairs, Neville twisted in his mother's clutches. "Papa! The carriage has thrown a wheel at the end of the drive. That was what we ran ahead to tell you!" he called.

The earl waved acknowledgment and turned to the butler. "Hudgens, call the proper men out. They'll dislike this weather but it cannot be helped. Promise them an extra pint."

"Yes, my lord." Hudgens left at once to set the task in motion.

Lord Ratcliffe chuckled. "Quite an exciting time we are having, eh, Greville? The unexpected casts a fine burnish onto the days. Enough to keep us all upon our toes."

Lord Dewesbury glanced toward Joan. "Indeed. One could wish for more comfortable times, however."

Lady Cassandra had come last to the drawing-room door and had stayed well back from the latest flurry of greetings. Now she moved forward, snorting her disdain. "Stuff and fustian! What a dreadful bore you have become, Greville! I had thought better of you. One should not curl up one's toes before the grim reaper ever appears! Miss Chadwick! You shall accompany me up the stairs. I am fatigued by the miasma of the hidebound and obstinate stupidity that emanates from a certain quarter!"

The earl's face and neck flushed. His mouth tightened. "You, madame, have always meddled in matters that are not yours to command. I have held my tongue, but no longer. Be warned, Lady Cassandra! I shall not sit idly by for more of your insults and sly maneuverings." He spun on his heel and strode down the hall until he reached his study. Entering, his lordship slammed the door with resounding force.

"Well! I am most impressed. Perhaps there is hope for Greville yet," said Lady Cassandra with perfect calm.

"Grandmama, I have also reached the end of my tether. Joan and I are agreed. There will shortly be changes made which will put a period to this pretty entertainment," said Lord Humphrey grimly.

Lady Cassandra's eyes narrowed. "I understand you, of course. Do as you think best, Edward! I have nothing to say about the matter, as Greville has so forcibly pointed out."

Lord Ratcliffe looked from the viscount to Lady Cassandra with a puzzled expression. There was obviously something being said of some moment, but the key eluded him.

Joan took the elderly lady's arm and drew her gently up the stairs. "Come, my lady. You will wish to rest before dinner."

"You will come to my room and keep my company," Lady Cassandra commanded.

Joan knew that her ladyship meant to weedle out of her whatever had been decided between herself and the viscount. She shook her head. "I think not, my lady. But perhaps later after the company retires, if you wish it, I shall come to your room and read to you from a book of poetry.''

Lady Cassandra smiled. She said dryly, ''Humoring the old woman, are you, my dear?''

Joan's eyes twinkled even as she inclined her head. ''Yes, my lady.''

Lady Cassandra chuckled, her good humor restored. ''I like you. I always have. You don't let anyone bully you about, including my grandson. You'll come through with flying colors, my dear.''

Joan looked at her ladyship, wondering exactly what Lady Cassandra was alluding to. ''What do you mean, my lady?'' But Lady Cassandra merely smiled in a secretive fashion and Joan understood that she was not going to have her curiosity satisfied so easily after she had decided not to confide in her ladyship. Joan laughed and shook her head.

22

THAT EVENING, dinner proved to be livelier and more congenial than at any other time since Joan and Lord Humphrey had arrived at Dewesbury Court. Joan looked around at those seated at the table. The company had swelled with the additions of Sir Thomas and Lady Athene and the viscount's younger siblings, Neville and Margaret.

The conversation practically sparkled with the fresh gaiety provided by the two youngest members of the Dewesbury clan, and affected everyone, bringing ready laughter to the surface. Even the earl and Lady Cassandra were able to set aside their skirmishing at each other.

Joan was profoundly relieved. She had become heartily sick of the constant tension and the sniping that had been carried on over her head and to her face. It was refreshing to be able to enjoy a normal dinner conversation with her partners, who happened to be Lord Ratcliffe and young Neville.

Joan found that she liked Lord Ratcliffe. He was a quiet gentleman of thoughtful expression, and if his opinions were delivered at times in a ponderous fashion, it was but an amusing quirk of his character. Joan decided that his lordship was at heart a good-natured and a fair-minded gentleman.

She knew that in regards to herself, Lord Ratcliffe had for reasons of his own made up his mind to accept matters for what they were and go on from that point. He apparently bore her no ill will for capturing the prize that by all intents was to have gone to his own daughter. In fact, his lordship made quite clear that his primary concern was not the viscount's aberration from obedience, but his fall from grace.

"I will not disguise from you, Miss Chadwick, my profound dislike of all this high drama over Lord Humphrey's betrothal to you. The earl and I have been friends nearly all our lives, and in the transport of celebration at the birth of my daughter, we exchanged a rash promise that I for one have come to regard as the silly mouthing of the moment, and certainly nothing that should have driven such a breach between Lord Dewesbury and the viscount," said Lord Ratcliffe.

"Your feelings do you justice, my lord. It is an ill thing, indeed, for there to be division between a father and his son," Joan said quietly. "But I do not know what can be done to heal the wound. Perhaps you, who have so much insight into the earl's personality, might suggest a proper course, my lord."

Lord Ratcliffe regarded her thoughtfully. "You speak gently, Miss Chadwick. However, the hint of steel in your own character makes itself well-heard." He smiled at her. "I shall endeavor to use what influence I may upon the earl. As the father of the maligned lady, I suspect that my opinion must carry some weight."

"Thank you, my lord," Joan said, smiling in her turn.

She felt a pluck at her sleeve and she turned her head to her other dinner partner. "Did you wish to say something to me, Mr. Dewesbury?" she asked.

The young gentleman flushed. "You may call me Neville, ma'am," he muttered.

"I am honored by the privilege," Joan said gravely.

He shot her a suspicious look to see whether she was ridiculing him, but her expression reassured him. Neville's

face cracked into a broad grin. "I say, I do like you better
than Augusta. That is what I wished to tell you, you see.
She is always handing me such set-downs. Not that I regard
it, of course. But I cannot bear the way that she has treated
my brother. She was always lording it over him and
positively crowed to the world that he was hers for the crook
of her smallest finger. Poor Edward could do nothing about
it, not when it was set in stone that he was to wed her. But
you have fairly quashed that!"

"However true that may be, I think it would be kinder
not to trumpet it about," Joan said, a pronounced twinkle
in her brown eyes.

Neville nodded sagely. "Aye, I understand, of course. I'll
not play the dastard and lord it over Augusta." His blue eyes
kindled and he said firmly, "No matter what provocation
she offers me, I shan't do it."

"Certainly that would be the course of a born gentleman,"
Joan said.

Neville's narrow chest swelled with pride. He picked up
his wineglass and looked about the table with a decidedly
cockish air. Joan had to turn away to hide her laughter.
Neville Dewesbury was young and idealistic and possessed
a strong sense of outrage at injustice. She knew that she was
going to enjoy watching him grow into manhood.

Still smiling with her amusement, Joan chanced to glance
across the table and met the unfriendly stare of Margaret
Dewesbury. The girl dropped her eyes to her plate. She
fiddled with her fork, not really eating.

Joan shrugged. She was sad that the viscount's young sister
had taken her in such instant dislike, but she was not going
to allow the girl's opinion to dismay her. Either she would
win Margaret over, or she would not.

Joan reflected that she had changed since coming to
Dewesbury Court. She had always been one eager for friendship with everyone she came into contact with and cast down
if that happy state was not achieved. In the beginning, the
level of hostility that she had encountered at Dewesbury had

made her actually physically ill. It had been a complete shock to her that anyone would regard her in the guise of an enemy. Lady Cassandra had attempted to prepare her in her own devious way, but her ladyship's hints and abrupt switch from confidante to acquaintance had fallen far short of armoring her against the reality.

Experience had taught Joan with harsh haste that she could not expect to receive the goodwill of all those with whom she became acquainted. It had been a series of painful lessons, but Joan had gradually come to understand that her own self-worth did not necessarily depend upon the opinions of others.

She had told the viscount that she was seen as an upstart, a seductress, and a baggage, and it had been true. Perhaps the words had not been actually voiced, but they had been there in the accusing eyes of those about her. Joan had been distressed and shocked by that slanderous image of herself. She knew that she was none of those things, but to defend herself had been impossible. She had had to accept what was thought of her and then shrug it away as unimportant. She would remain true to herself, and though it was a difficult road she walked, she remained hopeful that in some way she would find herself vindicated.

Lady Dewesbury and Lord Ratcliffe seemed to have changed their opinions about her already, and for that Joan was most grateful. Sir Thomas and Lady Athene, though they had not expressed enthusiasm over the so-called betrothal between herself and Lord Humphrey, neither had they condemned it. Neville Dewesbury had come down soundly in her favor. Joan hoped that she would be able to mend matters between herself and the earl, that she could somehow win over Margaret, and that she could become friends with the remainder of Lord Humphrey's immediate family. But if she could not, then she would accept the situation and find her friends outside the Dewesbury family.

Joan had not realized how long she had been reflecting until she saw Margaret's eyes rise to meet her gaze. There was frustration and hostility and unease in the girl's eyes, as though she was made uncomfortable by the length of Joan's regard. Joan smiled and looked away, but not before she had caught the quick look that Margaret had tossed down the table at Miss Ratcliffe.

Joan took a breath, at once and completely understanding the source of Margaret's hostility. She had assumed that the girl was reacting on her brother's and her family's behalf, but that had been erroneous. In that swift look of Margaret's, there had been a combination of adoration and a desire to be recognized. Joan glanced also at Miss Ratcliffe, seeing her as Margaret must—beautiful, sophisticated, and feted. Miss Ratcliffe embodied what every young maiden wished for herself, thought Joan. The girl positively worshiped the ground that Miss Augusta Ratcliffe trod.

The revelation was a disturbing one, encompassing as it did Miss Ratcliffe's spoiled nature. Miss Ratcliffe was obviously susceptible to flattery and certainly a young girl's adoration was that. She was also selfish and disregarding where others' feelings were concerned. Joan had been dealt personal experience at the lady's hands in that regard and she had no illusion about Miss Ratcliffe's sense of compassion. She could only hope that Margaret was not destined for a harsh disenchantment where Miss Ratcliffe was concerned.

When dinner was finished, the ladies withdrew into the drawing room to allow the gentlemen privacy over their port. They were not soon left to themselves, however, for the gentlemen all trooped into the room within the half-hour.

Joan elected to play softly at the pianoforte as an accompaniment to the conversation. She enjoyed music for itself, but in this instance it also served the purpose of gracefully excluding herself from the group. She preferred some quiet time in which to gather her forces of patience and civility, for every evening there was made some cutting or oblique reference to the ties that bound her to Lord Humphrey.

Vincent Dewesbury leaned his shoulder against the wall and observed his cousin's betrothed with the connoisseur's eye. Miss Chadwick was of passing good looks, but he thought there was nothing particularly remarkable about her. Her hair was brown, her eyes were brown, her skin the alabaster that so often characterized those of otherwise dark features; she was quick and graceful and ladylike.

Mr. Dewesbury's gaze left Miss Chadwick to travel across the room to Miss Ratcliffe's face. His mouth turned down in an odd half-smile. Miss Ratcliffe was a diamond of the first water and as unobtainable as the moon. His smile abruptly disappeared and he straightened from his negligent position to approach his uncle and engage the earl in conversation.

Lady Cassandra had badgered Lady Dewesbury in partnering her in a game of whist against Lord Ratcliffe and Sir Thomas and she was thoroughly enjoying the opportunity to show off her own trouncing skill at cards. Lady Athene stood at her husband's shoulder, recommending now and then a particular card with a whispered word. Sir Thomas gave no hint that he actually listened to his lady's advice, but played a game as unhurried and deliberate as his own character.

Lady Ratcliffe quietly embroidered while she listened to her daughter's sprightly discourse to Lord Humphrey and Margaret. The viscount's expression was one of polite interest, but there was a distance in his eyes that hinted Miss Ratcliffe's conversation was less than fascinating. His gaze strayed more than once to the young lady at the pianoforte.

The Harrington children had naturally been relegated to the nursery during the dinner hour, but they had been promised that they might be brought down later to the drawing room. When the door opened and the two boys spilled through it, followed by the nursemaid who carried the toddler, the sedate adult pace of the evening was shattered.

Lord Humphrey was at once dragooned by the twin five-year-olds into playing horse, which he laughingly obliged for first one and then the other. Neville volunteered to take on a rider and the towheaded boys squealed in delight as their

noble steeds played at jousting. The toddler howled his rage
at being excluded, but he was diverted to good effect by
Margaret, who chased him from one sanctuary to the next
in a course that crisscrossed the room.

Joan turned away from the pianoforte, greatly enjoying
the children's fun. She thought it particularly endearing of
Lord Humphrey not to care that his cravat had been pulled
out of its precise lines or that his hair had become mussed
by little hands.

A small force suddenly careened into her knees and she
looked down, startled. The toddler grinned up at her, his
innocent eyes alight as he clasped tight the folds of her skirt.
"Well, little man! Aren't you the bold one," Joan said,
chucking him under his soft chin.

The tiny boy chortled and ducked his head to one side.
He straightened and leaned against her again. "Din! Din,"
he demanded.

Joan obliged him and he ducked aside again, giggling. It
was a game that they played together for several moments
until Joan bent down to hug him. "You are a sweet boy,"
she whispered.

His little arms went around her neck and pulled tight about
her in a surprisingly strong hug. "You p'etty lady," he said.
Then he hared off after Margaret, who had withdrawn a short
distance away when she saw that her nephew had run over
to Joan.

The stir lasted for several minutes until all the adults
involved had been brought to an acknowledged point of
exhaustion. Then, while the toddler climbed up into Lady
Athene's lap, the older boys amused themselves by
pretending they were gallant soldiers. Their swaggers and
childish sallies brought laughter from all around.

Neville was inspired by his nephews' antics. "I say! Why
do we not hold a mummery? It would be grand fun."

"Oh, yes," exclaimed Margaret, her eyes shining. "We
could all have a part and put on costumes and masks. Oh,
do say we might, Mama!"

"Of course we must. It is a splendid notion," Lady Dewesbury said.

"But not one for this evening," said Lady Athene, rising with the sleeping toddler cradled in her arms. "It is time for bed, children. That is quite all right, Nurse. I shall carry little Ned upstairs myself. Come along, Todd and Theo. You must be very tired now." The twins vigorously denied it and campaigned to be allowed to stay up, but at a pointed glance from Sir Thomas, they subsided and allowed their nurse to herd them from the drawing room.

The children's reluctant exit proved to be but the precursor for the end of the evening's entertainment. It was not many more minutes before the company began to break up and seek their beds.

Neville and Margaret solemnly promised not to allow the mummery to be forgotten overnight. Lady Cassandra put in her own oar. "There is nothing I enjoy more than a good staging," she said.

"Yes, and we shall doubtless hear all sorts of outrageous plans for its denouement over breakfast," said the earl resignedly as he saw everyone out of the drawing room.

23

LORD DEWESBURY'S prediction came to pass, but even he did not reckon on the scope of imagination that would be unleashed. The summer days were long and warm and granted the feeling of ease necessary for the formation of such an entertainment. At any time one heard talk of the mummery.

The mummery proved to be so popular a notion that it began to be realized that there would be far more players than there would be members of the audience. "But I do not begrudge anyone the opportunity to declaim a speech," said Lady Dewesbury. "I am only glad that there is something to take attention away from your situation, Edward." As she spoke, she carefully set a long-stemmed rose among a score of others already gracing a large vase.

"As to that, Mama, I should like to speak to you and my father privately," Lord Humphrey said.

Lady Dewesbury threw him a surprised glance. "Do you, my dear? Is that wise? I mean to say, your father has been very disturbed these last few weeks."

"I know that, Mama. I, too, have noticed the frequency with which we dine on fowl," Lord Humphrey said impatiently. "It is partially for that reason that I wish to speak to you both."

"Very well, Edward. But at least wait until after the mummery. You know that must put his lordship into a jollier frame of mind. It will go so much easier then," said Lady Dewesbury.

Lord Humphrey agreed to his mother's condition reluctantly, feeling restless now that his decision to clear the air had finally been made.

The door opened and Miss Ratcliffe breezed into the room. She paused and exclaimed prettily, "Oh! I did not realize that you were here, Edward."

Lord Humphrey smiled a shade grimly. "Did you not, Augusta? Strange, I thought you were perceptive where I am concerned."

Miss Ratcliffe's lovely eyes smoldered. "Indeed! I was used to be, but matters have changed somewhat since, do you not agree?"

On her words, Joan entered. Her glance passed over Lord Humphrey's look of mild amusement and rested for a thoughtful second upon Miss Ratcliffe's expression of annoyance. Without a word to either, she turned to Lady Dewesbury. "My lady, I am the carrier of an urgent message from Lady Cassandra. She is making her way belowstairs now and her ladyship stated that unless you are able to speak reason to the cook, she will herself flay the woman alive."

"Oh, my word! Cook has rebelled again. Well, is it any wonder that she resents an arrogant stranger taking charge of her domain?" Lady Dewesbury exclaimed. "I must go at once, of course. Edward, do not dare to laugh! It is not at all amusing, I can tell you. Miss Chadwick, pray do me the favor of finishing with these roses. I am certain that you shall know just how to go about arranging them."

Joan's eyes riveted on the gloriously shaded gold and pink roses. "No, I could not possibly. That is, pray excuse me, my lady. I have just recalled a task of my own that cannot wait." Joan retreated hurriedly from the room.

Lady Dewesbury stared after her in astonishment. "What an odd start!"

Lord Humphrey was frowning. "Yes. I think that I shall go after her and attempt to discover the cause. I do not care to see Joan upset." He strode swiftly out the door.

"And I must go at once to the kitchen," said Lady Dewesbury. She still held the rose and she looked at it.

"I shall be happy to finish the roses for you, my lady," Miss Ratcliffe said.

Lady Dewesbury smiled at her gratefully. "Why, that is most kind of you, Augusta." She hurried out in her turn.

Miss Ratcliffe calmly and competently finished arranging the roses. When she was done, she stood admiring the effect for some time. "How odd it is that our Miss Chadwick does not care for roses," she murmured to herself. Then she smiled and went in search of Margaret.

Joan had escaped to the library. She spent a pleasant afternoon reading, and when the bell for tea rang, she reluctantly closed her volume. She emerged from the library and found herself instantly hailed.

"Miss Chadwick! I have looked everywhere for you."

Joan smiled in a friendly way at Margaret. She was surprised that the girl had approached her at all, considering how Margaret felt about her. "I was just coming to tea. Shall you come with me?"

"In a moment, but first I must tell you that I am the bearer of a gift," said Margaret. She was holding her hands behind her back. "It is to be a surprise, so you must close your eyes."

Joan laughed. "Very well. I am ready. May I look now?"

Something was thrust toward her. Joan caught an unmistakable scent. Her eyes flew open and she stared horrified at the pretty nosegay of roses. "Oh, no!" She stumbled back, but it was already too late. A violent sneeze shook her. "Take them—" Another sneeze, and another. Joan reeled away, fleeing, her eyes streaming and still racked by continuous sneezing.

Margaret stood rooted to the spot, absolute shock and consternation upon her face. Above her, a light laugh floated down. "Did not Miss Chadwick care for the posy, Margaret?"

The girl whirled swiftly, her face flaming. She stared at the beautiful young woman standing on the stair landing. "You knew! You used me," she accused hotly.

Miss Ratcliffe laughed again. "Come, Margaret. It was but a small joke. Surely you must see that?"

"I, for one, do not see the amusement."

Miss Ratcliffe's laughter was cut short. She looked down swiftly and met the twin gazes of the Earl of Dewesbury and her mother, where they stood outside the drawing-room door. Miss Ratcliffe was held by momentary consternation, but then she tossed her head. She turned on her heel and sped swiftly to the top of the stairs, disappearing as she turned into the upper hall.

"Come, Margaret. It is time for tea," Lady Ratcliffe said quietly.

"But Miss Chadwick! I did not know, Papa, I truly did not."

"No, you did not. I am sure that Miss Chadwick must realize that. She will undoubtedly accept your apology later. Now come into the drawing room."

Neville and Margaret appointed themselves stage managers and assigned each of several parts of the mummery production. Several days later the players pronounced themselves ready to tread from the makeshift stage that had been set up in the grand hall of the Tudor portion of the house. It was a felicitous stroke to produce the mummery in that location, for the large and ancient-beamed room contributed wonderful atmosphere to the endeavor.

Surprisingly, Lady Cassandra had loudly insisted that she

was to play a part, and she did so with a consummate grace
that won general admiration. When she was done, she regally
left the stage and took a prominent seat among the audience,
which consisted of Lord and Lady Ratcliffe, Lady Dewesbury
and the earl, and Lady Athene and her small family.

Miss Ratcliffe was naturally cast as a breathtakingly
beautiful and suitably virtuous princess. Vincent Dewesbury
seemed at first to have been miscast as the prince, but his
saturnine presence gave perfect effect to his poetic and futile
attempts to persuade his lady to her downfall. Joan was
content with her own small part, as it was played opposite
Lord Humphrey. Neville and Margaret played a noble couple
on pilgrimage to the Holy Land. Sir Thomas astonished
everyone by rendering a lengthy and moving speech as a
Roman centurion.

"I never knew the man actually possessed a tongue," said
Lady Cassandra caustically. She was loudly shushed.

After the mummery, refreshments were served to the
players and audience alike.

The mummery had concluded with a bloodcurdling account
by Lord Humphrey of the headless Tudor ancestor that had
held Lady Athene's progeny wide-eyed and awed to the end.
Candles had been set about to aid the shadowy appearance
of the main rooms of the Tudor section and the boys dashed
here and there in search of the headless moaning ghost. The
rest of the younger set sauntered off on their own explorations
of the old rooms, which had all taken on a shadowy life of
their own with the setting of the sun.

Mr. Dewesbury joined in the general fun, seemingly
moving at random, but always with a purpose. He had desired
for some time a few private moments with Miss Chadwick,
and with the mummery had come his opportunity. He finally
cornered Joan in the gallery. She was still wearing her mask,
as most of the players were, but there was no mistaking her
figure. He put a hand on each side of her shoulders where
she had pressed herself against the wall. "Ah, a fair masked
maiden! You have been fairly caught, my pretty one, and

now you must pay the price." His lips came down to hers.

Joan swiftly turned her face to one side. "No! Pray do not!"

"What, this?" His hand caught her chin, and as he spoke, he kissed her lightly. "Why, I hope to do much more, Miss Chadwick, and with your willing permission." There was a laugh in his voice.

Suddenly he was plucked away.

Spun roughly around, Vincent Dewesbury came into direct contact with a hard fist, well-placed and powerful. He crashed into the wall and slumped, shaking his head to clear his senses.

When Mr. Dewesbury saw who had hit him, he straightened abruptly. His eyes narrowed and his lean face flushed with temper. "My dear cousin, you are definitely *de trop*. The lady and I were just beginning a most pleasurable acquaintance."

The viscount stood with his fists bunched at his sides. "You will keep your damnable hands off of my wife."

Mr. Dewesbury's face turned ugly at the viscount's challenging tone. "If it is a mill you desire, Humphrey, I am most willing to oblige." Then the significance of the viscount's words struck him. "Did you say your wife, cousin?" There was a strange undercurrent in his voice. His eyes went from the viscount's hard face to Miss Chadwick's and back again. His whole countenance changed. "If that is true, I offer my sincere felicitations and apologies. An unavoidable misunderstanding, I am sure you will agree, since the lady is reputed to be only your betrothed."

"Pray say nothing to anyone, Mr. Dewesbury," appealed Joan. "For reasons quite unexplainable at present, we do not wish it known."

Vincent Dewesbury regarded her with an unfathomable expression. Then he turned his glance to the viscount. "I sense a heretofore unsuspected side of your character, cousin."

"Yes, well, that is neither here nor there," Lord

Humphrey said. His eyes were still hard and bright. He flexed his hands suggestively. "You had no business dallying with the lady at all."

"None whatsoever," said Mr. Dewesbury promptly. "The picture unfolded to my wondering gaze rapidly assumes untold possibilities. Again, my deepest apologies, my lady viscountess. Never fear, I shall not spill the ready." He sketched a bow and was gone.

"Well! He is a very strange fellow," Joan observed, her alarm already fading to memory.

"And hardly one that an unattended lady should be off alone with," Lord Humphrey said in a scolding fashion.

"So I have gathered, and much to my chagrin," said Joan with a spark of humor. She looked up at the viscount's still-frowning expression. The mask she wore seemed to grant her a boldness that was not ordinarily hers. "And you, Edward? Must a lady be on guard against you as well?"

Lord Humphrey regarded her in astonishment. If he did not know better, he would have sworn that she was flirting with him. He saw the flash of her smile and a light leapt suddenly into his eyes. "Oh, as to that, I am a most-feared rascal." He swooped down upon her.

Trapped comfortably in his arms, Joan was breathless as she gazed up at him. "My lord?" she questioned.

"What, no pleas or protestations, my lady?" he asked.

Joan cocked her head to one side and thought about it. "No, I do not think so," she announced.

Lord Humphrey grinned. He bent his head to kiss her. It was to have been a lighthearted salute, but the instant his lips touched hers, heat sprang between them.

The kiss deepened, became more insistent. His mouth possessed hers. Joan's head whirled. Without awareness that she did so, she slid her hands about the viscount's solid neck. Her lips parted softly, inviting him.

On a groan, Lord Humphrey crushed her against him. One of his hands slid roughly down her slender spine, fitting her to him. He tore his mouth free of her lips to seek the soft point between her neck and shoulder. She arched into the searing sensation. It was quite incredible and quite unlike anything she had ever experienced. The thought fleeted through her mind that she had not known Edward's kisses would have this effect on her, but then he was doing something else with his hands and his lips and she forgot everything else.

Slowly, he released her. They stared at each other, shaken.

The viscount swore. "I do not wish to be chaste with you, Joan. Do you understand, my dear lady? I want more than anything in this world to take you to my bed and love you until the sun rises."

His voice shook with his barely reined passion. Joan trembled in response. She could feel the heat rising in her face, in her body. She pressed her hands to her hot cheeks. Her confusion was startling to her. At one and the same time she was both frightened and thrilled by the viscount's declaration. "I do not think you should say such things, my lord."

"If I cannot say them to my wife, then to whom?" he asked sharply. He caught her wrists, but gently. He turned one hand and kissed the palm, then did the same with the other. He folded her hands against his chest. "I can feel you tremble, Joan. And I know that you must feel my heart pounding," he said in a low vibrant voice.

"Yes. I can." Joan looked up at him with a pleading expression. "Pray do not, Edward. Do not ask it of me, I beg. For I shall have to say yes, you know that I shall."

Lord Humphrey was silent. Then with a sigh he let go of her hands. "No, I will not ask it of you, my sweet lady. But I swear to you that I will not wait a day longer to declare you my wife. And I will not care whose sensibilities may be wounded." He smiled his twisted smile, his gray eyes still bright when he looked on her. "Then you shall not set me aside so easily, my lady."

Joan lowered her lashes to hide her eyes from the intensity of his gaze. "I will not wish to," she said in a low voice.

Lord Humphrey looked about them at the gathering shadows of the gallery. "I think that it is time that we leave this place. It seems to arouse the best and the worst in us all," he said.

There came suddenly a mournful and gathering wail. Joan caught her breath and she felt the viscount's sudden stiffening. The keening caught at her ears and raised the tiny hairs on her neck. "Edward," she whispered urgently, her eyes straining to see what might be moving in the shifting shadows.

The viscount's fingers were hard about hers. "Do not be afraid." There was an odd inflection in his voice and he seemed to be having difficulty in swallowing something. "I do not wish to alarm you, beloved, but I believe you are about to meet my unlamented and long-departed ancestor."

Joan cast a wild glance up at him. He was not looking at her, but was staring straight down the gallery. His face was expressionless and his complete immobility added to Joan's alarm. Another ghastly moan assaulted her ears. She turned to stare.

An apparition slowly advanced toward Joan and the viscount. It appeared to glide over the worn wooden floor, never quite deserting the edge of the shadows that were given life by the few flickering candles scattered in the wall sconces. The apparition was strangely lacking in shape and it seemed to carry an object tucked under one ghostly appendage. Joan realized to her horror that the object was roughly the size of a human head.

The apparition neared. It moaned anew. Joan felt ready to faint with fright. It did not comfort her to feel the viscount's own body shaking. "Edward," she uttered, clutching his arm tighter.

The viscount burst out laughing. He doubled over, holding his sides. "Ah, Joan! Joan!"

A choking sound emanated from the horrific apparition, then it seemed to fly apart. From its slowly collapsing depths appeared Neville, his hair spiked in every direction. His laughter joined with his brother's and he pointed a trembling finger at Joan. "She thought—she thought that—" He went into a fresh spasm of laughter.

Joan quietly and without fanfare slid to the floor.

The viscount and Neville were instantly silenced. They stared at her unmoving prone body and then at each other. As one, they went down on their knees beside her. Lord Humphrey raised Joan in his arms. He was alarmed by her limp unresponsiveness. "Joan! Joan!"

Neville was white-faced. "It was but a prank, a silly prank!"

"Indeed it was." Joan's voice was completely calm. She opened her eyes, a smile lurking about her mouth. "I think that I have my revenge, sirs."

Lord Humphrey turned her about and shook her halfheartedly. "You little fiend. A fair revenge, indeed!"

Joan pealed in laughter.

Neville's jaw had dropped when she first spoke. Now his mouth snapped closed. He grinned in delighted admiration. "You are a right 'un, Miss Chadwick. I knew it days ago."

Lord Humphrey stood up and aided Joan to her feet. "Indeed she is, Neville." He grinned down at her. "I was more fortunate than I knew when I tossed you into that watery ditch."

"As was I," Joan responded happily.

Neville looked from one to the other in rampant curiosity. "Ditch? You threw Miss Chadwick into a ditch, Edward?"

Lord Humphrey reached out to slap his brother across the shoulder. "Let that be a lesson in life to you, Neville. Never discount the worst of occurrences, for they may be true opportunities in thick disguise," he said cheerfully.

The trio began to make their way down the gallery. Neville bent to retreive the remains of the now-silent apparition, then hurried to catch up to his brother. "But I say, Edward! A ditch?"

Lord Humphrey and Joan merely laughed.

24

WHEN JOAN and her two companions returned to the grand hall, she was instantly asked by Lady Cassandra whether she would mind reading to her that evening. "Of course not, my lady. I will go down to the library and fetch up a volume that I espied on the shelves when I was in the room a few days ago," Joan said.

"Thank you, my dear. This evening's entertainment has stimulated me so that I do not think I shall sleep. A chapter or two, and I shall nod off," said Lady Cassandra, with a nod.

As Lady Cassandra moved off, Lord Humphrey quirked his brow as he slanted a glance down at the lady on his arm. "I hardly construe that as a compliment to your eloquency."

Joan laughed. "No, but it was not an insult either. It was simply Lady Cassandra."

Neville had deserted them upon rejoining the others, but now came back. "Papa has ordered that everyone is to leave the hall so that the servants may tidy up and put out the candles. I say, it was wonderful fun, wasn't it?"

Joan and Lord Humphrey agreed as they and the rest of the company left the older section of Dewesbury Court. Once returned to the lived-in part of the house, Lady Dewesbury inquired whether anyone would like to partake of coffee or sherry. "Hudgens has set up in the drawing room," she said.

Lady Cassandra declined, as did Lady Athene and Sir Thomas. Joan felt it incumbent upon her to decline as well, since she had promised to read to Lady Cassandra. "I shall also take my leave, Lady Dewesbury," she said.

"Very well, my dear. I trust that you shall sleep well," said Lady Dewesbury. She waved before she followed the earl, Vincent Dewesbury, and the Ratcliffes into the drawing room.

Neville and Margaret had said their good nights to their elders and were already traversing the stairs. Neville heard his mother's civil words and he paused to throw over his shoulder, "Aye, Miss Chadwick! I hope you do not dream of our headless ghost."

"Thank you for your concern, Neville," Joan said.

Lord Humphrey laughed. He caught up Joan's fingers and carried them to his lips. His eyes gleamed at her. "My brother is an incorrigible scamp. But it was a superb performance, was it not?"

"Quite," said Joan with a mock shiver.

Lord Humphrey flicked her cheek softly with his finger. "Sleep well, my dear," he said softly. He turned and went into the drawing room.

Joan stood still a moment, her face and heart warm. She had learned so much about herself and the viscount that selfsame evening. Her lips curled in a small happy smile. His lordship had actually called her "beloved" while they talked in the old gallery. And as for the rest, those moments were best recalled in the privacy of her bedroom. But first she must attend her duty and find that book for Lady Cassandra's reading.

Joan turned and went into the library. A few candles had been left burning and there was the remains of a dying fire on the hearth that cast enough of a glow that she could see. Joan found quickly the volume that she had recalled, but she lingered. Books were a passion and it was rare that she could enter any library without exploring for a few moments among the bookshelves. She rounded the corner of one bookshelf. Here the light was poorer and she had to bend close to be able to read the spines.

While slowly perusing titles, Joan heard the library door open. Her first inclination was to step around the bookshelf to see who might have had the same inclination as she had, but then she hesitated. She was reluctant to bring herself to the attention of the earl or anyone else who was still not resigned to her presence. It was so very late and she felt quite incapable of behaving with civility if her pride was to be verbally assaulted yet again. So she remained still, hoping that whoever it was would go away. More than likely it was but a servant come to snuff the candles, for she had noticed previously that the library was not well-frequented.

"I had no notion that you were so missish. Do you suspect me of laying a trap, my dear lady?" There was bored amusement in the gentleman's tone.

Joan stiffened, instantly recognizing Mr. Dewesbury's voice. Fresh to her memory was the manner in which he had manhandled her in the gallery. She was caught in a fine dilemma, not wanting to be guilty of eavesdropping, but neither did she want to bring herself to the gentleman's unwelcome attention.

While Joan hesitated, she heard Miss Ratcliffe's peevish voice.

"I do not know why you have insisted upon this meeting, Vincent." There was a rustle of skirt and restless movement toward the bookshelf behind which Joan was secreted. She stepped back, horrified. She looked wildly around for some means of escape, but there was none. She knew herself to be caught and it was too late to declare herself.

"You have been rude and inopportune and rag-mannered. But you have always been so, haven't you, Vincent? Really, I cannot imagine what the London ladies find so charming in you. Surely your reputation as a rake and dangerous ladies' man must be grossly inflated," said Miss Ratcliffe, turning to glance at the gentleman as he closed the library door.

"Put a damper on it, Augie," Vincent recommended, sauntering toward her.

"Augie? Augie!" gasped Miss Ratcliffe. Her bosom heaved in indignation. "Positively no one has called me that repulsive name since I was in the schoolroom. I shall not allow you to do so now. Do not *ever* call me by that detestable name again!"

She swept toward the door, but he reached out and caught her wrist. Miss Ratcliffe's beautiful eyes shot daggers at him. "Let me go, sir."

Vincent Dewesbury appeared not to hear. Instead, he said ruminatively, "The old nickname brings back such memories. Do you know, I have been in love with you ever since you were a fat little cherub with golden ringlets and I pulled you out of the millpond after you had fallen in." He smiled reminiscently. "As I recall, you boxed my ears soundly and burst into tears."

"I was never a fat cherub, and if I boxed your ears, you undoubtedly deserved it. You were always detestable to me," Miss Ratcliffe said in a low trembling voice.

"I was detestable because my love for you was, and always has been, hopeless," Vincent said harshly.

Miss Ratcliffe gave a trill of astonished laughter. "Next you will say that not one of those expensive lady-birds of yours have ever meant a thing to you," she said with a sniff.

"They haven't. I may have been with them, but I always carried you in my heart." It was not altogether true, but Vincent Dewesbury thought it sounded well and he repeated it firmly. "You were always in my heart, Augusta."

"Oh, stuff!" Miss Ratcliffe dismissed his declaration with a disbelieving toss of her head, but she was flattered, nevertheless. After all, the Honorable Vincent Dewesbury was the quintessential man-about-town, and his slightly dangerous admiration was always considered a coup for any lady. He had released her, but she was not in such a hurry as before to be gone. She lingered on the chance of hearing more. She drew her finger across the edge of her low bodice in the pretense of smoothing it.

Vincent was too experienced not to recognize her susceptibility. He held himself still, knowing well how to tease in his turn. "Knowing that I could never have you, I consoled myself with those others," he said softly. To his surprise, he discovered that he had spoken with complete sincerity. His own hitherto-unsuspected vulnerability gave him pause and a frown of confusion crossed his face.

"Really, Vincent!" Miss Ratcliffe's contempt was visible in her abrupt gesture. "I am not one of your unseasoned misses that I may be dazzled by such blatant claptrap." She started to turn away.

Mr. Dewesbury flushed angrily. Her quick arrogance touched him on the raw. He had exposed too much of himself and her contempt was like salt in a fresh wound. With a swift step, he reached her and spun her around. His hands bruised her upper arms and he put his face but inches from her own. He said sharply, "You shall not dismiss me so lightly, ma'am. Think you that I have willingly stood by without uttering a word? But you were not mine to woo. You were destined for my cousin Humphrey."

His voice thickened with his suppressed jealousy and he shook her, once and quite hard. "For Lord Humphrey, who is too thickheaded to realize his golden fortune. But I forget you, do I not, my fine ambitious lady? You never looked beyond my cousin. In your complacency you never saw me."

His barely checked rage frightened Miss Ratcliffe. She had never seen such a furious fire in his green eyes. Instinctively she leaned away from him as far as his hold on her would allow. "Vincent, pray! You are hurting me."

He laughed harshly. "Humphrey has never hurt you, has he?"

"Of course not," flashed Miss Ratcliffe. "His lordship is always the gentleman. He has never—"

Wanting to put an end to her infuriating words, Mr.

Dewesbury crushed her to him. He rained possessive kisses upon her face and throat and shoulders and breast. When at last he stopped, he said with low savagery, "Humphrey never made you feel like that, Augie. He never will. But I can. Remember that tonight in your cold bed, my lady."

He released her abruptly and wrenched open the library door. It slammed behind him.

Staring wide-eyed at the door, Miss Ratcliffe put her hand out to the bookshelf for support. She slowly became conscious that her gown had been ripped from her shoulders and her breasts were exposed to the night air. But her skin was so heated that she felt no chill. She fumbled with her torn bodice, repairing the damage as well as she was able, and then turned to the library door.

A loud bang sounded behind her. Miss Ratcliffe whirled. "Who is there?" she hissed.

For a long moment there was no answer. Then Joan emerged from between the bookshelves. "It is I, most unfortunately," she said quietly.

"You heard," breathed Miss Ratcliffe. "You heard and saw everything."

Joan reluctantly nodded. "I am afraid so. I do apologize. I was fetching a book for Lady Cassandra when Mr. Dewesbury came in. Not wishing to bring myself to his notice, I—"

Miss Ratcliffe advanced on her swiftly. "I do not care for your feeble excuses, Miss Chadwick. They are meaningless. You deliberately eavesdropped on me—on *me*!" She breathed quickly, her nostrils flaring. "I do not know what you hope to gain, Miss Chadwick, but I promise you that you will regret ever having interested yourself in my affairs." She smiled, but it was not a friendly expression. Her eyes moved disdainfully over Joan. "You are nothing but a vulgar eavesdropper, Miss Chadwick."

Joan's pride burned, but there was nothing that she could say to defend herself. It was all too true. She should not have remained hidden like some craven. Instead of protesting, she started to turn aside. "As you say, Miss Ratcliffe."

Miss Ratcliffe sucked in a wrathful breath. "Oh!" She grabbed the other young woman's arm and spun her back around. A slender chain slipped free of Joan's bodice. "How dare you speak to me in that impertinent fashion. As though you were dismissing me."

"If I have given offense again, believe me, Miss Ratcliffe, it was unintentional," Joan said evenly.

"And you expect me to accept that?"

Miss Ratcliffe's eyes were suddenly caught by the glittering chain that hung from Miss Chadwick's neck. "What is that you have on your chain?" she asked sharply, her hand coming up.

Joan moved quickly. Her fingers protectively covered the ring that was suspended on the chain. But she was not quick enough, for the other woman had already realized what it was she had seen.

Horrible comprehension entered Miss Ratcliffe's eyes. She stared at Joan's hand, then her eyes lifted to Joan's face. "That is a wedding band," she accused.

Joan said not a word. Her mind had gone completely blank and she could not think of anything. She saw the hatred in Miss Ratcliffe's eyes and for an instant she thought that the young woman meant to strike her, but at the last second Miss Ratcliffe whisked herself about, wrenched open the library door, and ran out.

After a moment, Joan also left the library, but more slowly.

Vincent Dewesbury was mildly surprised when his bedroom door abruptly opened. He was standing on the open balcony, his coat discarded, his cravat untied, smoking a cigar. He turned his head, and instantly he threw the cigar over the balcony's edge and strode back into the room. "Augusta," he exclaimed in astonishment. "What are you doing here?"

Miss Ratcliffe closed the door and stood quite still in front of it. "Vincent, what did you say to me in the library?"

Mr. Dewesbury's eyes narrowed. He gave a negligent shrug, his countenance satirical. "I said a good deal of nonsense, as I recall. What in particular had you in mind, my dear?"

Miss Ratcliffe went to him slowly. She did not touch him, but lifted up on her toes. Her lips brushed his mouth. "Do you want me, Vincent?" she whispered.

His breath shortened. "Want you?" He laughed hollowly. "I suspect that I gave you too much insight into my hell-ridden soul, Augie." He grasped her arms suddenly. His eyes blazed down into hers. "What do you want of me? Why do you taunt me? I warn you, I am not one to be toyed with. You will get burned at whatever little game you seek to play."

Miss Ratcliffe was breathing quickly. There was a wild glitter in her eyes. "It is no game, Vincent. If you want me, then take me for your wife. Fly with me. Now, tonight!"

"What are you saying?" Vincent asked hoarsely.

"Don't you yet understand? I want you to take me away with you, at once. I don't care where we go, just take me away from this horrid place," exclaimed Miss Ratcliffe.

Vincent Dewesbury stared down at her for several long moments. A slow smile dawned on his face. It was cruel in its knowledge. "You have discovered that Humphrey is already wed," he said.

Miss Ratcliffe's eyes slid away. Then she threw back her head. Her indigo-blue eyes flashed magnificently. "Yes. But if that troubles you, do pray forget that I have ever been here." She would have pulled free then, but he tightened his grasp.

Vincent shook his head. His green eyes held a strange expression. "Oh, no, Augusta. I shall not forget. And neither shall you." He thrust her from him. "Go and get your things. I shall meet you at the stables in fifteen minutes. Mind, not a word to your maid."

Miss Ratcliffe had already gone to the bedroom door. "Do you think me a complete nodcock?" she hissed disdainfully before she whisked herself through the door.

Mr. Dewesbury regarded the spot that she had vacated. "What I think of you, my dear, you have yet to discover," he said softly.

25

THE FOLLOWING MORNING Joan was dressed early and she hovered downstairs near the breakfast room, hoping to waylay Lord Humphrey before he went in. She kept herself hidden from other risers and waited anxiously for the sight of the viscount. When at last Lord Humphrey sauntered down the stairs, Joan came out of hiding to rush up to him. "Edward! I must speak to you."

Lord Humphrey was astonished and alarmed. There was that in her voice and her expression that instantly conveyed dire tidings in the making. He caught her hands. "Joan! What is it? What has overset you so?"

"Not here. Come into the library," exclaimed Joan, urging him with her hands.

Lord Humphrey took her arm and rapidly escorted her into the library. He shut the door. "Now, what is it?" he asked quietly.

Joan clasped her hands together. "I fear that we are undone, my lord. Miss Ratcliffe learned last night that we are wed. If she were to tell anyone before you have the chance to talk with the earl—"

"Good Lord," exclaimed Lord Humphrey, appalled. He understood at once her fears. "Augusta will pillory us. My father—Lord and Lady Ratcliffe—and Mama! None of them will ever be able to forgive me for that humiliation.'' He put his hand on the knob. ''I must go upstairs at once and catch the earl before he comes down.''

''His lordship is already at breakfast! And so is Lady Dewesbury,'' Joan said despairingly.

Lord Humphrey looked at her, a grim set to his mouth. ''The Ratcliffes? What of Augusta?''

Joan shook her head quickly. ''No, not as yet. But the Harringtons and Lady Cassandra came down only moments before you did yourself.''

''We have time, then. Come. I mean to request an immediate audience with the earl and my mother.''

Lord Humphrey and Joan left the library. He swiftly escorted her straight into the breakfast room, finally stopping beside Lord Dewesbury's chair. ''My lord, I wish to speak with you and my mother at once,'' he said.

The earl stared up at the viscount. His lordship was taken aback by Lord Humphrey's abrupt tone, but he was conscious that the viscount would not violate the respect due to himself for a small cause. ''Of course, Edward. You have our undivided attention,'' Lord Dewesbury said evenly.

He spared only a fleeting glance for Miss Chadwick. He was not nearly so against her as he had been at the first, and he was slightly ashamed of his rude treatment of her. He had been cynical in the beginning of Miss Chadwick's genteel manner, suspecting her of disguising her true character, but he had gradually come to realize that she was not the grasping harpy that he had so strongly believed. In addition, certain observations that his old friend Lord Ratcliffe had presented to him, as well as Miss Ratcliffe's own appalling disintegration into jealousy and malice, had gone far in reconciling him to his son's engagement to Miss Chadwick. It was only his pride that now prohibited him from openly acknowledging her right to a place in his family.

Lord Humphrey said tightly, ''Forgive me, my lord. I did

not make myself clear. I should like to address yourself and my mother in private.''

There were several interested and curious gazes trained on the viscount from around the breakfast table. Neville, who had come down along with Margaret while Lord Humphrey and Joan had been closeted in the library, sharply nudged his sister. She flapped her hand at him, never taking her wide eyes from Lord Humphrey's face.

''Of course you may speak to us privately,'' said Lady Dewesbury, throwing a glance at the earl. ''We shall go into the study straight after breakfast, won't we, my lord?''

The earl nodded. He saw the denial that sprang into the viscount's eyes and he held up his hand. ''After we have finished breakfasting, Edward,'' he said firmly.

Lord Humphrey stood irresolute, then he reluctantly nodded. His face set, he handed Joan to a chair at the table before he seated himself. At the footman's query as to his preferences from the sideboard, Lord Humphrey made a short reply.

Queried in her turn, Joan refused everything but hot tea.

''Black or white, miss?'' asked the footman.

''White, please,'' Joan said, attempting a smile. It was not her best effort and it quickly faded as her eyes strayed to the door of the breakfast room. When the footman placed the tea, to which had been added a generous portion of cream, she concentrated on stirring it so as to keep herself from staring too obviously at the door.

Lord and Lady Ratcliffe entered far too quickly for Joan's taste. She held her breath as she carefully studied their faces. But she saw nothing untoward in either of their expressions. Lord Ratcliffe nodded congenially all around and even Lady Ratcliffe had a friendly word for the company.

''Isn't Miss Ratcliffe joining us for breakfast?'' Joan asked, unable to bear the suspense any longer.

Lady Ratcliffe looked at her in astonishment. ''My daughter never breakfasts.''

"Of course. How silly of me," murmured Joan. Her eyes met the viscount's gaze. He offered her a tight smile and she began to breathe a little easier. It was going to turn out all right, after all. Joan signaled the footman and requested from him a bowl of fresh ripe blueberries covered in thick cream.

The breakfast-room door opened and another footman entered. He conveyed a folded note to Lady Dewesbury. She read the missive with astonishment. She looked up and exclaimed, "Why, Vincent has gone. He extends his apologies for his abrupt departure, but he says that a pressing matter has arisen that demands his attention. How very odd!"

The Earl of Dewesbury shrugged. He continued to make inroads into his steak and kidneys. "Vincent was always the brooding sort, too restless by half. Depend upon it, he merely became bored with us here at Dewesbury and has hared off to find better sport."

Lady Dewesbury sighed, but she could not fault her husband's opinion of his nephew. She was also aware that the kind of hospitality to be found at Dewesbury Court was not the sort that could long hold one of Vincent Dewesbury's saturnine temperament and libertine propensities.

"He has probably returned to London to that opera dancer of his," Neville said casually.

"Neville," exclaimed Lady Dewesbury. She regarded her youngest son sternly. "And what do you know of the matter, young sirrah?"

Neville reddened as he cast a glance at his father's interested expression. "Why—why, everyone knows Cousin Vincent's reputation. I just assumed—"

"You shall not assume again, Neville, if you please," Lady Dewesbury said frostily.

Neville hung his head. "Yes, Mama." He slid another glance toward his father, expecting similar condemnation from that quarter, but instead he was astonished to be given a sly wink.

"Leave the boy alone, Charlotte. He but parrots his elders," said Lord Dewesbury.

Nothing more was thought of Vincent's abrupt departure until Miss Ratcliffe was discovered to be missing.

Miss Ratcliffe had never come down for breakfast, preferring always to have a cup of chocolate brought to her in bed, if she desired anything at all. She had not rung her bell for the chocolate to be brought to her, and so her maid assumed that her mistress was sleeping late, which was not an uncommon habit.

Miss Ratcliffe's maid came running into the breakfast room, screeching at the top of her lungs for Lady Ratcliffe. "My lady! My lady! Oh, my lady!" She threw herself on her knees beside Lady Ratcliffe's chair and burst into noisy sobs.

"What is all that racket about? Here, stop that. It's enough to curdle one's stomach," Lady Cassandra exclaimed irritably.

Alarm showed in Lady Ratcliffe's expression. "What is it? What has happened? Is it Augusta? Stop that bellowing at once, do you hear?" Her command had no effect. Smartly she slapped the maid.

The maid's hysteria was reduced to dismal sniffles. She held out her trembling hand and offered a small note. "She's gone, my lady."

"Gone! What do you mean, gone?"

"What is the wench babbling about?"

"I say! Perhaps she has leapt into the millpond."

"Oh, no, no! Edward, do you suppose—"

"Neville, do be quiet. Margaret, pray close your mouth at once. A young lady should not resemble a fish."

Among the varied exclamations, Lady Ratcliffe snatched the note out of the maid's hand and her eyes swiftly ran over the few words. She turned pale. "Augusta has gone off with Vincent Dewesbury!"

"C'mon," exclaimed Lord Ratcliffe. He grabbed the paper

from his wife's limp fingers. When he looked up, his face was expressionless. "It is true."

Stunned silence fell over the company. They all looked at one another with expressions of astonishment, shock, and appallment.

"Oh, dear God. She will be ruined," Lady Dewesbury said faintly. "Vincent, of all people! Vincent!"

"A most worthy young lady, indeed," Lady Cassandra said bitingly.

Lord Dewesbury had flushed dull red with rage. His narrowed eyes glittered in their depths. "Yes, Vincent. My nephew has done this thing." From between his teeth, he repeated, "My nephew!" He threw aside his napkin and leapt from his chair. "They cannot have gone far, John. We shall go after tham at once."

Lord Ratcliffe passed a hand over his eyes. "I thank you, Greville. Yes, we must go after them, of course."

"I will have the horses put to," said Sir Thomas tersely. He pressed Lady Athene's hand and then left the breakfast room.

Lord Dewesbury took hold of Lord Ratcliffe's shoulder in a gesture of rough sympathy and apology. "We shall catch them, John. Never fear. And when we do, I vow to you that your daughter's reputation will not suffer." He expelled his breath heavily. "Vincent will marry her, I swear to you."

"Marry," exclaimed Lady Dewesbury. She had left her own chair and come around the table to put her arms about Lady Ratcliffe's shoulders.

The earl looked around at his wife impatiently. "Of course, what else? It is a question of honor—Augusta's honor as well as the Dewesbury honor."

Lady Cassandra cackled. "That's rich, by heaven! When all along, on your own doorstep—"

"That will be enough, my lady," warned Lord Humphrey. He stared meaningfully at his grandmother.

Lady Cassandra grimaced, but she shrugged dismissively.

"But why? Why ever would Augusta do such a thing?" wailed Lady Ratcliffe, wringing her hands.

Lady Dewesbury patted her shoulder, murmuring consolingly.

"I believe that I may know," said Joan quietly.

All eyes swiveled in Joan's direction. She was regarded with astonishment.

"Joan," exclaimed Lord Humphrey.

She looked at him and gestured helplessly. "Well, Edward? What else can we do?"

Lord Humphrey gave a short bark of laughter. "Indeed! What else?" He reached for her hand and held it in his firm grasp. "Joan is not my betrothed. She is my wife."

Lady Ratcliffe gave the faintest of moans. Her lids fluttered and she slid out of her chair.

The maid, who had stayed kneeling beside Lady Ratcliffe's chair during all that had been said, gave a frightened squeak and promptly burst into renewed sobs. Lord Ratcliffe and Lady Athene went at once to Lady Ratcliffe's succor. Lady Athene appealed to the hovering footmen to stop idling by and to carry Lady Ratcliffe up to her room.

Lord Humphrey stared the earl straight in the face. "I am sorry, my lord. I should have said so from the start."

Lady Dewesbury stared at her son, quite unnoticing of the commotion about her feet. "But why, Edward? I do not understand. Why such subterfuge?"

"That was my contribution, daughter. I persuaded Edward and Joan that the hasty marriage would never be accepted," said Lady Cassandra. A smile formed on her lips. "I suspected that it would all be highly entertaining, and so it has proven."

"You are a wicked and awful old woman, Lady Cassandra," said Lady Athene angrily, at the same time holding open the breakfast-room door for the footmen who were burdened with Lady Ratcliffe's supine form. Lord Ratcliffe watched his wife carried off and then turned back into the room.

"And you, my dear Athene, shall be much like me," retorted Lady Cassandra.

"I say, Edward, did you wed Miss Chadwick because you tossed her into the ditch?" asked Neville.

"In a manner of speaking, Neville. I wed Miss Chadwick because after I had run her down with my carriage, I abducted her with the intention of carrying her off to Gretna Green," said Lord Humphrey. He was the object of several pairs of disbelieving eyes. He flushed. "I was drunk as a wheelbarrow at the time."

"So I should hope," Lord Dewesbury said forcibly. He went up to Joan and took her hand. "My son has much to apologize for, my dear ma'am. And so must I. If I had known that a point of honor was at stake, matters would have gone far otherwise for you here at Dewesbury Court. When this other matter is attended to, we shall have the leisure to begin anew and become properly acquainted."

"I should like that very much, my lord," Joan said, smiling up at her father-in-law.

At that moment Sir Thomas returned. "The carriages are ready, my lord."

The earl gave a sharp nod. "John, Thomas, we are off at last. Edward, I shall leave you to handle whatever other domestic crisis might arise during our absence." Followed by Lord Ratcliffe and Sir Thomas, he strode out into the entryway. An instant later he was heard to utter a curse. "Charlotte, my dear. Here are our neighbors, come to pay their respects to Edward and his betrothed."

"Oh, no," moaned Lady Dewesbury, putting her hand to her head.

Lady Cassandra chuckled cheerfully. "Oh, yes!" She tucked her hand into her daughter's arm. "How I do adore a lively party! Come along, Charlotte. We must go greet your new guests. And the rest of you may as well come also. No, not you, Edward. I think it best if you and your delightful wife were to stay away until the first shock has died somewhat."

The breakfast-room door swung closed and Joan and Lord Humphrey were alone. The room seemed incredibly quiet of a sudden. They looked at each other, and spontaneous laughter burst from both.

Lord Humphrey turned up his wife's face with one hand. "We have at last achieved a measure of peace, my lady."

"Yes, but I doubt for long. At any moment that door must be pushed wide and ourselves caught up in long explanations," Joan said.

"Then we must make good our escape while we may," said Lord Humphrey. He grinned down at her. "Have you ever found the center of the maze, Joan?"

"Why, no. I should like to, however," she said, her eyes beginning to gather an answering twinkle.

"Then we shall. As soon as the new arrivals are safely into the drawing room, we shall dash through the entry and take ourselves off to the maze," said Lord Humphrey. He touched her lips with his finger. "But I think that the time intervening can be put to good effect."

"Indeed, my lord?" Joan asked. She lifted her lips in daring invitation.

Lord Humphrey laughed softly. "Indeed, my beloved lady." He bent his head to prove it to her.